MURDER IS ACADEMIC

When revered Ivy League college president Dr. Amos Loeb is murdered, prime suspicion falls upon an alumnus who has raged against the president's admission of women to this historically all-male institution. Loeb, as a survivor of Auschwitz, a renowned scholar, and a heroic humanitarian seemed a very unlikely target for assassination. But as his long-concealed personal misdeeds come to light, he is revealed to have been a far from perfect man, imperfect enough to suggest that several others in addition to the disgruntled alumnus could very well have wanted him dead.

The Loeb murder is baffling the local police when a journalist arrives in town to pursue his own investigation toward writing an account of the affair. This journalist, a would-be Truman Capote writing a would-be *In Cold Blood*, produces the book *Zänker* in which he is both a focal character and narrator of events. As the former, he is less an objective reporter than an active player in the college community's combustible social life, sparking interpersonal tensions before ultimately solving the case.

Editorial Reviews

"Set in a beautifully rendered northern Vermont college town, this terrific page-turner centers on the murder of the school's president, an academic superstar seemingly beyond reproach. But was he really?

The characters are a vivid if unsettling mix of locals, academics, and townsfolk. One of them is obsessed with the Holocaust. Another is obsessed with homicide…committing one, that is.

So curl up and get started. Just make sure all the doors are locked."—*Sebastian Stuart, author of The Hour Between, The Mentor, To the Manor Dead, Dead by Any Other Name, and What Wasn't I Thinking?*

D1218309

i

Excerpt

The next day's edition of *The New York Times* reported the ghastly assault upon Dr. Amos Loeb, the president of Ballyvaughan College. Under the headline "Heroic College President Victim of Knife Attack" was an account of the dreadful deed and a sampling of community reaction to it. The deed was not a mere stabbing, it was the severing, apparently by intention, of the victim's male member.

ZÄNKER
Peter Maeck

Moonshine Cove Publishing, LLC
Abbeville, South Carolina U.S.A.

Second Moonshine Cove Edition March 2023

ISBN: 9781952439520

LCCN: 2022915894

Cover illustration and design by Peter Maeck.
Interior design by Moonshine Cove staff.

About the Author

Peter Maeck is a novelist, poet, playwright, and photographer. His narrative poem *Remembrance of Things Present: Making Peace with Dementia* (Shanti Arts 2017), illustrated with his own photographs,  celebrates his father's brave, good-humored journey through Alzheimer's disease. Peter has presented *Remembrance of Things Present* at multiple TEDx events and international mental health conferences. His latest poems are collected in *Aperture* (Shanti Arts 2022). *Zänker* is his first novel.

Peter's stage plays and dance scenarios, including for Pilobolus and MOMIX Dance Theatres, have been produced in New York City, Europe, and Africa. Peter served as a U.S. State Department American Cultural Specialist in Tanzania and Morocco. He is currently a destination and enrichment speaker aboard cruise ships of Holland America, Royal Caribbean, Celebrity, and Regent Seven Seas Cruises.

Peter's award-winning photography is in galleries and private collections. He was named one of the "Hot 100 Photographers of 2021" by the Duncan Miller Gallery in Los Angeles. He has created training and motivational programs for corporations worldwide, and has ghostwritten books on business and healthcare, published by McGraw-Hill and Oxford University Press.

Peter holds a BA in English *magna cum laude* from Dartmouth College and an MFA in Playwriting from Brandeis University. He is a member of The Authors Guild, The Dramatists Guild, The Academy of American Poets, The World Dignity Project, and the World Federation for Mental Health.

More at: http://www.petermaeck.com

For Kristen and Alexandra

Ζώμεν γαρ ού ως θέλομεν, αλλ' ως δυνάμεθα.

—*Menander*

PART ONE

The Place

The village of Glenfarne snuggles in the high green forests of northern Vermont, a lonesome area that other Vermonters call "up there." Some fifty miles east of Montpelier, twenty miles south of St. Johnsbury, this locality with its early frosts, limpid sapphire skies, and arctic-clear air feels rather more Yukon than New England. The native accent is barbed with a woodsman-cum-lobsterman "Down East" twang. The terrain is hilly, verging on alpine, and the views from the higher elevations are Olympian. Elk, bear, and moose appear frequently, often on town sidewalks. And the great clock tower of Ballyvaughan College's Founders' Hall is visible long before the traveler reaches it.

I was that traveler recently, and, aside from the tragedy that drew me there, I was enchanted by the boreal, Arcadian outdoor milieu; charmed by the town's quaint main street with its storefronts like a stage diorama for a play set in colonial America; cheered by the happy shoppers toting cratefuls of backcountry curios and gallon jugs of Vermont maple syrup. I marveled at the seeming millions of enticing volumes on the college bookstore's shelves; I ogled the co-eds emerging from the college co-op, each sporting a green hooded sweatshirt with a big, bright letter B on the front; I promenaded the hallowed campus common, saluting tweeded dons and hallooing fresh-faced matriculants too blissfully self-absorbed to acknowledge the greeting of someone thrice their age. No matter, time melted on those wondrous afternoons, rousing me to feel, if only for the nonce, what it was to be on the cusp of life, fresh-faced, free, and incorrupt.

"You'd love it here," says the real estate agent who catches me perusing the photos of for-sale properties in her front window. Indeed, who could not love a place with such spirit, merriment, and enlightenment; a realm where education and recreation are interlaced; where the air buzzes with lofty concepts, profound insights, and groundbreaking thoughts? Leaders are molded here, leaders of industry, military battalions, commerce, science, art, music, architecture, even abstruse, abstract thought. For the moment I am my younger self, imagining that I, too, could achieve such eminence. It might not be too late.

Until one evening in November of 1988 Glenfarne was for most Vermonters, indeed for most Americans, a pristine natural sanctuary, a fabled intellectual retreat, a collegiate cloud nine, a weathertight, stormproof safe house for our best and brightest young peoples' spirits, minds, and hearts. Like the south-flowing waters of the nearby Connecticut River, like the motorists speeding along the Interstate highway just west of town, like the freight trains rumbling up toward or down from Montreal on century-old tracks, drama of the macabre kind had never abided here. Aside from petty pilferage by youth come over in darkness from the neighboring state, Glenfarne and the college it cradled were crime-free. But then, on that clear, frigid evening in November, the slash of cold steel on one man's flesh maimed an entire human community. Thus, Eden was breached and all within it were poised for a dizzying, sickening fall. *Après moi, le déluge* as much as declared this Zion's destroyer, as henceforth, where pennies from heaven had long sprinkled, the acid rain of fear and recrimination would now pour down in a flood.

The Man

The November 2, 1988 edition of *The New York Times* reported the ghastly assault upon Dr. Amos Loeb, the president of Ballyvaughan College. Under the headline "Heroic College President Victim of Knife Attack" was an account of the dreadful deed and a sampling of community reaction to it. The deed was not a mere stabbing, it was the severing, apparently by intention, of the victim's male member. I am not a devotee of true crime, but I was fascinated by such savagery erupting in such a civilized enclave and thus I was moved to set aside all other literary projects and travel to Glenfarne to investigate the matter further. This project was for me, initially, a merely journalistic undertaking, but immersion in the lives of my subjects would lead me to reconceive it as an exploration of human dynamics in conditions of abnormal stress. In fact, I was weary of journalism, and sought to fulfill a lifelong aspiration to tell a tale that in its lyrical telling became truer than its elemental truth; to produce a book-length emotionally true fable founded on hard fact; to write a "nonfiction novel," to use what I believe is the proper term of art, and in so doing to achieve my long overdue presence on the *Times* bestseller list.

I arrived in Glenfarne just three days after the attack. The town and the college within it were in shock. Dr. Loeb was under critical care at Glenfarne Hospital, lapsing in and out of consciousness as doctors labored round-the-clock coaxing his vital signs, replacing the blood he'd lost, staving off infection, and arguing over how to reattach the severed organ.

Amos Loeb was sixty-one years old at the time. He was not quite six feet tall but his professional stature was that of a giant. And while bedecked and beribboned for his heroic scholarly and humanitarian work, he was beloved for his simple human kindness.

He was, to be honest, not a traditionally handsome fellow, with his fleshy lips, sleepytime eyes, and ragged scar from his right cheekbone down to his chin from a wound sustained defending valiantly though alas unsuccessfully his mother's life. Despite Loeb's less than Apollonian physical aspect, his mien was galvanic to men and aphrodisiac to women, millions of whom were smitten by his image on a *Time* magazine cover in 1988. The accompanying article reported that Loeb was born in 1927 in Leipzig, Germany. He was six when Hitler became German chancellor. Loeb's parents Asher and Ruth Loeb opposed Hitler and spoke out publicly against the Reich. In 1942 they were involved in a thwarted plot to kill *der Führer* in Berlin. The plot's failure sent them into hiding where Loeb's father fell into a deep depression and committed suicide.

Loeb and his mother were found and arrested soon after that and his mother, after spitting in the SS guards' faces was, despite her son's ardent defense, shot to death on the spot. Amos, crazed with rage and grief, kicked and punched the guards with such fury and force that these guards, impressed by his strength, sent word ahead to Auschwitz-Birkenau that he should not be killed immediately but instead put to work laying roads and digging drainage ditches. Ultimately he worked so well that he was spared from execution and thus he survived, starved and nearly frozen to death, until January 1945 when the camp was liberated by the Soviets. Amos then returned to Germany, attended university, did splendidly well, then traveled to the United States and earned a Ph.D. in European History at Stanford, specializing in the Nazi era.

Dr. Loeb became a professor at Ballyvaughan soon thereafter and while teaching he became famous writing books and lecturing nationwide and worldwide on the Holocaust. In 1970 he was named Ballyvaughan's president. The 1988 *Time* magazine feature made him a national and international celebrity. "But my greatest accomplishment," as he would say to his rapt audiences, "was convincing Lucy Stickeen to be my wife." Lucy was never present at these speaking engagements and was rarely seen on campus or in the town. Her own photograph in the magazine depicted a braided, pale-faced, walleyed woman wearing wooden clogs and a granny skirt from the Woodstock era. "I'm so proud of my man," the caption under the image read.

Loeb, for his part, was not prideful in the least, forbearing the acclaim verging on worship he inspired, deflecting all personal honor toward the Holocaust victims whose memories he championed. His chronic self-effacement led many to see this Holocaust survivor as a prime exemplar of the affective syndrome known as survivor's guilt.

Dr. Loeb awoke on Friday November 1, 1988 at four a.m. as he always did. Lucy had arisen earlier to prepare his oatmeal and toast and when he was shaved, showered, and dressed he consumed this provender with one hand flipping pages in the morning newspaper and the other gripping his mug of steaming tea.

All as per routine. Nothing out of the ordinary. Except for the fact that this particular Friday was the first day of Autumn Inferno Weekend, the very extraordinary annual celebration of Ballyvaughan's grand and glorious academic, social, and especially athletic traditions. Literally thousands of alumni would be arriving on campus to join the three thousand undergraduates for the festivities. And these alums would all want to shake Dr. Loeb's hand for bestowing such honor upon their beloved alma mater.

Well, most of the alums would. A persnickety few would denounce him for "modernizing" this venerable institution; for imposing a parvenu political correctness that rejected what had made the college great. Indeed, several dozen of these disaffected old grads were already gathered outside the administration building when Loeb arrived this early dawn for work. "Top o' the morning, gents!" he greeted them, receiving their hoots and hisses with affable grace, little knowing that the most extreme of these negative sentiments would later this day amalgamate into sharpened steel and bring about his death.

The Plot

Leaning on crutches, his left foot in a walking boot, thirty-eight year-old Tom Dunraven was raking leaves on the pasture-broad lawn of his Connecticut faux Tudor mansion fronting the whitecap-flecked gunmetal gray plane of Long Island Sound. Each time he mustered a small heap of leaves a wind gust dispersed them and Tom limped off to rake them back up. Last week he had climbed a ladder to replace a roof shingle and on his way back down had missed a rung and fallen to the ground. He'd landed on his feet and had felt fine for awhile but then his left foot swelled and an x-ray revealed that he'd sustained a hairline fracture of the third metatarsal.

"You could have cracked your spine and been paralyzed," said Charlie Cubbage, Tom's longtime best friend who was accompanying Tom around the lawn. Paralysis was Charlie's personal phobia. He often dreamed of being pinned to a board like an insect specimen, with scientists over him jotting notes on clipboards. "Hell, Tom, you even could have died."

"I'll die when it's my time, Charlie," Tom said, "and not a minute sooner."

The wind finally subsided long enough for Tom to achieve a good-sized leaf pile which he then set ablaze with his cigarette lighter. The men watched in rapt silence as the flames warmed the slate-cold October sky. But this bonfire was a mere flicker compared to the massive blaze they would behold tomorrow night at the traditional Autumn Inferno homecoming rally up north on the campus of Ballyvaughan College.

Charlie and Tom were proud Ballyvaughan alumni from the Class of 1971. Nostalgically inclined Charlie contributed annually to the alumni fund and went back for Autumn Inferno every year. He always asked Tom to go with him but Tom always refused. "The past is the past," Tom said, "and goodbye to all that." But Charlie knew Tom was really just angry that it was gone. Charlie was angry, too, but he got over it. Then he was just heartbroken.

Tom was angry in particular at the college's president Dr. Loeb for shutting down fraternities. Tom didn't approve of binge drinking and hazing pledges though he'd done his share of both when he was a house brother back in his day. He accepted that the frat system needed reforming but he was against abolishing it altogether. Some of Tom's sweetest days and nights, he loved to recall, were losing at beer pong in the basement of Kappa Kappa Nu.

Tom's other gripe, in fact his main gripe, was Loeb's approval of coeducation. Ballyvaughan was founded for men only and it stayed proudly all-male for two centuries until Dr. Loeb upset the tea kettle in 1970. "Why fix what ain't broken?" is how Tom put it in phone rants to the president's office and letters to the alumni magazine. Tom remembered the friendly little school in the pines where you could grow to be a man among men. "Me, too, Tom," Charlie agreed, "I remember, too, but for everything turn, turn, right? There is a season under heaven, and a reason, as the folk song has it."

It wasn't that Tom hated women, he loved women, after all he married one, Svetlana from Novosibirsk, a sizzler, and his daughters Masha and Zasha weren't exactly homely. Charlie said to Tom, "If your two little girls end up applying to Ballyvaughan I'll bet you'll be tickled when they get in."

"They won't apply, Svetlana's pegged them for goddamn Moscow State."

Tom wasn't just frustrated with life, he was furious at it. And more than furious, he was deeply depressed. Until recently he'd led a blessed life: baseball star in college, Phi Beta Kappa, Yale Med, then a thriving practice at Yale New Haven where he was the presumptive future chief of OB/GYN. At home were a beautiful wife and two beautiful kids.

Then the trapdoor flew open. First he was sued for medical malpractice and lost the case; then he watched his hair go gray overnight then his wife ditched him and took the kids with her. He'd abused her, she claimed, but she showed no bruises to prove it. Abused her mentally, she clarified, but how do you prove that? By quoting some peevish remarks? Where's the tape recording? Who took notes? It was a classic 'he said/she said' case. At the end of it all Tom drove his El Dorado off the end of the Martha's Vineyard ferry, steered onboard, gunned the motor and just shot out the other side right through the safety chain. He said the gas stuck but Charlie knew he was simply overwhelmed by his turn of bum luck. At the bottom of the harbor Tom just opened the car door and stepped out like he'd parked at the curb. The Coast Guard fished out the Caddy but once salt gets in that motor it's scrap.

After a while Charlie stopped inviting Tom to go with him to the Autumn Inferno weekend. He realized Tom would never come and he took it very personally when Tom rejected him. But now in the fall of 1988 with Tom so down in the dumps Charlie called him again, thinking that a trip back to the alma mater might cheer him up. "Forget it, Charlie," is what Charlie expected to hear from Tom.

"Okay," Tom said instead.

"Why the change of heart, buddy?"

"It's time to go head-to-head with that bastard,"

"What bastard? You mean Loeb?"

"It's useless writing and phoning in my complaints. It's time to go settle the score once and for all, mano a mano, head-to-head."

"You're going to talk to him in person?"

"I'm going to kill him in person."

"Ha-ha."

"Seriously."

"Kill him how?"

"Cut him."

"With words? Good luck."

"I'm through with words."

"If words could kill I'd be a dead man myself."

"What do you mean?"

"I mean your words, Tom, are sharp as a knife sometimes."

"What do you mean?"

"They hurt."

"I know. I'm sorry."

"It's all right."

"I always take them back."

"You do, which I appreciate."

"I never stay mad at you, Charlie, you're too nice."

"My saving grace."

"But other people ..."

"Like Loeb, I know."

"Like my wife."

"Forget her, Tom. Forget your wife."

"I try."

"Forgive her. Forgive her and forget."

"Some people I can't forgive."

"Then just forget."

"I will, but only when they're dead."

"Okay, that's enough of that."

"I don't mean you, Charlie, I mean Loeb."

"I know you do."

"I've got to do this, Charlie, I've waited long enough."

"Great, do it, grab him by the collar, give him a piece of your mind, get it all off your chest."

"Oh, I'll do that. But that won't be enough."

"Of course not, you need to kill him, like you said. Sure, that's just a splendid idea, sane, efficient, and if you leave no fingerprints and drop the murder weapon down the Mariana Trench, there's no chance in the world you'll be caught."

"Exactly."

"You're funny, Tom."

"Nothing funny about it."

"What's your murder weapon?"

"A knife."

"Why not just shoot him?"

"I don't own a gun."

"Where's the knife?"

"Right here." Tom patted his left front pants pocket.

"Let's see it."

Tom pulled out a banana.

"You're a scream, Tom."

"No, the knife is in my suitcase, I forgot."

"Well, get your suitcase or we won't make it to Glenfarne by sundown."

The men had to reach Glenfarne before sundown since Charlie couldn't drive at night having scarred his retina glancing at an eclipse, and Tom couldn't drive with his broken foot. Tom turned and hobbled away.

"Wait, what about the fire, Tom?"

"The fire's dead."

"It's still smoking. Maybe we should douse it."

"Then douse it." Tom motioned to the garden hose coiled by the tool shed, and went indoors. Charlie got the hose and turned on the water and doused the ashes until they were a sodden hissing pile of black muck. Then he re-coiled the hose.

"You missed a little," said Tom upon returning with his suitcase. A patch had flared back up. Charlie picked up the hose. "Piss on it," Tom said. Charlie aimed the hose at the ashes. Tom grabbed the hose from him. "Piss on it," Tom repeated. Charlie refused, politely. "Piss on it!" Tom all but shouted. Charlie didn't respond and Tom said, "What's the matter with you?"

Charlie told him the matter was that he couldn't piss in the presence of another person. Tom said why not? Charlie said forty-two percent of men have that problem. Tom said, "But why you?"

"Ask my shrink."

Charlie didn't have a shrink but Tom didn't press him on it. "But I'm not another person, Charlie, I'm your old friend."

Charlie said friends, strangers, it didn't matter.

"What do you do in a public restroom?"

"I go in a stall."

"You're a weird one, Charlie."

"About half as weird as you."

The men shared a good laugh then they got in the car and shoved off for the great north.

The Attempt

Charlie loved driving Tom's brawny new Camaro. Up the Interstate, cruise control, he was flying. In the old days before the Interstate was completed Charlie rode the bus from New Jersey up the state roads through the little towns and the thick stands of pine along the big river rising out of the hot mean urban and suburban jungles into the soft, cool, deep green of higher education. Green, in fact, was Ballyvaughan's official color. Founded by an Irishman and named after his Irish hometown, the college decked its sports teams in green, inspired by the Emerald Isle's verdant hue.

Ballyvaughan's glorious sporting tradition was, is, and always will be on fullest and proudest display on Autumn Inferno weekend. The homecoming football game is on Saturday and the rally around the bonfire is Friday night. Freshmen work all week stacking up old railroad ties to make a giant pyramid. On Friday night it's soaked with gasoline then it's torched and it blows up to something like the burning of Atlanta in *Gone With The Wind* while all the undergrads and the grads who've flown in from around the world stand hand-in-hand in a great circle singing "Boys of Ballyvaughan" which had to be changed to "Boys and Belles of Ballyvaughan" after they started letting in women. That first class of women didn't want to be called fresh*men* so the college decided to lump men and women together as "greenhorns." The Kappa Kappa Nu bro became known as the Greenhornies, for reasons easily surmised.

The college mascot used to be a lunatic Irishman with a pipe in his mouth, a mug of Guinness in his left hand, and a Celtic battle axe in his right. He was more or less a leprechaun except leprechauns are pixie size and this mascot stood ten feet high on stilts. His name was Seamus, or Shimmyin' Seamus when he did his jig at the 50-yard line during halftime of football games. He was Shitfaced Seamus when he chugged his whole mug of Guinness and rolled around on the grass playing dead drunk. Pretty amusing.

The girls in the first coed class had a different name for Seamus, though: *Shame*-us. They didn't like his guzzling and mock upchucking and the twin basketballs and pogo stick under his zipper that looked like jumbo private parts.

The female students lodged a formal protest and were supported by most of the faculty. Grudgingly, the college agreed to choose a new mascot more acceptable to touchy modern sensibilities but that still honored the school's old Irish heritage. Candidates were chosen and everybody could vote on them including alumni. The candidates were all Irish saints: Patrick, Ciarán, Malachy, and Oliver Plunkett. Patrick won and so the boys' teams would henceforth be called The Pats and the girls' teams The Patties. Ballyvaughan t-shirts, mugs, and hoodies would have Saint Patrick's picture on them, complete with snakes and a green gold-buckled miter for a hat. Booze-loving alumni, however, griped over Saint Patty's prissy reputation as "temperate and abstemious" and rejected him. They caved though when the mug of Guinness was stuck back in his left hand to balance the scepter in his right and his belly was fattened to symbolize the famous Dublin brewery's "Stout." Protests that a saintly mascot made secular Ballyvaughan College appear to be a Jesuit school were dismissed with the affirmation that Ballyvaughan shared with Jesuitism only the core prinicples of ethics, leadership, and community service. And Saint Patrick, by this time in history, was less a religious symbol than an Irish national icon.

Rich traditions like Autumn Inferno were what had attracted Charlie and Tom to Ballyvaughan. As freshmen in 1967 they'd helped build the bonfire pyramid. On Friday night they joined with all the other Ballyvaughan students and alumni in singing "Boys of Ballyvaughan" as the pyramid was set on fire. This was before coeducation compelled the addition of "Belles" to the song's title, though a lot of alums continued thereafter singing just "Boys" and left out the "Belles," either because that's how they'd learned it and by now it was automatic, or they were protesting women on campus. It didn't matter, with people's teeth chattering on these cold November nights the song's words were pretty garbled and the hooch being swilled all around didn't exactly promote clear speech. But the words mattered less than the memories for these proud and loyal Ballyvaughanians as they stood before that mighty blaze, arms locked, swinging left and right, the tears streaming down their faces, looking in those flames at all the blessings of their lives.

The day Charlie graduated from Ballyvaughan was the proudest day of his life. Nobody in his family had gone to college before and here he was with an Ivy League degree. For Tom, graduation was the saddest day of his life. He wanted to stay on campus forever. Time to get out in the world and make your mark, Charlie said to him. Time to start real life. Tom said Ballyvaughan was real life.

But Tom went and made his mark anyway. Charlie made his mark, too, though not as bright a one as Tom's. Charlie's academic and athletic record couldn't match Tom's so his mediocre accomplishments after college were no surprise. He sold things for a series of manufacturers whereas Tom blazed a comet's trail across the medical firmament. Most people are jealous of their more talented best friends but Charlie took pleasure in Tom's successes. He often wondered why Tom had ever befriended such a lesser classmate. But Charlie wasn't complaining.

It was five o'clock and the sun was nearly gone when the Camaro rolled into Glenfarne. Tom requested a quick spin around the campus before they went to the president's mansion where Tom would give Dr. Loeb a piece of his mind. So Charlie drove them around the big common where the almost-finished pyramid stood waiting for the torch tomorrow night. Then they passed by the football stadium, the tennis courts, the observatory, the heating plant, the library, then wended through the cozy neighborhoods where the faculty walked their dogs and raised their kids. Right now a horde of those kids were out in the street, dressed in hobo rags and hangman's masks and astronaut suits, roaming like pack wolves, howling, setting off firecrackers, and pelting houses with raw eggs. They collected around Charlie and Tom's Camaro and forced it to stop. Charlie beeped the horn but they didn't scatter. Instead, they banged on the car windows, begging for handouts, rich spoiled professors' kids playing gutter rats for a night. Charlie shifted into neutral and gunned the engine to scare the urchins. The urchins just laughed and began pounding on the hood. "Put 'er in gear," said Tom. "Mow 'em down." His signature sense of humor.

Charlie opened his window and tossed out a few coins and the kids fought for the loot like sharks over bloody hunks of meat. With the youngsters distracted, Charlie drove on to the end of the street then turned left onto Founders' Avenue until he reached the president's mansion where he pulled over and stopped behind a parked Toyota Corolla.

"Shit," Tom said.

"What's the matter?"

"Someone's in that car ahead of us."

"So what?"

"So he'll be a witness."

"To what?"

"To what I'm going to do."

"You're going to speak to Dr. Loeb."

"I mean what I do after I speak to him."

"Right, I forgot, you're going to draw and quarter him."

"Just cut off his dick."

"Oh, is that the plan? My mistake."

The driver of the Corolla, Ben Marble, shifted in his seat. Ben was a former Boston policeman who, after he was kicked off the force for questionable reasons, was hired by Dr. Loeb to be his personal bodyguard. Loeb had received many nasty threats from alumni

21

enraged by the changes he'd made to the college, especially closing fraternities and admitting women. Their pressure had gotten him to re-open the fraternities but on the coeducation issue he'd stood firm. He loved that song "Woman Is The Nigger Of The World" by John Lennon and Yoko Ono which came out in 1972. He said it proved what he'd been saying all along that women weren't treated as equals to men and that his mission on earth, or one of them, was to fix the situation. He sang the song to alumni groups but the grads didn't applaud when he finished and half walked out.

Initially, Loeb had been excoriated by alumni in general terms, but recently he'd been receiving precisely worded death threats. Loeb didn't trust the local police to protect him effectively so he went and found a big city cop with the lethal skills and crime-busting experience who could. Now when Loeb was out walking Ben tailed him on foot, treading softly, quiet as a cat, keeping to the shadows, eyes peeled for threats. When Loeb was driving his Porsche Ben followed him in the Corolla, as he'd done tonight while Loeb tooled about town, dodging the swarms of bratty kids and finally arriving home at the president's mansion. But Loeb wasn't totally safe even within his brick-walled residence so Ben kept watch from the street, alert for anyone arriving with malign intent, like perhaps the two men who had just parked their car behind his own. Except that Ben was not aware of the car behind him because, as Charlie observed to Tom, he was asleep.

"How can you tell?" Tom said.

"His head is flopped sideways."

"I'm going to check."

Tom exited the car, grabbed his crutches from the back seat, and hobbled to the Toyota. Then he hobbled back. "Snoring, you're right." He glared at the mansion. "Well, this is it, Charlie. Wish me luck."

"Don't forget your knife," Charlie mock-reminded him.

"Got it right here," Tom said, patting his right front pants pocket. He headed toward the mansion. Meanwhile, a taxi pulled up and Kandy Roby, wife of Grayson Roby, Glenfarne's Chief of Police, got out. Kandy wore a fox coat beneath which she was dressed like a flapper from the Jazz Age. She sashayed toward the mansion, overtaking Tom immediately. "Going to the party?" she asked him.

"What party?"

"Dr. Loeb's Halloween party. You're not in costume. Unless you're going as a grumpy old grad. Ha-ha."

Tom sneered.

"I meant that in a good way. You look great!"

Ben had awakened by now. He exited his car and rushed to Tom. "Can I see your invitation, sir?"

"What invitation?"

"To the party."

"I'm not going to the party."

"Damn right you're not."

"Who are you, the police?"

"That's right."

"Where's your badge?"

Ben tapped the Licensed Security Guard badge pinned to his shirt. Tom hobbled back to the Camaro.

Ben followed Tom. "You and your friend out for a drive?" Ben said as they reached the car.

"That's right."

"Doesn't look like you're driving. Looks more like you're parked."

"Is this a no parking zone?" asked Charlie.

"It sure is."

"I don't see a sign."

"No sign needed, it's understood."

"Not by me."

"That's the president's mansion right there, fellows. Parking's not permitted within fifty yards of the mansion, the whole town knows that."

"We're not from town," Tom said.

"We used to be," said Charlie. "We were students here, Class of '71."

"And back then," said Tom, "you could park anywhere you damn wanted."

"Times change, fellows."

"Yeah," Tom snorted, "and mostly for the worse."

Kandy was now being greeted at the front door by Dr. Loeb who wore a red satin smoking jacket reminding one of Hugh Hefner at the Playboy mansion. He even had a Playboy pipe in his mouth. On his feet were slippers of the kind a fat financier wears by the fire puffing a cigar and reading the Wall Street Journal with his brandy at his side and his twin bloodhounds at his feet. Loeb kissed Kandy's hand then waved her into the house with a theatrical gesture.

"You gents move on along now," Ben said to Tom and Charlie.

Tom said, "And if we don't?"

"I'll have to ticket you."

"You can't, you're just a security guard."

"I can ticket you on campus grounds."

"And if I tear up the ticket?"

"I'll arrest you."

"How? You're not a real cop."

"A security guard can make a citizen's arrest then turn the lawbreaker over to the municipal police."

"And if I resist arrest?"

Before Ben could answer that question the driver of a just-arrived Ford Fiesta cried out, "Amos, wait!" From the car bolted Freddy Krueger complete with right-hand four-bladed glove straight out of that *Nightmare on Elm Street* slasher picture where Freddy attacks young people in their dreams.

"Hello, Avi," Ben said to the gruesome figure as it passed him on its way to the mansion.

Freddy was actually Avital Mittelman, a cocktail waitress at the Ballyvaughan Inn bar who'd been flirting with Ben for several months

24

now, vainly of course since Ben was spoken for, although Ben was flattered by her affectionate attention, even tempted to return it, especially since he found himself dreaming affectionately about her every night.

"Welcome to my party, Avi," Loeb said to her when she reached the front porch.

"The party's over, bastard," she said back, extending her finger blades for him to shake.

"*Touché!*" he said, play-parrying her thrust with his pipe.

Now a police car siren wailed and four Firestones screeched to a halt on the street. The car was a town police car and its driver was Chief Grayson Roby. Loeb used the distraction to slip inside the house as Roby bounded toward the mansion. "Halt!" Roby yelled, attaining the porch as Loeb, closing the door, shut him out. Loeb had invited Kandy Roby to his party but not her husband Grayson Roby. Loeb and Kandy were having an affair and Loeb feared that if Grayson, a famously violent man, caught them nuzzling their jig would be violently up.

"Avital Mittelman," snorted Roby to the Krueger impersonator. "Jesus Christ, he's doing you, too?" Roby pounded on the door. "Open up!"

Loeb opened the door. "You came as a policeman, Grayson," Loeb snickered to his uninvited guest. "How creative."

"Where's my wife?"

"Right this way, Chief."

The two men entered the mansion. Avital got halfway in but they shoved her back out. So Kandy Roby wasn't Dr. Loeb's only mistress. He was screwing Avital Mittelman, too, and here she was disguised so no one would suspect her. Well, Ben did more than suspect her, he pronounced her a brazen Lorelei, luring boatman Loeb to ruin on the rock of adultery, albeit Loeb had been on that particular rock since Ben first knew him.

Was Ben jealous of Loeb's appeal to Avital? Such jealousy would mean that Ben wanted Avital all to himself which, despite the implied betrayal of his own marital vows, he did. However, while Ben was married he was now legally separated from his wife and so he could reasonably, albeit not legally, dally with another woman. That might not stand up in a court of law, but for his personal conscience it made a sound enough self-defense.

Or was the alluring shoe on the other foot? Did Loeb seduce Avital? Yes, that was it of course! How dare he, the rat! She was a no-name tavern wench and he was the esteemed president of a world-famous educational institution. Talk about power differentials. And he was so much older than she. Who did he think he was, Humbert Humbert? Avital could be Dr. Loeb's daughter for God's sake.

Hold on. Wait a minute. Ben wasn't thinking straight. Dr. Loeb was his friend, perhaps his best friend. Loeb was an honorable man. But so was Caesar and look who got skewered in that scenario.

All of which made Ben wonder about Lucy, Loeb's wife. Was she home? Doubtful, since he was welcoming his two paramours here tonight, and God knows how many others amongst the faculty wife pool. Correction, Loeb was welcoming Kandy but turning away Avital. But tricked out as a Wes Craven character, what did Avital expect? As for Kandy, Ben surmised that Chief Roby was about to find her starkers on Loeb's bed.

"*Guten Abend, Polizist!*" crowed someone at Ben's back. Ben whirled around, hand clenching his pistol's grip. "*Ach, schieß nicht!*" the someone added. It was a man in a fully inflated Pillsbury Doughboy suit. One hand was raised in surrender, or on second look, in a Nazi salute. The other hand held a half-full bottle of *Spaten Oktoberfest*. "*Ich komme in Frieden,*" the man slurred with beery breath.

Ben knew no one named Frieden and there was no Frieden on the list he kept of Dr. Loeb's trusted acquaintances. "This is a private party, invitation only."

The man showed Ben a printed invitation to President Loeb's Halloween costume party. "This could be addressed to anybody," Ben challenged him. The man turned it over and showed it was addressed to Professor Anton Wohlgemuth of the Ballyvaughan Drama Department. "How do I know it's you in this Pillsbury Doughboy getup?"

"*Ich bin der verdammte Michelin-Mann, du dummer Dummkopf!*" the man snapped, which scarcely needs translation.

So Ben let him in, and after him he admitted a whole stream of fiends, trolls, hobgoblins, Typhoid Marys, Lizzie Bordens, and Incredible Hulks whom he identified as faculty members despite their faces disfigured by gaudy smears of greasepaint and smudges of burnt cork. Avital slipped inside with the mongrel crowd. Two latecomers straggled up whom Ben did not recognize: a middle-aged and a younger woman, so he asked them for identification.

"I'm Faye Foxley," said the older one, "and this is my daughter Piggy."

"Do you have invitations?"

"Oh, I'm an old friend of Dr. Loeb. I don't need an invitation."

"If afraid you do tonight."

"Wait, I know you. You're Ben Marble."

"How do you know me?"

"We met at that book signing at Barnes & Noble this past summer. Jasmine Elm gave a talk then signed copies of her book. Then you and I went out for drinks."

"Jasmine Elm, Jasmine Elm ... " Ben mumbled, pretending not to recognize the notorious name.

"The Holocaust denier."

"Oh, right, her." Ben remembered Ms. Elm perfectly, a small, trim woman wearing a body-hugging way-above-the-knees lime green and pink dress of dragon-embroidered silk. Her lips were bright red, her eyes sea-blue, and the ringlets of her hair platinum blonde. A hint of rouge warmed her porcelain cheeks. On stiletto heels she'd stepped briskly to the lectern like a political candidate about to give a stump speech. "Yes, Jasmine Elm," Ben said, "such a pretty lady but such an ugly speech."

"Was it ugly? I couldn't follow most of it. I looked over and saw you hanging on her every word so I was glad to meet you afterword to ask what it was all about."

"Did I tell you?"

"I ended up not asking, I was too shy. You intimidated me."

"Really? I didn't mean to."

"You had this tough-guy look."

"I'm a cop."

"But you had a soft side I found out, when we had drinks. You asked for my phone number, remember?"

"No."

"Well, you did and I gave it to you but you never called me."

"Sorry."

"You said you'd stay in touch."

"Sorry."

"Doesn't matter, we're in touch now, right?"

"Right."

"So let us go into the party."

"Can't do that."

"Come on, I'm best friends with the host."

"Sorry."

"Look, go in there and tell Amos I'm here. He'll probably come out and let me in personally."

"You're not in costume."

"So what?"

"This is a Halloween party. You've got to be in costume."

At that instant an egg struck the back of Ben's head. Spinning around, he saw the horde of candy-grubbing, egg-tossing trick-or-treaters approaching the mansion. "Hold it right there!" he shouted but they kept coming and when Ben finally halted them with a spritz of pepper spray, Faye and her daughter slipped into the house.

The party was really erupting now. Through the open front door came a madcap symphony of corks popping, glasses clinking, dogs barking, cats hissing, yodelers yodeling, and a stereo blaring some mix of Hendrix and the theme from Captain Kangaroo. The scene was blurred in marijuana smoke whose sickly sweetness gave Ben a contact high as he inhaled it and drew it down his throat so that his memory from that point forward as the Siren scent pulled him bodily in through that door was a distended, distorted, Mad Libs-inspired Looney-Tunes-in-Disneyland tableau of acid-dropping animalia, all fantastically *déjà vu* as if Ben had seen this scene before somewhere, or God willing or not, he someday, somewhere would. But while the outer optics flashed and flimflammed before Ben, his inner eye was filming everything in slo-mo for later frame-by-frame review. In his profession, what you saw was what you got.

Tom, now back in the Camaro, was fuming in frustration.

"Cool down," Charlie said. "You can talk to Dr. Loeb tomorrow."

"I might lose my nerve tomorrow. I've got to do this tonight."

"Then do it, damn it. I'm exhausted, I want to get to bed."

"I can't do it with the cop still here."

"I don't see him."

"He went in the house."

"He's not a cop, he's a security guard."

"He's got a gun."

"Some guards go armed though most never fire their guns. I doubt they'd know how."

"I'll bet this one used to be a cop, in a big city somewhere. He looks the part, he's got a tough-guy look. He'll know how to shoot."

At that moment Ben came back out of the house. On wobbly legs he walked back to his car, got in, and shut the door. Within moments his head was flopped sideways again.

"I think he conked back out," said Charlie. Loud snores like the snorting of a horse came through the cop's open car window.

Tom exploded out of the car and bounded to the mansion without his crutches, striding with his good foot and galumphing on the walking boot. "Loeb!" he shouted as he pounded the front door. "You can't hide, Loeb! Show yourself!" He continued pounding until Loeb appeared.

"Can I help you?" Loeb said.

"I'm Tom Dunraven," Tom yelled. "I was a student of yours way back when. I took your history course."

"That would be before I became the college's president."

"Right. And you flunked me."

"You skipped half of my classes."

"You remember?"

"That's something I wouldn't forget."

"I skipped them because I was sick. So the college erased the failing grade and let me make up the credit with another course later. Otherwise, thanks to you, I wouldn't have made Phi Beta Kappa."

"You were sick. Was I alerted to that?"

"Sure you were, you must have been. But you didn't care. Just like you haven't cared about all the things that made this college great."

"If you resent my sanctioning coeducation—"

"Damn right I do. And here's what else I resent:"

Tom tongue-lashed Loeb for his multiple additional crimes against the college's sacred traditions. To Loeb it was the usual alumni beefing, by now pretty much standard. Tom was probably a harmless blowhard and in his semi-crippled condition probably didn't pose any physical threat. But better safe than sorry. "Ben!" Loeb called out. Ben, snoring in his car, opened his eyes.

"You're going down, Loeb," said Tom.

"Excuse me?" said Loeb.

"Down, way down."

"Thank you for your input, Tim. Enjoy your weekend."

"I will after I do this." Tom reached into his pants pocket but before he could pull out whatever was in there he felt the hard jab of Ben's nightstick in his back.

"Mission accomplished?" said Charlie when Tom returned to the Camaro.

Jaw clenched, Tom spat out, "Not yet."

The Ascent

The next morning at the Ballyvaughan Inn Tom was still sleeping while Charlie Cubbage was on the phone to the National Weather Service for current meteorological data. Charlie made this call on the first of every month. It was a little ritual of his to affirm the structure of passing time lest time seem like clear, fresh water flowing doomed to become brine in the oil-slicked ocean. In the November 22 square of his calendar he had already marked the upcoming 25th anniversary of John Fitzgerald Kennedy's tragic demise in 1963. Charlie revered JFK and had cried over his murder all day every day for a week while Tom had let it roll off his back, being a Nixon man. "The higher they fly, the harder they fall," Tom had said so flippantly that Charlie wanted to slap him hard across the kisser. He didn't slap him, though, because that would have killed their friendship as surely as Oswald's bullets had done a beloved president, albeit the shots came from the grassy knoll as Charlie was mostly sure they did.

But time healed all wounds, surely. It did on a college campus like this one in New England where, although the maples were bare by now, their once-resplendent leaves fallen and burned to ash in the slash pit behind the heating plant, the noble evergreens stood high, mighty, and sempiternal, sheltering their flock of tiny mortal scholars below.

After Tom woke, showered, and shaved the two men had breakfast then strolled across the vast mid-campus greensward. Their pace was slow since Tom leaned heavily on his crutches. "I didn't think I'd say this, Charlie," said Tom, "but I'm happy to be in this precise place at this precise moment in time. Thanks for asking me." Then he spit out the gum he'd been chewing.

Tom led Charlie straight to the Methodist church where he'd been married to Svetlana. Inside, Charlie looked around at the stained glass windows while Tom stood at the altar in deep contemplation. Finally joining Tom at the altar, Charlie stumbled and Tom steadied him with a strong, warm hand. Charlie felt like a bride. Then he thought of Tom's ex-wife Svetlana and he was ashamed.

A man all in black came in the door and offered to answer any of Tom's and Charlie's questions. Tom said, "Are you the rector of the church?" The man said this wasn't a church anymore it was a gay and lesbian student center. "But I was married here," Tom informed him.

Charlie saw that he was still holding Tom's hand from when Tom steadied him and he wondered what the gay and lesbian fellow might be thinking. "I was the best man," Charlie said. The fellow gave Tom and Charlie some brochures which they dropped in a trash can as soon as they were back outdoors where the air wasn't so musty.

Next stop was the river. It was wide and still here but farther down it narrowed and there was a bridge across it and a half mile or so farther on there was a dam where the water backed up and poured over the top and plunged down to the rocks below like Niagara Falls and just about as loud. Townie boys used to jump from the bridge and float downstream with the current. One boy dropped over that dam one day. He shouted for help but his pals couldn't hear him with the thundering water.

In the boathouse it was quiet and the canoes were up on their racks. Tom tried taking one down but its weight was too much for his bad leg so Charlie helped him. In the old days Tom hefted these canoes with ease, laughing off Charlie's offers of assistance.

The river was a mirror, the realm of heaven upon its surface with a dark, drowned world below. In the canoe the two men were like water bugs, poised by surface tension between the two.

Tom eased the canoe out. He and Charlie had paddled up to the river's source in the autumn of their senior year. Or rather Tom alone paddled since Charlie lost the feeling in his arms after twenty minutes' straining against the southward flow. But Tom stroked on like an Iroquois. It turned out that Charlie had a heart condition.

"How can a church go out of business?" Tom now said. In his mind he was still back on that altar with Svetlana his bride. Great gal, Svetlana, an exchange student at Skidmore when he met her, now the lion keeper at the world famous Novosibirsk Zoo. Tom lost his heart to her at a mixer dance after it had snowed two feet the day before. The advent of coeducation stopped the mixers but in the old days buses rolled up to Ballyvaughan on Saturday nights from the women's colleges and the young men stood outside the buses and the women walked through the men like through a medieval gauntlet. The men didn't say a word, they just ogled all those beautiful women in their muffs with their breaths puffing white and hot in the wintertime air. At Tom and Svetlana's wedding Charlie dropped the ring, watched it roll down the floor toward a heating grate, dove, grabbed, caught it! Beautiful ceremony, perfect marriage, gorgeous family. Then Svetlana got disenchanted and walked out. The best laid plans, eh? Charlie never married, fearing he couldn't take what might happen, not with his heart.

"She wasn't a mail order bride, you know," Tom said apropos of nothing.

"Who?"

"Svetlana. I get that all the time: 'Oh, you answered a magazine ad for hot, lonely Moscow cuties, didn't you, Tom.' Hell I did, Charlie!"

"I never said that, Tom."

"These jealous bastards don't know Moscow's nowhere near Novosibirsk." Tom paddled on upstream, but listlessly now, with doleful, grieving strokes, as if the river ran with the thick congealed blood of his ex-wife's faithless heart.

"At least the church you married her in is still standing," Charlie said blithely. "They didn't tear it down."

Tom said, "Better if they did."

Tom paddled a while more then stopped paddling and the current brought the canoe downstream again. Back onshore the men went to the alumni luncheon. Curried chicken was served. Why? That was Indian food, why serve Indian food at an American college with deep Irish roots? Tom ate a few bites then stopped eating. He offered Charlie what was left on his plate, except for the mango chutney which he gobbled. Charlie's tongue was throbbing from the curry he had already eaten so he declined his friend's offer of more curry. Finally the plates were taken away and coffee was served with a good American crêpe suzette dessert.

Licking his lips and clearing his throat, Dr. Loeb, at the place of honor in the middle of the head table, stood up, went to the podium, and started to speak. "As Hitler rose to power in the 1930s my Jewish parents refused to leave Germany," he began. "All their friends in Leipzig were fleeing the country and they begged my parents to depart also. My parents told them: Some of us must stay behind to show *der Führer* that we will not be destroyed without a fight."

The room was silent. Usually, speakers at a banquet start off with a joke but Dr. Loeb wasn't joking. "Can you all hear me?" he said. His voice boomed through the speakers. Everybody nodded. "You see, my parents were in the German Resistance. In 1942 they aided German conspirators in a plot to assassinate Hitler. But the plot was discovered by the Gestapo and its leaders were imprisoned and executed. My parents, though, evaded capture and took me with them into hiding.

"We lived then for several months in a tiny basement somewhere in the city. No windows, no toilet. We relieved ourselves in the small yard in the back, spending just a few minutes out there in the darkness of the night.

"My mother was a marvel. She'd brought fabrics and an oil lamp and made a little home out of the place. But my father grew more and more depressed. He lay on the floor most of the day, his eyes milky, his lush dark brown hair going suddenly gray. When he did stand he paced in a circle for a long while in one direction then turned and went the other way. What little food we had came from a sympathetic and courageous German woman who dropped a packet down the air shaft every couple of days. But my father barely ate. Such a strong, brave man now so hopeless and weak. He'd put so much into the plot to kill Hitler, he'd staked his whole life and hopes on that, and when the attempt failed he lost all interest in staying alive."

Dr. Loeb stopped talking and took a drink of water. He dabbed his eyes with a finger like he had moved himself to tears. He looked at the water glass like it was a crystal ball then resumed his sorry saga. He was still droning on a half hour later when Charlie checked his watch, wondering what in hell point this man was trying to make. Charlie had expected a fundraising tub-thumper or a musing on the educational ideal. This was folklore instead, and of a particularly morbid type.

Tom sat red-faced, shaking his head. His face streamed sweat. He inhaled repeatedly with a hee-haw sound like he was having a heart attack. "Loeb's a liar," Tom whispered. "His father wasn't in the German Resistance."

"What do you mean?"

"There wasn't any German Resistance. In France, Poland, Holland, Norway there was resistance, highly organized and coordinated. But in Germany it was just intellectuals here and there and a few impotent little groups. To call German resistance a Resistance movement with a capital R is wrong, just wrong. What happened to the Jews in Germany the Jews let happen. They lay down one by one, they didn't stand up together and fight."

Charlie's belly squawked. Damn curry. He wanted to bolt the premises but he couldn't move right or left as he and Tom were in the dead center of a long row of grads all perched forward, enraptured by this rehashing of a world conflict long since resolved.

"Then one day a wondrous thing happened," Loeb continued, his voice suddenly tighter and higher pitched. "My father awoke, jumped to his feet and asked me to go on a walk with him. A walk? I said. Where? I was puzzled because we never left that basement except for those brief backyard outings. 'We live in a beautiful city, Amos,' Abba said to me. 'We have never appreciated it as we should. It has probably grown more beautiful since we have been dithering away our time in this grotto of ours. It is winter now and the streets will be glazed with frost and the lindens will be decked in snow. Let us go and have a look.' I didn't argue and he opened the door and led me up the stairs and out the front door of the building. Well, it wasn't winter, it was July and the lindens were decked with pulverized stone and plaster dust from the Allied bombings and the rubble-chocked streets were piled with corpses. Abba looked around and smiled. 'Ah, home,' he said. Then he took off his cap which his own father had given him and he threw that cap high in the air and it flew in a great arc and came down and landed on a lamppost, the only still-standing lamppost as far as I could see. 'Dead ringer, Abba,' I said to him as he stood there grinning with real pride like a kid who'd won a carnival game. And so here was this man, just a week before he committed suicide, who was finally catching some luck."

Tom cackled snidely, loudly enough so everyone in the audience could hear. All eyes turned toward him. Dr. Loeb made no sign that he'd heard the rude sound. He just stood gazing beatifically over his now-hushed flock.

"Now," Tom said through clenched teeth.

"Now what?"

"I've got to do what I came here to do. I've got to do it now."

"He hasn't finished his speech. Catch him afterward."

"No! Now!" Tom bolted toward the aisle, clambering over two dozen pairs of knees, shins, and feet. In the aisle he charged toward the dais, his right hand in his right pants pocket. He was a yard short of Loeb when Ben grabbed him from behind.

"Where the hell are you going?" Ben said.

"Me?"

"Get back to your seat."

"In a moment."

"Siddown. Now!"

As Ben pulled Tom away from the dais, Dr. Loeb dropped his microphone and without another word stepped away from the lectern and walked out the exit door.

"Who are these people?" Tom said as he and Charlie filed outdoors with their jowly classmates and their plain wives. Loeb roared by them in his Porsche 911, rushing back to the president's mansion. "Midlife crisis," Tom snarled, flipping off the rakish vehicle, which was a bit self-righteous considering Tom's own flaming red muscle car.

Tom and Charlie wandered onto the campus green where a big crane was hoisting railroad ties and the nimble freshmen were bounding up and down the rising bonfire pyramid like ape men. It was late fall but the sun glared like July. Charlie shielded his eyes from the sun but Tom stared straight at it. "You'll scorch your retina," Charlie clucked like a hen. But he'd learned his lesson peeking at that eclipse the year before and that was why he couldn't drive at night anymore.

"What did you say?" Tom said.

"I said batter up," replied Charlie, leading Tom away from the pyramid, past the college museum (mastodon bones and Indian artifacts mostly), around the tennis courts, and finally to the baseball diamond. Here Tom perked up a bit. He bounded to the pitcher's mound and toed the rubber. Charlie scooted to shortstop. "He's a whiffer!" Charlie chirped like a damn Little Leaguer which is all he ever was. Tom looked in for a sign. As a college senior he'd pitched three no-hitters and the scouts had showed up in packs. The Red Sox offered him a contract but he turned it down. "How can you turn down a major league career?" Charlie asked him at the time.

"You know what kind of lives ballplayers lead, Charlie? On the road all the time, never seeing their kids?"

That's when Charlie realized Tom's main goal in life was to be a family man. He became one but then it all went bust. What if he'd stayed with his pitching? A sports team is a family of sorts, he might have been very satisfied. Charlie thought Svetlana was behind Tom's reluctance to turn pro. On his own Tom would have played ball. Still, Charlie's hat was off to all family men, it was the noblest and gladdest adventure going, he'd just never gotten the call.

The minutes went by and Tom kept looking in for that sign. It was like life itself was in the batter's box and last time up it had clipped his heater for extra bases. Now he didn't know what to throw. Rain started falling, out of nowhere. "Game called," Charlie said, patting Tom on the rump.

They sat in the dugout and Tom unwrapped a new stick of gum. In college he'd chewed tobacco. He'd chewed it until he met Svetlana who outlawed it. Tom now tore the gum wrapper in two pieces then tore these two into four. "You know how my dad died, Charlie?"

"He died? When did he die?"

"Last month, he killed himself, bullet through the head."

Two fathers killing themselves, Dr. Loeb's and now Tom's. "He was a ballplayer, you know," said Tom. "A pitcher, he played pro." Charlie did know this, Tom had told him many times and had shown him photos of his father in the uniform of a Red Sox minor league affiliate. "He killed a man once with a pitch."

"No." Tom had never told Charlie *that*.

"Dad was a fireballer, short relief. The Sox were in a pennant fight, they were going to call him up for the stretch drive. His life's dream was coming true." Tom had now torn the gum wrapper into sixty-fourths, at least. "You don't want to hear this, Charlie."

"Yes, I do."

"In his last game in Triple-A he gave up a home run and his manager told him to bean the next batter. He said no. The manager said then forget about going up to the big leagues. So Dad drilled the guy in the ear, Dominican guy, had a wife and two kids. Good base-stealer, great glove, now he was dead."

"No."

"I will never lie to you, Charlie."

"Was your dad charged?"

"Not officially, but he was guilty in his head. And he thought he had to pay. He figured you take life from one man, you've got to take your own someday. Bullshit, eh? I could've told him that was bullshit, I *should've* told him but I didn't. If I'd have slapped some sense into that sonofabitch I wouldn't be an orphan today."

"Did he make it to the majors?"

"For exactly one day."

"What happened?"

"Tore his rotator cuff, had surgery, but his old fastball was a floater afterwards. So he quit the game, figured this was how the ending for a sinner like him should be. But he didn't believe that obviously. A sore shoulder didn't end things like they needed to be ended so last month with his Bauer Automatic he found a better way."

What a disaster this trip was turning out to be. And all Charlie's fault. Reminding his friend of the good old times was only showing him what he'd lost. Charlie should have known it would. "We're out of here," Tom said.

Charlie thought Tom meant they should drive back home immediately but Tom headed for the campus green where a huge construction crane was hoisting the last railroad tie for the topper to the pyramid. The rain had stopped and the sun had come back out.

"Who are these assholes?" Ben Marble wondered about the two men as they passed his car on their way to the pyramid. He recognized the bigger of the two as the nut who'd rushed up the aisle a half-hour ago at the banquet. He was the same guy who'd harangued Dr. Loeb last night at the mansion until Ben stopped him with a jab of his nightstick while the guy in the Camaro blipped the throttle like a getaway driver keeping the revs up for a quick escape.

40

Right now the big guy, still in his walking boot, leaning on crutches, waved at the kids up on the pyramid. "Need a hand?" he shouted.

"Sure!" they shouted back.

Ben figured what was this old gimp going to do, skitter up there like Spiderman? "Hold these," the gimp said and handed his pal his crutches.

"Don't do this," the pal said but the gimp started climbing, hopping up with his good leg and dragging the other behind. If he fell, which looked likely, he'd be a dead man.

"Get back down here!" Ben shouted as he jumped from his car. It wasn't Ben's job to monitor the pyramid construction, the campus police should be doing that. Ben was a private security guard with one mission, to protect Dr. Loeb. But if this nutcase alpinist fell off the pyramid and died, Dr. Loeb, as president of this institution, could be sued for criminal negligence. It was Ben's sworn duty to protect Loeb from that. He gripped his holstered gun.

"Don't shoot," said the climber's accomplice.

"What's your name?" Ben asked him.

"Charlie Cubbage, Class of '71."

"Who's Spiderman up there?"

"He's my friend."

"What's his name?"

"Tom."

"Tom, get off that pyramid!" Tom kept climbing. Maybe he thought Ben was barking at some other Tom. "What's his last name?" Ben asked Charlie.

"Dunraven."

"Tom Dunraven!" Ben hollered as Tom reached the halfway point. Charlie said Tom Dunraven was deaf in one ear so he probably couldn't hear Ben calling him. Ben called louder: "Tom Dunraven, get down here this minute!" He felt like a mom calling her kid home for dinner.

Charlie feared that Tom would fall and land on his head. He wouldn't die but he'd be paralyzed. Charlie would move in with him as his nursemaid. Tom would pee through a rubber hookup into a receptacle. He'd be unable to swallow food so Charlie would feed him through tubes. Charlie would sponge bathe him and change his pajamas and read him the news at night. And each day doctors would poke needles into Tom to test his nerve endings.

Tom reached the top. He stood with his feet spread wide, pounding his chest like the ape on the Empire State Building. The crane was now hoisting the last railroad tie and it dangled near Tom's head, about to brain him. Charlie couldn't look. He turned away but turned back when the freshmen cheered Tom as he corralled the railroad tie and set it in position without assistance. Now the pyramid was finished. Tom whooped. A wind gusted up. Tom teetered in the gust but kept his balance and began dancing a little jig. The freshmen danced with him. They all sang "Boys and Belles of Ballyvaughan," Tom omitting the "Belles." It was almost mystical. The sun was a ball of molten lava and the pyramid glowed red like it was burning already. Tom stood proud and tall on the summit like a colossus. Then the students started back down and a couple of them helped Tom descend.

"What are you, crazy?" Ben said to him when he was on terra firma.

"Ask my friend Charlie. He knows me better than I know myself."

Tom's pants were ripped, he'd lost a shoe, and he stank of creosote. The sunset had turned purple like beef liver. Charlie explained to Ben that he and Tom had been roommates all through their years at Ballyvaughan. Now two decades later, they were still best friends.

Ben asked Tom if he'd been drinking. Tom shook his head. Ben asked if he was on any medications.

Charlie answered for his friend: "Tom doesn't take any medications. He doesn't even see doctors because if you go in for one thing they always find something worse."

"He must have seen a doctor about his foot," said Ben, indicating Tom's crutches and walking boot.

Charlie said, "Yes, and it was only sprained when he went in."

"There was a hairline fracture," said Tom.

"On the x-ray," said Charlie. "But whose x-ray? Maybe it was switched, or the doctor doctored it."

Tom patted Charlie's head and said to Ben, "My friend is a cynical bastard."

"Skeptical," Charlie corrected him. "Healthily skeptical."

Ben asked Charlie if he himself had been drinking. Charlie said he hadn't had a drop. Tom chuckled. "It was a Virgin Mary," Charlie snapped at him.

"Time for a real one," said Tom. He suggested the three of them go to the Ballyvaughan Inn bar for cocktails. Charlie said it was too early for cocktails. Tom said it was never too early. Ben told the men he was on duty so he couldn't drink. Ten minutes later they were at the bar drinking.

"What the hell was last night all about?" Ben asked them.

"Last night where?" Tom responded.

"At the president's mansion, you ripping into Dr. Loeb like that."

"He and I are old friends, we go way back."

"You looked like mortal enemies, I thought you were going to take him down. You're lucky I didn't shoot you on sight."

"You ever do that?" Charlie asked Ben.

"Do what?"

"Shoot someone on sight."

"I used to be a cop in a big tough city, what do you think?"

"What's it like being a cop?"

"If I told you I'd have to kill you."

"No, really. I've always wondered about the life of a law enforcement officer."

"You tell me your life first."

So Charlie did, in brief, with emphasis on his years at Ballyvaughan and his lingering fondness for the place which brought him back to Autumn Inferno year after year.

"What about you, Tom?" said Ben.

"I don't come back anymore."

"You're back now."

"This is my first time since Loeb became president."

"Why did you stop when Loeb became president?"

"Because he fucked the place up."

The Attack

Back in their room at the inn Charlie had to pee badly from the cocktails but Tom was in the bathroom. He'd been in there for ten minutes. Charlie knocked on the door. "You coming out?"

No answer.

"I'm coming in." Charlie opened the door and went in. Tom was on the can. He was shirtless. On his stomach was a tattoo of a peach blossom. What that signified Charlie couldn't begin to fathom. So close to this man and still so much Charlie didn't know. Then Charlie saw the knife in Tom's right hand. It looked about a foot long. "My God, Tom, what's that?"

"Full tang Damascus steel Bowie hunting knife. Beauty, eh? Rosewood handle, crazy engraving all over the sides of the blade. Have a look."

"What are you doing with it?"

"I haven't done it yet."

"Done what?"

"What I said I'd do. As you've seen, I've been trying but so far no luck."

"I thought you were kidding."

"I don't kid."

"That crap about hurting Dr. Loeb, I assumed that was a joke."

"I never joke."

"I didn't think you were serious."

"I'm always serious."

"Have you gone crazy?"

"Maybe."

"Are you off your meds?"

"They do no good."

"All right, enough. Stop. You are not going to hurt Dr. Loeb."

"Not until I get the angle."

"Give that to me."

"Later."

"Now, Tom. Give me that knife."

"I'll give it to you when I come back." Tom stood and flushed the toilet and left the bathroom, still holding the knife.

Charlie followed him. "Where are you going?"

Tom waved out the window at the rally. "Where do you think?"

"No."

"I came here to do one thing, Charlie."

"No!"

"One more try, Charlie. One more try."

Tom bolted from the room. Charlie dashed after him and glimpsed him disappearing into the elevator. Charlie took the stairs to the lobby but when he got there Tom was not to be seen.

Charlie ran outdoors. The bonfire leaped at the sky. The glee club was crooning on the steps of Founders' Hall and Dr. Loeb, ablaze in floodlight, standing on a little platform and holding a microphone, was leading the roistering throng in singing the college anthem. Charlie ran toward Loeb.

"You again," said Ben, darting out of the crowd and blocking Charlie's way.

"Stop him!" cried Charlie.

"Who?"

"My friend Tom! He's got a knife!"

Now Chief Roby appeared. "What's the trouble here, Marble?"

"Nothing, I've got this covered."

"He's got a knife!" Charlie spluttered to Roby.

"Who does? Marble?"

"No, my friend Tom Dunraven, and he's going to use it!"

"Use it on who?" Roby said.

"On Dr. Loeb!"

Tom's head bobbed above the crowd. "Look!" Charlie said, pointing. "There he is! Get him!"

Ben broke toward Tom but his way was blocked by the tightly packed crowd. Charlie tried to bolt but Roby held him fast.

"Amos!" Ben shouted. Dr. Loeb saw Ben and waved. "Get away! Run!"

"What, Ben?"

"Get out of there, Amos!"

Loeb was cupping his ear, grinning.

"Right now, Amos! Go!" Ben made a last, desperate thrust to reach Loeb, cleaving the crowd with his fists and elbows before disappearing in its midst.

After a moment Ben reappeared, leaping onto the platform and yanking Loeb out of his spotlight then shoving him off the little stage, out of harm's way. A few seconds later Ben followed Loeb into the surrounding darkness to assure his safety.

Abruptly, there was a cry—Loeb's cry, shocked, agonized. The crowd surged toward the appalling sound, and from the crowd then burst sickened, horrified shouts: 'No! Oh, *no! Oh, NOOOO!"*

A flashlight beam, Ben's, illuminated Loeb flat on his back, blood oozing at his groin area through a ragged tear in his pants. Loeb groaned, fluttered his eyelids, gasped for breath—was he reviving? No, his eyes remained dilated in Ben's light and his breathing slackened.

Ben cursed himself aloud for arriving too late to thwart Tom Dunraven's assault. Where was Dunraven right now? Had he escaped? No, he was surely tight within Chief Roby's iron grip.

A violent tremor jolted Loeb. He coughed, he choked. Ben cocked open the stiffened jaw, thrust in his thumb and forefinger, pulled up the tongue that had slid back down the pharynx. Loeb's pulse was barely discernible. His eyes said "Save me, Ben" but as Ben gave him lip-to-lip resuscitation he upchucked in Ben's mouth.

Ben deserved the fetid rebuke. Protecting the college's president was his one and only responsibility and he had failed to meet it utterly, and potentially fatally. Worse, he had betrayed the trust that Loeb had placed in him to safeguard his life. If Loeb died, Ben would almost feel that he himself was the killer.

An ambulance's siren wailed. Ben saw its red flashing lights. Two medics arrived with a stretcher. "Get away," said one. Ben refused to leave Dr. Loeb. The other medic hoisted Ben to his feet and shoved him aside. Ben shoved him back and they tussled until Chief Roby appeared and pulled them apart. "Go home, Marble," Roby snapped.

"You get him, Chief?" Ben said.

Roby didn't answer.

Ben persisted: "The man with the knife, Tom Dunraven, you got him, right?"

"I said go home, Marble."

"Where is he? And his friend Charlie? Did you let him go? They were in this together. I know because they told me."

Loeb was on the stretcher now but the gawking crowd blocked the medics' way to the ambulance. Roby barked at the people to disperse but they just crammed in tighter, parting only when Roby brandished his nightstick like a machete as if hacking away jungle undergrowth.

The End

Roby had not captured Tom Dunraven. The man had simply vanished and Roby, who'd been holding onto his accomplice Charlie, had for some reason let Charlie go. As for Loeb, he'd been castrated but was still alive in the ICU at Glenfarne Hospital.

Ben haunted the hospital in ensuing days, cadging tidbits of news on Dr. Loeb's condition as they leaked out. The gist was that Loeb was critical but stable. The medics had recovered his severed genitals and the hospital had deep frozen them and would try reattaching them when Amos was out of the woods. The only problem was that none of the hospital surgeons had done one of these reattachments before. They would have to get somebody from Boston or New York but even then the procedure would be chancy. A reattached member was sometimes completely without feeling. Sometimes it withered from insufficient flow of blood. Sometimes it became infected and the patient died of septic shock. These were not hopeful prognoses but Dr. Loeb, in addition to being a towering intellect, was endowed with very great physical strength. Best case he'd be up and fully functioning in a few weeks' time. Worst case they'd fit him with a catheter and he'd be moderately inconvenienced but in no way unable to continue as college president. Ben's money was on best case. If Ben knew Amos he'd pull through good as new, maybe better. One could pray for such an outcome if one was so inclined. If not then one could live on hope.

On December 1, 1988, one month after Dr. Loeb was attacked, Ben received a call from the hospital: Loeb wanted to see him. It was urgent. Ben rushed right over.

The desk directed Ben to the fourth floor. He found Loeb lying unconscious on his bed. He looked dead but Ben trusted that he was merely sleeping.

The doctor walked in. His name was Dr. Oufkir. Ben said Oufkir was a strange name. The doctor said it was Moroccan. He'd been born in Marrakesh but had moved with his family to Rabat when he was six years old, possibly seven years old. Had Ben ever been to Morocco? No, Ben said, but he would like to go. But more importantly, how was Dr. Loeb?

"Up and down," said Dr. Oufkir. Ben thought he meant up walking then down sleeping but he meant up and down with his vital signs. He hadn't done any walking yet.

Dr. Loeb remained inert while the doctor and Ben were talking. He wasn't in a coma, Dr. Oufkir said, he was just asleep. "He asked me to come to him," Ben said.

"Yes, he did," said Dr. Oufkir. "And then he conked out."

"Can he hear us?" Ben asked.

Dr. Oufkir said who knows what people can hear while they are sleeping? There are medical researchers who study that sort of thing but he was not one of them.

Ben leaned down to the bed. "Dr. Loeb?" he whispered. "Amos?" Loeb's right eyelid fluttered. "I think he hears me, Dr. Oufkir."

"His face twitches irregularly," said Dr. Oufkir. "It's reflex, from his medications."

A nurse brought in a tray of food—a single slice of white bread, a pat of margarine, and a tiny paper cup of apple juice. Ben didn't know why Dr. Loeb was being brought solid nourishment while he was on an IV drip. Dr. Oufkir didn't know either. "Who's that food for?" he snapped at the nurse.

"Room 402," she said.

"This is 502," Oufkir said which surprised Ben since Ben knew they were on the fourth floor not the fifth. "Are you new here, nurse?" said the doctor.

"No."

"How long have you worked here? I don't recognize you."

"I've been here fourteen years."

"Take this away." The nurse left with the tray. She seemed about to cry.

Dr. Loeb's eyes opened at that moment. Ben touched his hand. Loeb muttered something that sounded like "food." Ben asked him if he'd said "food." Loeb seemed to nod his head. Ben asked Dr. Oufkir to bring back the nurse with the tray. The doctor refused. "Amos?" Ben said, breathlessly. "It's me, Ben."

"Hello, Ben."

Ben gasped with relief.

"I'll leave you two," said Dr. Oufkir. But before he left he checked the drip and the other monitors then took off his blue surgical gloves and his mask and dropped them in the waste receptacle. He looked at the clock and checked it against his watch. He smacked his watch as if it wasn't running. "What time is it?" he asked Ben. Ben hadn't the faintest. His own watch had stopped long ago. "Nurse!" the doctor shouted out the door. No one answered. Dr. Oufkir departed the room, cursing in Arabic.

"I'm hungry, Ben," said Dr. Loeb.

"A nurse was just here with food."

"Where did she go?"

"She took it away. The doctor told her to."

"Why?"

"Because you're on a drip."

"What doctor?"

"Oufkir."

"Who?"

"Oufkir, he grew up in Marrakesh then moved to Rabat."

"That guy." Dr. Loeb seemed to have an opinion on the doctor in question but he didn't share it with Ben.

The nurse returned. She still had the tray with the bread etc. "I had the right room after all," she said. She set the tray on Dr. Loeb's bed table.

"What's this?" Loeb said. The nurse said it was his dinner.

"This is *dinner?*" She shrugged and hurried back out of the room. Dr. Loeb fingered the bread.

"Easy, Dr. Loeb," Ben said. "Lie back down."

"How long was I out?"

"I don't know."

"It's morning now, right?"

"Yes. No. It doesn't matter. How do you feel?"

"Great."

"Nurse!" No nurse. Dr. Loeb picked up the bread. "It's poisoned."

"What is?"

"The bread."

"How could it be poisoned? This is a hospital."

"Then you eat it."

"I've had my dinner."

"Liar." Loeb was right, Ben hadn't had dinner and he was hungry because it was dinnertime. "Who ordered this shit?"

"You don't want it? I'll call for something different."

"Good luck."

Ben stood and went to the door and looked out in the hall to find Loeb's nurse or any nurse. The hall was deserted, including the nurses' desk. Ben returned to Loeb. "You're feeling fine now, aren't you? You look fine, like nothing happened, like nothing happened at all. You look like you could jump out of that bed and walk with me right out the door and then you know what we'd do?"

"This is insulting." Dr. Loeb was still fixated on the bread. "Who do they think they're feeding here, a rodent?"

"You have an appetite, that's a good sign."

"Of what?"

"That your condition is improving."

"Tell my dick."

"You'll feel better when you eat."

"I could eat a bucket of General Tso's Chicken with a side of Kung Pao Shrimp."

"Ha-ha, you must be feeling better."

"What do *you* want, Ben?"

"I'm not hungry." Ben was starving.

"Get yourself some bean buns, my treat."

"Bean buns, mmm, like you made for me once."

"When?"

"Remember? When I came over that night?"

"Oh, yes. You hated them."

"I did not *hate* them."

"You took one bite and spat out the rest."

"I was car sick."

"You were not in a car."

"I'd been in a car all day, my patrol car."

"It probably needs new shocks."

"Hey, I'm disturbing you, keeping you from sleeping. You need your sleep."

"I need food."

"I'll call the nurse for more bread."

"Fuck the nurse. Fuck more bread." His medications were untethering the poor man. "Ben. Go get me some food. Real food. Hunan style, hot as it can get so it scalds my tongue and burns holes in my gut. And get me a beer."

"When you're better."

"Now. Tsingtao. Tsingtao Beer."

"They won't let you drink beer."

"Pour it in my drip bag."

"I'll see what I can do."

"Get going."

But Ben didn't dare get going, Dr. Loeb might expire before he returned so he had to keep watch over him. Of course Loeb couldn't really eat anything solid yet anyway. "NOTHING BY MOUTH" was right there on his chart. And yet they'd brought him bread and butter. Well, that could have been meant for another patient. It would be a

53

typical hospital slipup, no wonder there was such a high rate of iatrogenic illnesses in these places. Or maybe the chart was wrong and Dr. Loeb could eat what he wanted, though that probably didn't include Chinese takeout.

"There's a place called Jade Wok on Larch Street," said Dr. Loeb. "Where's Larch Street?"

Ben named a town south of Glenfarne and said Larch Street was just off the main drag there. That was a good long way from the hospital, down the road by the river and over the bridge a mile or so before the dam then a few more miles down the other side of the river.

"Dr. Loeb, your doctor needs to sign off on what you can and can't eat."

"Jade Wok makes killer bean buns. The best I ever ate."

The thought of bean buns made Ben literally salivate. "You're shaking, Dr. Loeb."

"So are you."

"You look like you're having a low blood sugar attack."

Ben was the one having the attack. He needed calories quick. Eating Dr. Loeb's bread was no option as by now Loeb had pulled it apart and kneaded it into doughy clumps. "All right, I'll go," Ben said. But he just stood there.

"Well? Get a move on."

"I'm afraid to leave you."

"I'll be fine."

"What if you need something?"

"I'll call the nurse."

"What if you fall unconscious?"

"I'm wide awake."

"You could have a seizure." Ben's stomach growled.

"You're the one having a seizure."

"Oh, that's so *you*, Dr. Loeb. Worrying about *me* when *you're* the one in the hospital bed."

"It's because I love you, Ben."

Ben blushed. "No, you don't."

"I do."

"I'm not worthy."

"After what you did for me in Boston? You're worthy."

"I appreciate that but—"

"Chopsticks, Ben. Don't forget chopsticks."

"Okay, Amos, okay, I'll be quick."

"Jade Wok closes early on Sundays, hurry."

"It's Saturday."

"Hell it is."

"Okay, I'll hurry."

Ben shook Dr. Loeb's hand then left the room.

The Jade Wok was a dumpy little joint. Several sections of its sign's neon tubing were blown out so that "JA OK" was what it now said, which made Ben want to enter the place goose-stepping.

He ordered the General Tso's Chicken and two bean buns then remembered the Kung Pao Shrimp and added that to the order. They were out of Kung Pao Shrimp, though—the first time a Chinese restaurant had ever been out of anything in Ben's experience—so he substituted Orange Flavored Shrimp but was told they were out of shrimp period so he went for the Szechuan Scallops. They didn't have bean buns, either, and they didn't have anything to substitute for that so Ben just forgot about getting something sweet. He ordered a Tsingtao beer but was told they didn't sell beer because they didn't have a liquor license but Ben could get beer at the liquor store around the block. Ben reminded them to put chopsticks in the bag.

Back in the car Ben took the two fortune cookies out of the bag and ate them both. He had to, he was feeling hypoglycemic. He'd tell Dr. Loeb that they'd forgotten to give him fortune cookies. Ben didn't usually read the fortunes in fortune cookies but this time he did. One said, "Only three things woman need in life: food, water, compliments." The other said, "The bigger the voice, the smaller the brain." Lame! Those weren't fortunes, they were aphorisms. In the old days fortune cookies foretold the future, they didn't just fob you off with some cheesy observation. Back then they hired respected Chinese writers to write the fortunes and they'd be pithy gems of prophecy, auguring sudden fortune or looming calamity, always with a tinge of classic Oriental wit. As a result they were tickling and chilling, allusive and elusive all at once. Now the cookie makers didn't care, they paid five bucks for five hundred "fortunes" to any unemployed copywriter off the street, whether he was Chinese or not. Hell, Ben himself could do this work right now and he wasn't even a published writer, just a washed-up ex-cop.

Ben drove to the liquor store but couldn't find it. It wasn't around the block, or at least the block Ben thought the JA OK woman meant. Finally after a long drive he found a liquor store but it was boarded up and cordoned with yellow crime scene ribbon. Ben didn't know this neighborhood. In fact he barely knew this town at all, it was way south of Glenfarne, outside his professional bailiwick. Maybe this wasn't the town Loeb had directed him to at all. It might be in a different county. Ben felt light years from Glenfarne by this point even though he could still hear the water thundering over the dam on the river and that dam was only a mile south of the college. Ben didn't have GPS in his car because GPS hadn't been invented yet and he didn't feel like asking for help from the two hooded bruisers huddling in a doorway smoking something that certainly wasn't filter-tipped cigarettes. So he drove on, trying to retrace his route back to JA OK, not to consult them again but just to return to more familiar, somewhat less threatening territory where he might ask better directions from a fresh, attractive young couple pushing a baby carriage, or a good Irish policeman walking his beat.

No luck. After ten minutes of driving in what he thought was a beeline back to JA OK Ben found himself back upstream where the mill pond piled up wide, deep, and still behind the dam before it crashed over it. Somehow Ben had left the main route and taken a side road toward the riverbank. There was no barrier here blocking him from driving into the drink and no lights anywhere so he didn't see the river until it was almost too late. This little road, which was now just a dirt track, didn't end here; it continued and became a downsloping put-in ramp for boats. Why wasn't there a barrier or at least a sign warning the unwary motorist? Ben was partway down the ramp before he realized he was heading for the water. He burned rubber full-throttling in reverse to safety.

Someone tapped Ben's car window, a man in a black suit and black tie with a bright red pocket square, and wearing a French style beret. The man's presence was so incongruous and even menacing that Ben didn't open the window, even though as a Boston cop he'd faced and neutralized much worse menaces hundreds of times.

The man spoke but Ben couldn't hear him from his side of the window so it was lucky that he was instinctively an expert lip reader. "Need some help?" Ben saw the man say.

"Liquor store," Ben mouthed exaggeratedly.

"Two blocks back, first right, under the overpass, then first left after the third set of lights."

The man was right. The LIQUER (sic) LOKCER (sic) sign welcomed Ben with a flickering phosphorescence. Ben knew he could get in and out of this place quickly because the parking lot was totally empty.

He took a single bottle of Tsingtao from the cooler and brought it to the checkout counter. "ID?" the kid there said.

"ID? Are you serious?" Ben was about to ask him for his own ID, the whelp looked twelve or thirteen at most. "I'm a policeman, I'll have you know, young man."

"You got proof?"

Ben tapped his Security Guard badge. He noticed by the clock on the wall that he'd been gone from the hospital for almost an hour. Dr. Loeb could have died and gone to heaven and returned from the dead in less time than that. While the boy scrutinized Ben's badge Ben felt like a naughty adolescent buying booze under false pretenses. And then he felt like a cop again, or a security guard who used to be a cop, and it was all he could do not to clout this little prick with his nightstick on his greasy head. The boyo sold Ben the beer.

Ben chugged that beer in the car, he was so parched and in need of its sedative effects. But they weren't sedative enough so Ben went back in the store and bought a whole six-pack. The brat looked at his badge again like he hadn't just been in here already. In the car Ben drank two more bottles which made him sure he could navigate his way back to the hospital without having to stop for directions at every other streetlight.

He drove fast so the Chinese food wouldn't be cold when he got back to Dr. Loeb. At the hospital he took the elevator to Loeb's floor. When he entered his room he saw a new nurse drawing the curtain around the bed. "What's happening?" Ben said.

"Nothing, I'm taking his temperature."

"Is he worse?"

"He'll be fine, you have a seat." The nurse went behind the curtain.

"Let me see him."

"In a minute."

"Now."

A doctor came into the room, not Dr. Oufkir. "How are we doing?" he asked Ben.

"*I'm* not the patient." The doctor chuckled and went behind the curtain. "Hey! Doctor! What's going on? Is Dr. Loeb all right?"

An orderly came in with a clean, shiny bedpan. He sniffed the air. "Mm, Kung Pao Shrimp."

"No, they were out of shrimp." The orderly went behind the curtain. Another orderly appeared wheeling a large monitoring device of some sort. He also went behind the curtain. Now the whole world was behind that curtain. You'd think this was a ship's stateroom in a Marx Brothers movie.

The monitor started beeping. A chaplain entered the room. Ben blocked his way to the bed. "Why are you here, Father?"

The cleric tapped his Bible. "I'm late," he said, and joined the others behind the curtain.

Ben was freaking out. He had to pee from the beers. The monitor's beeping was speeding up and Ben heard the chaplain administering the Sacrament of the Anointing of the Sick. "He's not Christian!" Ben shouted out.

The beeping stopped. After a few moments of silence the doctor came out from behind the curtain. "How is he?" Ben asked him. The man just smiled and patted Ben on the shoulder. Ben tore back the curtain. The priest was making the sign of the cross as he, the orderly, and the nurses huddled around the bed, obscuring Dr. Loeb from Ben's view. The first nurse saw him. "Don't worry, he's not suffering," she said. The second nurse leaned down and put her ear to Dr. Loeb's chest whom Ben still couldn't see clearly. He stepped forward to get a better look at him but the orderly—the *orderly* of all people—held him back. The nurse took a pulse reading then turned to Ben and, brushing away a curl of hair that had fallen across her eye, told him the patient was dead.

That was the end of the world for Ben. Luckily, the dead guy wasn't Loeb after all so the world started up again. Loeb had been moved out of Room 402 and this new guy had been moved in while Ben was out for food. Now Loeb was in Room 502 one floor above. Ben didn't wait for the elevator, he ran up the stairs to the fifth floor and arrived breathless but overjoyed that his friend hadn't bought the farm yet. He was sitting up and watching television. "Guess what just happened," Ben said, giggling.

"Sit down, it's *The Golden Girls.*"

And so all that beautiful Chinese food went cold while Amos fixed on the sitcom and Ben in his chair beside him fell asleep in the soporific TV glow.

It was snowing. Snow usually falls silently but this snow had a loud fuzzing sound ...

Ben bolted awake. The fuzzing snow was the ash storm on the television screen that comes on when the last show of the day is finished. Ben turned off the television. The fuzzing stopped then there was another, softer sound. It was Amos inhaling and exhaling as he slept. Ben sat again at his side. His breaths were like a little bird's. But he wasn't asleep at all, his eyes were wide open but he wasn't looking at anything. Ben took his hand. It was papery, cool, and limp. "Come on, Amos," Ben whispered. "You're going to make it. I'm here. I'll always be here."

Yesterday Loeb's condition had been upgraded from critical to serious but today it was back to critical. His area of injury had become infected and the infection had spread. They hadn't performed the reattachment surgery because he was too weak to survive it. A surgeon from Cornell Medical Center in New York City had agreed to do the reattachment surgery but it wasn't yet time for such surgery and perhaps it never would be.

"Come on, Amos. Come on, Amos." The line on the heart monitor was barely wavy. There should have been doctors in this room but only Ben was in this room. There should have been cardiologists, there should have been infectious diseases specialists, there should have been at least a nurse. Would Ben alone watch this man die?

He would not die. He was Amos Loeb. He hadn't died at Auschwitz. He wouldn't die in Glenfarne, Vermont. "But if you do die," Ben said, "I will catch your killer because I know who he is."

Now the line on the heart monitor was a flat line. And Ben alone saw it. Loeb's hand was quickly cold and his eyes rolled back into his head.

Ben swam out of the room, through a rip current of scrubs-wearing healthcare "professionals" rushing in. Ben meant to tell them they were too late, too late, goodnight ladies, too late, but he didn't bother.

In the car Ben sat frozen stiff in grief. He was silent but there was a tortured howl that was stuck behind his clenched teeth so he flipped on his siren to release it heavenward.

He drove away from the hospital. He aimed toward home but he didn't aim straight, he veered left then right then around and around, rolling by the football stadium, the heating plant, the observatory, and then he was down at the river and he had an idea to get out of the car and walk into the current and float downstream so that eventually, in fact rather soon, he'd swan-dive over the dam and be scooped up by the waterwheel then dumped into the tail race to slide from there to the sea.

But he thought better of it and he drove back up the hill to the campus and his car steered itself past Founders' Hall to the church where the gays God bless their grit and their immaculate hearts took over from the straights. He walked by the check-in desk. The clerk said, checking in, sir? Ben said no, he was here to drink and he beelined to the bar and ordered from Avital Mittelman a double Laphroaig neat and she brought it to him and he drank it in one gulp and he ordered another and when Avital brought the refill she said, "Happy Birthday," and Ben said, "Why did you say that? It's not my birthday." And she said, "You looked depressed, I thought it might cheer you up." And he said yes, he was depressed and she asked him what was wrong and Ben said everything was wrong, and she sat down and said, "I'm guessing something broke your heart," and he said she was right although he knew he shouldn't admit to a broken heart because once a cop did that, once he let his feelings rule his head, he was dead.

"Do you want to talk about it, Ben?"

"The man who attacked Dr. Loeb is now a murderer."

"Dr. Loeb has died?"

Ben nodded.

"Oh, God."

"I'm sorry, Avi."

"Oh, God, oh, God, oh, God."

"It was peaceful."

"You were with him?"

"Yes."

"What did he say?"

"At the end?"

"Was he conscious? Did he speak?"

"Yes, he spoke."

"His last words, what were they?"

Ben had to think. Loeb had told him to be quiet so he could watch a show on television. The show was *The Golden Girls*. "Sit down, it's *The Golden Girls*," Loeb had commanded then had said no more after that.

"He said your name," Ben lied to Avital.

"No. My name? Really?"

"He whispered it."

"You're sure that's what he said?"

"As God is my witness."

Avital dropped her head, first to her hands then into Ben's lap where she broke into sobs. Moments later she straightened back up and wiped her cheeks dry. "You were his friend, Ben."

"You were his friend, too, Avi. A very close one, I know that."

"How did you know?"

"I'm a detective, don't forget."

"You're not a detective anymore."

"The old dog still knows a few tricks."

"How did your friendship with Amos come about?"

Ben was curious about Avital's own bond with Dr. Loeb but he told his story first, about the time he met Loeb in Boston in the Combat Zone which at that time was his beat.

"What's the Combat Zone?" asked Avi.

Ben told her that today it was bright with chic cafés, co-ops, and fashion shops but back then it was where the hookers, pimps, and pushers roamed the streets and therefore where the druggies and the sailors and on some occasions Dr. Amos Loeb hung out.

"He was a junkie?"

"No. Oh, no, not that."

"He frequented the prostitutes?"

Ben nodded. Was Avital not aware of Loeb's philandering? Ben was sorry to be revealing it to her.

"So what happened in the Combat Zone?"

"I think I've said enough."

"Amos argued with a pimp?"

"A little more than that."

"They fought."

"Perhaps."

"Who won?"

"Let's say that he escaped."

"The pimp?"

"No, Amos escaped, with my help."

"And the pimp—"

"—was not so lucky."

"You saw to that."

"I did."

"How? With force?'

Ben nodded.

"What kind of force?"

"I don't want to talk about it."

"Did you put him in a chokehold or something?'

"I should have."

"So what force did you use?"

"More than was needed, it turned out."

"You hit him with your stick."

63

"I should have stopped at that."

"But you didn't. What did you do then? Shoot him? You didn't shoot him."

"He was just a teenager, a scrawny kid."

"You shot him. Did he die?"

"What's the difference?"

"He died. Didn't he."

"What's done is done."

"Was that the first person you ever killed?"

"No."

"How many were there before?"

Ben shrugged.

"Is that why they fired you?

"That's what they said."

"But policemen carry guns for a reason. They have to use them sometimes. That's their duty. It's their right."

"I abused my right, they said."

"Did this teenager have a gun?"

"I thought so."

"So you were in mortal danger."

"I wasn't in danger."

"But he threatened you with a gun."

"He wasn't threatening *me*."

"Who was he threatening?"

Ben didn't answer.

"Dr. Loeb?"

Ben nodded.

"Why? Because Dr. Loeb had threatened *him*?"

"Because Dr. Loeb had threatened his sister."

"His sister, you mean his –"

"His sister, his sister was his prostitute, he was her pimp, that's correct."

"Loeb had threatened her physically?"

"With words."

"So the teenager was defending her."

"Yes."

"With a gun?"

"I thought it was a gun.

"What was it?"

"His finger."

"Finger?"

"Under his coat. It looked like a gun."

"But you felt your life was in danger."

"I felt Dr. Loeb's life was in danger."

"So you did what you had to do."

"It turned out I didn't have to."

"But you didn't know you didn't have to."

"I should have known."

"How?

"The kid was laughing. 'Pow!' he said."

"In that situation that was a risky thing for him to do."

"He was just a kid."

"A pimp. A criminal."

"'Pow! Pow! Pow!' He was pretending. 'Gotcha,' he said." Ben was breathing heavily. He closed his eyes. As if to deny the truth of what he'd just told Avital, he started shaking his head.

"Ben."

"What?" Eyes still closed, head still shaking.

"Come here."

"Where?"

"Here, up close."

She took his head in her hands, stopped its motion. Ben's eyes opened. She pulled him to her. He resisted then relented. Then she kissed him. They separated and then Ben grasped her head and pulled her to him and kissed her in return. They were kissing when a policeman's nightstick whacked the table. Above them stood a sneering Grayson Roby. "Last call," the chief said.

Darkness had fallen and as Ben flipped on his headlights for the drive home he realized he had to find and capture Dr. Loeb's killers himself. Chief Roby was noodling along in his own investigation, pursuing one false lead after another with no significant result. Well, Ben had all the lead he needed: Tom's self-declared intention to attack Loeb and Charlie's warning at the rally that Tom was about to carry out his threat. Ben owed it to his now-dead friend Amos Loeb to bring his killers to justice. He owed it to himself to atone for failing to prevent that great man's death.

Ben was halfway home when another car's headlights appeared in his rearview mirror. They followed him each turn he made. Who was this jerk who was blinding Ben with his high beams? Ben flipped the mirror up and down to send the beams back at him so he'd wake up and switch to low beams but all it made him do was speed up until he was almost up Ben's tail pipe. If Ben braked hard now the jerk would end up in Ben's trunk. The two cars zipped along for another half a mile as if conjoined. It creeped Ben out. Okay, he'd pull over to the shoulder and the other guy could pass him if he wanted. But the other guy didn't pass Ben, he pulled over, too, stopped, got out, and came to Ben's window. "Driver's license and registration."

"Roby?"

"You heard me."

Chief Roby was charging Ben with reckless driving although Ben had been right at the speed limit, below it actually, and he hadn't once crossed the center line. Roby wrote up the ticket and handed it to Ben. Ben ripped it up.

"That'll double your penalty."

Ben flipped him the fat budgie. "Double *this*, you crooked cop."

"I know what you did for Loeb in the Combat Zone."

"You were listening to me and Avi just now in the bar?"

"I knew it already."

"Well, so what?"

"So I wouldn't call *me* a crooked cop."

Ben didn't dignify this insult with a reply, he just barged into first gear and peeled away.

Shortly before Ben's home street was a bend in the road where it was easy to slide off onto the shoulder if one was speeding. The shoulder was hardly a shoulder just a strip of sand a couple of feet wide at most beyond which was an embankment sloping down to the river. There was no guardrail. Ben was approaching this bend when Roby's high beams exploded in his mirror again. Ben sped up, Roby did likewise. Ben goosed it to fifty then sixty mph where thirty was the posted limit.

Now Roby was on Ben's bumper, love-tapping it at first then ramming it so hard that Ben couldn't steer straight and his car was fishtailing and he was counter steering, but he was all over the road and then he was off the pavement and onto that skinny sandy shoulder then he was in free fall over the cliff and then he faded to black until he awoke upside down hanging by his seat belt in a diminishing pocket of air in his car-turned-submarine sluicing toward that waterfall ahead.

Ben belonged to no church but right now he was praying to God to let him live so he could make good on the promise he'd made to Dr. Loeb back at the hospital as he was fading out, that he would find and capture Tom Dunraven, the man who took Loeb's life. Ben promised aloud that he would do this if God saved him from his present dire predicament. "Hell, Lord," Ben spluttered into what remained of his air pocket, "I'll do it even if You don't."

PART TWO

A Bad Review

"What have you been smoking?" squawked Ben regarding my account of his nightmarish odyssey for Chinese food and beer. As a courtesy I'd provided him an early draft, just a preliminary sketch really, of Part One of my book. Actually, I wasn't just being courteous, I wanted Ben to review my account for accuracy, at least as far as his involvement in the story was concerned. I expected from him a quick thumbs-up but that's not what I got. He declared my rendering of his activity on Dr. Loeb's last night too fanciful. He claimed he'd told me a much simpler story, to wit: One, he'd called the order ahead; two, he'd arrived to pick it up; three, he'd driven straight back to the hospital. All in about twenty minutes. And as for Roby forcing him off the road and into the river, all that was true but wouldn't the reader want to know exactly how Ben had survived the dunking? That would be the best part of the book.

"Leave the book writing to me, Ben," I said politely, as politely as possible given his insult to my professional competence, and his denial of a creative nonfiction writer's right to make a complex true story assimilable by means of a lyrical narrative approach.

But what did I expect? As a cop Ben was necessarily and understandably ignorant of the penetrating power of artfully chosen and arranged dramatic events and figures of speech. His life's total written output was a stack of dry police incident reports—just the facts, M'am, and nothing but the facts. My own more ardent prose, while no less factual, delivered a keener and thus more memorable version of the truth.

While dismissing Ben's critique of my manuscript-in-progress, I remained in admiration of his experience and expertise in his own field. Ben's service as a law enforcement officer in one of our biggest and most dangerous cities beggared Roby's as a small town cop. Ben had taken down more dope kingpins and mobsters than Roby had written parking tickets. Thus I took seriously Ben's assertion that Messrs. Dunraven and Cubbage had conspired to kill Dr. Loeb, and I understood his zeal to capture them. Dr. Loeb had not trusted the local police to protect his life and Ben didn't trust the police to find those who took Loeb's life. Bringing the killers to justice would be more than Ben's duty as a lawman, it would be his sacred mission as a dear friend of the deceased. It would also help assuage Ben's personal guilt in the matter, guilt which burned so hot that it made Ben consider ending his own life.

Did I myself believe Dunraven was a murderer and Cubbage his accomplice? I didn't know the men personally so had no opinion on the matter. I was a writer not a detective and so had no right to judge a suspect's innocence or guilt, just as Ben the law enforcement professional was out of bounds in judging my own work. It was odd that Chief Roby had ignored Ben's plea to apprehend Tom Dunraven and Charlie Cubbage at the crime scene, and had not seemed to be pursuing those two since that time. But maybe Roby was hot on their tails and not telling anyone for fear that Ben would find them first and get credit for rounding them up. Possibly, Roby thought Ben was too stupid to have identified the right suspects in the first place. Perhaps Roby was certain of someone else's guilt, or he had a full roster of usual suspects whom he would grill mercilessly until one of them cracked. In any case, it was certainly best that the culprits not know they were being hunted, lest they flee the country to avoid being caught. So I accepted Roby's secretiveness. As a man at the top of his profession, albeit in one of its backwoods outposts, he deserved the benefit of the doubt. Thus I could not, would not, and should not say, as Ben did, that he was full of shit.

While stung by Ben's disapproval of my writing, I was nonetheless sensitive to his own feelings, and lest I'd seemed dismissive of his exegesis of my work, I pretended to appreciate it. "So I exaggerated your plunge into the river, did I?"

He repeated, with unnecessary vehemence, that I'd gotten the river stuff right except for his escape which I'd wrongly left out. The part I'd exaggerated, he said, was his run for Kung Pao Shrimp which he'd done in twenty minutes flat round trip.

"You're forgetting the beer," I said.

"What beer?"

"The Tsingtao. You consumed several cans."

"One can."

"It's a wonder you weren't pulled over for drunken driving."

"I was. I passed the breathalyzer test."

"Who tested you?"

"Who do you think?"

Obviously Chief Roby. However, Ben hadn't mentioned any breathalyzer test in his initial account to me of the event. But even if Ben had passed the test, Roby certainly would not have admitted it. With what I now knew of his and Ben's relationship, if Ben had indeed been sober Roby would have fudged the results to show that he'd been over the legal alcohol limit. "The simple outline of events you are now insisting upon, Ben, is simply incomplete."

"It's the truth."

"It's the core of the truth but it's missing the lyrical detail you supplied during our original interviews."

"What do you mean lyrical?"

"I mean the color and the nuance, the sounds and the scents, the emotional soundtrack playing inside your head."

"How do you know what was inside my head?"

"Because you told me."

"I did not."

"I fear that you have forgotten that you did."

"You made tape recordings of our conversation, didn't you?"

"Did I?"

"I know you did. I remember we had to go over the river part twice because the first time the tape stopped running because the battery went dead."

"We went over it twice because I didn't believe you the first time."

"But then you did."

"Because your second rendering confirmed the first."

"So you do have me on your tapes."

"Fine, so what?"

"So you can play them back for me right now. We'll see what's lyrical or not."

"I'm afraid I can't play them for you."

"Why not?"

"They're proprietary."

"What does that mean?"

"They are mine and mine alone."

"But they're my words."

"Your words on tape. That's different."

"Not to me."

"It would be to a judge." This got Ben's attention. No doubt he imagined himself on the witness stand, being asked to recall verbatim what he'd told me in our sessions and finding his mind totally blank.

"Fuck it," he said after another long pause during which his breathing accelerated while his jaw muscles clenched and unclenched. "You want to write it your way? Go ahead. I'll do my investigation and you write your damn book. It'll never be published anyway, not from what I've read so far."

Being a thorough-minded professional, Ben admitted the very dim possibility that someone other than Dunraven had killed Dr. Loeb. The attack had happened so quickly that all witnesses, slaphappy in the sentimental uproar and deep in their cups, could not describe the assailant who disappeared within an instant like some avenging ghost.

So before launching a full-throttle pursuit of Tom and Charlie, Ben would make a pro forma check of Loeb's old office for evidence, such as a threatening letter, of anyone else's guilt, however unlikely.

Of course, Loeb had received many threatening letters from many old grads so Tom's and Charlie's would be just one in a tall stack. But it would be the only one with a Southport, Connecticut postmark. No chance Ben would find it, though, since Loeb had very publicly burned these malign missives. "To danger I am indifferent," Loeb had proclaimed as his ill-wishers' ill wishes went up in smoke, "and to those who threaten me from afar I have only contempt."

Ben had dreaded returning to Loeb's office, fearing that stripped of all the great man's pictures and books and multifarious tchotchkes it would feel a grim, cold, haunted space and Ben would plunge back into the swamp of grief from which, with doubled dosages of Old Crow and daily deep breathing exercises (which reactivated the smoker's cough he'd long thought he'd licked), he'd only just emerged.

Ben's worries were unfounded. The office turned out to be untouched, with everything exactly as it had been on his last visit. This surprised Ben until he remembered that Provost Lou Pinto who'd become acting president had opted to stay in his own provost's office until the trustees officially chose a new chief executive, preferably himself. Lou didn't want to appear too presumptuous of his own prospects. He could wait.

Meanwhile, Loeb's widow Lucy was granted her request that her late husband's office not be disturbed in any way until his successor was installed. She wanted to be able to go in there and imagine him still at his desk, still savoring the roast beef that she'd always brought him for his lunch.

Ben wasn't a big reader but he did love Ernest Hemingway, at least the bullfighting stuff. Ben had once visited Hemingway's old house on Key West. In the writing studio above the carriage house Ben had felt the great writer's presence, as if he had just left to take a leak. On the wall was a stuffed and mounted antelope head. On the round table lay an open book with a sharpened pencil on it. The typewriter, with a half-typed sheet in it, sat beside a ream of virgin typing paper, behind which purred a six-toed cat. Ben had half-expected Papa to wander back into the room at any second zipping up his pants. When he did Ben would bow and scrape. I'm not worthy, he would think.

Today in Vermont, the same feelings roused by similar office items overwhelmed Ben in the Ballyvaughan College presidential suite where Captain, O My Captain Amos Loeb so recently had helmed the ship of academic state.

In the coat closet Ben found four milk crates filled with mail addressed to Dr. Loeb. Ben perused the hate-filled contents of several envelopes which had clearly been sent by disgruntled alumni. Why had Loeb kept these particular poison pen letters and burned all the rest? As fuel to fire his efforts to show up his critics? If Ben was pained to read them, imagine how Loeb must have felt. Ben had received reproachful notes from relatives of miscreants he'd busted but he hadn't read beyond their first few lines, and then he'd burned them just as Loeb had done with his own, except for these four crates' full. Ben now considered burning the letters in these crates himself, but decided to take them home and read them all instead. If Tom Dunraven turned out to be innocent of the attack on Dr. Loeb, one of these letters might hold the damning clue to whoever else was the attacker.

In the closet also were Loeb's beaver coat, his snorkeling gear, six dozen nail clippers (Ben counted them), a blood pressure monitor, an empty box of Wheat Thins, an unopened box of condoms, two badminton racquets and a shuttlecock, an uncapped bottle of Pepsi, and a Special Delivery package to Loeb postmarked October 5, 1988 from Jasmine Elm, presumably the Holocaust-denying Jasmine Elm from the Barnes & Noble book-signing event. In addition, there were a stack of videocassettes, all travelogues judging from the two on top, a biography of Beethoven, sheet music for Beethoven's Piano Sonata in C Minor opus 13 (the "Pathétique"), and a bust of Beethoven with one ear chipped off. If Ben had known anything about music he would have thought it odd that Loeb, a man brutalized by Germans, had worshipped a German composer, albeit Beethoven was of Flemish stock. Even odder were the great number of nail clippers Loeb had possessed. Had he been a collector? What an odd thing to collect. Why not old coins or first day cover postage stamps? Numismatics and philately were perfectly normal leisure time pursuits. Hoarding personal grooming tools was not.

But Loeb had not been a normal man, and that had been his glory. What other glorious abnormalities might Ben find if he extended his research into, say, the medicine cabinet in Loeb's private lavatory? Or to the drawers in his desk?

The medicine cabinet was just aspirin, Ban Roll-On, and a styptic pencil flecked with dried blood. The desk drawers were another story. Ben riffled through tax returns, scholarly essays, and scolding letters not just to major city newspapers but also to fishing and hunting magazines, the *Journal of the American Medical Association,* and *Cosmopolitan.* The one positive letter praised to the skies a do-it-yourself feature in *Boys' Life.* So Amos was a Scout. No, of course he wasn't, he'd have been too old when he reached the United States. Right? But did the Boy Scouts have an age limit? Ben had no idea. Ben had never been a Boy Scout, he'd spent his youth as a public safety cadet at his local Boston police district.

Ben couldn't picture Loeb as a Boy Scout and so was further astonished to find among the badges the Scout Code, neatly typed in bold italics:

On my honor I will do my best:
1. To do my duty to God and my country;
2. To obey the Scout Law;
3. To help other people at all times;
4. To keep myself physically strong,
    mentally awake, and morally straight.

Before each of the first three things Loeb had evidently vowed to do for God and country he had put a check mark and a date, presumably of its achievement. There was no check mark or date on number 4, though, indicating that Amos had seen strength, wakefulness, and moral rectitude as lifelong pursuits, never fully achievable but accruable over one's lifespan toward an ultimate winning tally at time of death.

Ben was pained to imagine Loeb thinking he had failed to reach all of his goals and that he might therefore face stern judgment in the afterlife. *You've done plenty, Old Friend,* Ben scribbled at the bottom of the sheet. *More than most.* Loeb had checked off the Scout Code's first three mandates. With a bold stroke, Ben now check-marked the fourth.

Believing he'd now scanned every single document, cocktail napkin doodle, and note-to-self scrap contained in the desk Ben started to close the last drawer but then he glimpsed yet one more item in its recesses. It was an envelope addressed to Dr. Loeb, postmarked this past October 15th from Southport, Connecticut. There was no return address. It had been slit open then resealed with Scotch Tape. Ben slit the tape. Inside was a piece of paper folded origami-style to make a swan. Ben unfolded the swan. "Greeting:" It began. The last time Ben had seen "Greeting:" was on his draft notice which was a death warrant during the Vietnam era, and for Ben at Khe Sanh, was very nearly that. This letter to Dr. Loeb seemed itself to be a death warrant:

```
Oh, the shark, sir, has such teeth, sir,
And it shows them pearly white.
```

Ben heard Bobby Darin singing in his head ...

```
Just a hunting knife has old MacHeath, sir,
```

75

And he keeps it out of sight.

Hunting knife. This was a murderous threat.

You know when that shark bites with his
teeth, sir,
Scarlet billows start to spread.

This was ghoulish. The hairs stood up on Ben's neck ...

Fancy gloves wears old MacHeath, sir,
So there's never, never a trace of red.

The assassin was foretelling his fatal attack. He was hiding in plain
sight ...

Now on the campus green, frosty evening,
Lies a body just oozin' life,
And someone's sneakin' 'round the corner.
Could that someone be Mack the Knife?

That someone was Tom Dunraven, there could be no doubt.

Oh, the line forms on the right, sir,
Now that Macky's back in town.

It was Tom Dunraven who was auguring his own return to town for
Autumn Inferno with his alumni brethren, most of whom hated Loeb
for the changes he'd made to Ballyvaughan and many of whom had
sent him death threats. But none except Tom was rash enough to
make good on their threats.

Look out, old Macky is back!

If Dunraven hadn't smelled of guilt before, right now he fairly reeked of it. Chief Roby had been dead-ending up blind alleys sniffing for smoking guns—well, this letter was as good as a bloody knife. Ben couldn't wait to show the letter to Roby and then watch the chief lick the egg off his face.

On second thought, why get Roby all riled up? He'd probably forbid Ben from hunting down the culprit, not that he legally could. So until Ben had Tom Dunraven cuffed and booked, he'd keep the letter to himself.

Ben left Dr. Loeb's office, locked the door behind him, and walked toward the grand staircase with a new spring in his step. He was about to descend when a strange sound caught his attention, a *swish-swishing* from behind some door farther down the corridor. He ignored it and started down the stairs. The *swish-swishing* continued and with this sound wafted the distinct scent of roast beef. Ben's curiosity got the best of him and just as well because curiosity was the best thing a cop had since it led him into abandoned, overgrown alleyways most people overlooked—the roads not taken, so to speak.

Swish-swish, swish-swish. Ben returned upstairs and tried a few doors, all locked. Finally a door opened and there was Lucy Loeb in the executive kitchen, a platter of steaming roast beef before her, *swish-swishing* her carving knife over a knife sharpener. "Excuse me, Mrs. Loeb," Ben stammered.

"You're excused," Lucy said.

The Hell You Say

Ben told me he'd gotten Tom Dunraven's Connecticut home address from the college alumni office and was going to drive down there and make him confess.

"And if he doesn't confess?" I asked him.

"I'll use force."

"What kind of force?"

"Leave the force to me, you write your book."

In fact, I'd been neglecting my book of late, enjoying schussing down the Ballyvaughan Skiway slopes and hiking the ice-glazed trail up majestic Mount Passumpsic. (The Indians had held sway in these parts before the Irish civilized them with "five hundred gallons of Dublin's strong waters," as allotted in the college charter.) My literary agent Bebe Spinoza was phoning me frequently at my motel, leaving messages with the desk clerk that I should send her some draft chapters and a provisional outline or at least my research notes. Why hadn't I been updating her on my progress? Had I gone to Vermont just on a lark? She wanted to start thinking about which publishers to approach.

I resented that she thought I was loafing. But she wasn't a writer and couldn't acknowledge that writers keep their minds fresh by keeping their bodily sensations at their peak. And so after a day shredding the relatively easy terrain at the Skiway, easy for me, anyway, if not for the college ski team, I got back to work, focusing on Dr. Loeb not just as a heroic figure, but as a man of flesh and blood.

I started in his office in the administration building. There I found everything that had conjured for Ben Ernest Hemingway's writing studio: a typewriter, an open book with a sharpened pencil, a tray of virgin white sheets. Loeb's stuffed and mounted elk's head stood in for the head of Hemingway's mounted antelope. Loeb was seriously allergic to cat hairs, though, and so there was no purring feline on his desk, six-toed or otherwise.

In the coat closet I affirmed the sundry paraphernalia that Ben had inventoried—the swim fins, nail clippers, condoms, cracker box, one-eared Beethoven, and all that. Loeb had been a world traveler, thus the stack of videocassettes with labels like Tonga, Phuket, and Surabaya. I had always wanted to visit such places so after asking the college's permission I tucked the tapes under my arm and carried them to my car. The college actually didn't grant my request for permission but they'd never know I took the tapes as I would have them back in the office closet by first light the next day. Of course, I hadn't brought a videotape player with me to Glenfarne so I rented one from the local electronics store. On the way to my motel I picked up a ten-pack of Slim Jims and a quart of Old Milwaukee then settled in for my vicarious South Seas adventure.

My hard, lumpy motel bed became a rope hammock strung between coconut palms as I basked in the tropical sunshine of the first three tapes. The fourth one, though, snapped me back home. It was unlabeled. When I pressed PLAY I wasn't whisked to a blue lagoon but to a television studio where the well-known morning talk show host Darlene Shine was interviewing a woman who called herself the world's greatest skeptic. This sassy, brassy debunker of conventional wisdom, of both the politically correct and incorrect types, was making the media rounds promoting her latest canard-blasting book *The Hell You Say!* which, as the dust jacket proclaimed, cast serious doubt upon the efficacy of prayer, shot down the Mediterranean Diet as a preventive of Alzheimer's Disease, and in its climactic chapter, razed beyond hope of reconstruction the "already tottering" myth of the Holocaust. Jasmine Elm, of course, was the author's name.

As a non-churchgoer, I wasn't too sure of the power of prayer either, and with no family history of Alzheimer's I wasn't too worried about developing it myself. But deny the Holocaust? On a recent ski trip to Austria I'd side-tripped to Poland to visit Auschwitz and believe me, I saw the ghosts.

"Have you been to Auschwitz yourself?" Shine asked Elm.

"Have you?" Elm countered.

"I've seen the photographs."

"They're doctored."

"By whom?"

"Read my book, you'll see."

"Fine. Now about the Mediterranean Diet—"

"Hold it, we're still on the Holocaust. You don't want to talk about the Holocaust?"

"To be honest, I'd rather not talk about it with *you*."

"Then why did you invite me on your program?"

"I didn't, my producer did."

"Smart producer."

"All right, let's move on to the healing effects of prayer."

"Smart producer, dumb host."

Shine bolted up out of her seat. She seemed on the verge of smacking Elm with the back of her hand but held back. Wow. Shine's interviews were usually gushing, fawning, and cotton candy light as befitted the dippy name of her show, *Rise 'n' Shine*, but here she began ripping into Ms. Elm's book like a human paper shredder. "Your shaming the Jews as pretenders to martyrdom," she said, "puts the true shame on you."

"What about you?"

"What do you mean what about me?"

"Your own shame."

"What shame?"

"About your name."

"I'm proud of my name."

"Then why don't you use it?"

"What do you mean?"

"You use Shine instead of Schine."

"My name *is* Shine."

"But you misspell it."

"What are you talking about?"

"You drop out the 'c.' Your real name isn't S-h-i-n-e, it's S-*c*-h-i-n-e. Which is Jewish, which comes from the Yiddish S-c-h-e-i-n. Are you ashamed of your Jewish-Yiddish roots? Are you afraid that a few of your three million Gentile viewers might not tune in to a Jewish-Yiddish happy-talk host?"

"We are through here."

Ms. Elm thanked Shine for such a thoughtful, probing interview then walked off the set as Shine cut to a commercial.

After rewinding the tape to the beginning I brought it and the other videocassettes back to campus and replaced them in Dr. Loeb's office closet. Why, I wondered, had Loeb made and saved a tape of Jasmine Elm so cruelly and spuriously refuting his own very real personal ordeal? Why, after watching that interview once did he preserve it for further review? Why not just ignore the woman entirely? Out of sight, out of mind, I would have thought. But no, shame on me, how presumptuous could I get? I'd suffered a lifetime of editors' rejection letters but I hadn't survived a death camp. Jasmine Elm had struck at the heart of Amos Loeb's personal experience of transcendent evil, and the record of her doing so would fire and re-fire his zeal to strike back.

When I arrived back at my motel room I noticed that an envelope had been slipped under the door. Presuming it was from management regarding my missed payment of last week's bill, I slit open the envelope and took out the sheet within.

I KILLED AMOS LOEB.

read the first line. It continued:

I will sign a confession for you with my real name
for a ten percent cut of your book royalties and
fifteen grand upfront.

No signature, no return address. So the sharks were out, smelling the blood of a writer desperate for information on the Loeb case. Except sharks weren't bottom feeders like these Deep Throat wannabes were. I knew their scam. They'd swindled me before but wouldn't again.

The note concluded:

Turn the lights off and on three times right now if
you agree to this deal. Just turn them off and leave
them off if you don't agree.

I replaced the sheet in the envelope and dropped the envelope in the trash basket. Then I took it out of the trash basket. I didn't want the cleaning people to find this note and give it to Chief Roby, or worse, send it to the FBI who would trace it back to me. It was unnerving to think the sender of this letter was staking out my room to see what I did with the lights in response to his proposition. So I flossed and brushed my teeth to settle my nerves then I switched off the lights and left them off, smugly imagining how my darkened room was dashing the hopes for easy money of the so-called assassin out in the street.

I was never scared of the dark as a kid but the blackness of this room suddenly terrified me. I heard noises. Was someone tapping at my door? *"Quoth the raven, Nevermore!"* Christ, I was wetting my pajamas. Immediately, I switched the lights on and off three times. I took ten deep breaths. That was better. Was I caving to a blatant fraudster? No, I was just having some nasty cat-and-mouse fun with him by feigning acceptance of his gambit, cunningly stringing him along. If I could catch him returning here to leave me another note I could collar him and demand that he pay me money not to give him up to federal authorities. If he refused to pay I'd turn him in with great glee. If the note's sender really was Dr. Loeb's killer, which he almost certainly wasn't, I could keep him in play by promising him payment then withholding it over and over, thus buying myself time to discover his true identity which, when found, would set the keystone of my now sure-to-be bestselling book. A win either way.

Champagne and Old Milwaukee

I confess that I wasn't totally sure that Dr. Loeb had kept the Jasmine Elm tape merely as motivation to avenge her vicious libels. He had decades' worth of motivation to stand up to such malign individuals, he didn't need another spur. So why keep an unlabeled videotape of her malignity? Thinking that Ben might have an answer, I drove to see him at his home, hoping he hadn't left on his vigilante mission yet. As I've said, I neither accepted nor denied that Dunraven was Loeb's killer, but by supporting Ben in his supposition I would keep him relaxed in my presence and willing to confer more privileged information for my book. I therefore brought with me a bottle of champagne to toast the success of his impending trip.

Ben's car was still in his driveway. Through the front window I could see him packing his suitcase. I knocked on the door and he opened it. "Fuck me," he said.

"Why?"

"I was this close to that bastard Dunraven that night but I missed him."

"Water under the bridge, Ben."

"So Loeb's blood is on my hands."

"The blood is on that bastard Dunraven's hands. And you'll nab him, won't you? And his bloody knife."

"I'm leaving tonight. I just hope I'm not too late."

"You think he might have absconded?"

"I'll find out."

"You have time for a little drink before you go?"

"No."

"*Veuve Clicquot.*" I showed the bottle.

"What's that?"

"Champagne."

"Sure, why not."

I popped the cork and the geyser shot up festively. Ben got two coffee mugs and I filled them. I sipped mine and Ben drained his in one gulp. I refilled his mug. "What are these?" I said, pointing to a shelf full of crudely carved birds and fish.

"My hobby."

"You whittle?"

"My dad gave me a whittling knife as a kid." Ben rummaged in a kitchen drawer and pulled out the very tool. "I never used this 'til I moved up here. Vermont's got a lot of great wood. Elm, Ash, Red Maple."

"Elm."

"Spruce, birch, hickory."

"Tell me about Elm."

"It's a firm and tough wood, hard to work, requires a very sharp blade."

"Jasmine Elm. Tell me about Jasmine Elm."

"Her? Why? She can go to hell." Ben snorted.

"You don't want to talk about her?"

"I don't want to *think* about her."

"This'll be quick. Dr. Loeb made a tape of her TV interview. I want to know the reason."

"He was hot for her."

"No, really?"

"Can you believe it? That bitch?"

"Why do you call her a bitch?"

"Did you watch the tape?"

I nodded.

"You don't agree?"

I did agree but apparently Dr. Loeb hadn't agreed. Ben said Loeb had been so smitten with the woman—intellectually, not romantically— that he brought her to the college to debate him onstage before a student audience. Jasmine Elm was human scum but she was brilliant human scum and Loeb couldn't figure how such a highly intelligent woman could harbor such benighted views. Well, maybe he could figure it. Maybe she didn't harbor the views sincerely, she just made a grand show of doing so for fame among the very sizable racist and anti-Semitic book-buying public, and the fortune such fame brought her. Uh-huh right, and maybe the Germans didn't hate Jews sincerely but just made a grand show of exterminating them for their anti-Semitic *Führer* and the *lebensraum* that would bring them. Actually, maybe they did, and maybe Jasmine Elm was just a conwoman extraordinaire. In his bafflement Loeb was losing sleep. If he couldn't yet solve the pan-German accession to the Final Solution, maybe he could crack the Jasmine Elm nut and reveal whether she was truly evil or not. A face-to-face public encounter with her, Loeb decided, was the best way for him, and since this debate would be highly publicized, for the whole world to find out. And once Elm was found out she could be neutralized. "The debate was scheduled for the first day of October," Ben said.

"Exactly one month before Loeb was attacked."

"Nice timing, right?"

"You think there was a connection?"

"Nah, just coincidence."

"Might be worth checking into, though."

"Why? We know who the attacker was."

"I mean just as background material for my book on Dr. Loeb. As they say, you can know a man by the company he keeps."

"Who says that?"

"Aesop."

"Then it's just a fable."

"You're up on your ancient Greek culture, I see."

"I thought he was French."

"Well, Ben, I won't delay you any longer."

"One more swig." He wagged his mug at me and I poured more in.

"Did you meet Jasmine Elm when she was here at the college?"

"I met her before she was here at the college."

"On what occasion?"

"She came to the Barnes & Noble to sign her book."

"There's a Barnes & Noble in little old Glenfarne?"

"It's in Montpelier."

"That's an hour's drive away."

"Not how I drive."

"Why did you go see her at Barnes & Noble?"

"Same reason you would."

"But I wouldn't."

"Then you wouldn't get why I did."

I tipped the champagne bottle to refill Ben's mug but the bottle was empty. Luckily, I'd brought a second one. Ben smacked his lips as I popped its cork.

"I went to see her just for fun," he said then gargled his new mouthful of bubbly. The hooch had unwound him to the point where Jasmine Elm was no longer a taboo subject.

"What do you mean, 'fun?' Ben?"

Ben reaffirmed that Elm was an odious woman who held appalling views and that he'd had no desire to see her in person. However, the spectacle of verbal and maybe physical violence she was likely to provoke at the gathering made her a must-see attraction. Plus, as a cop, Ben could help restore order if things got too unruly.

A throng was massed in front of the store when Ben arrived for the event. As he waited in line someone breezed by and identified himself to the armed guard at the door. Now Ben saw the person's face: it was Dr. Loeb. The guard let Loeb right in.

When Ben himself finally gained admittance, Ms. Elm was just sweeping in and taking her place at the lectern before the clearly loaded-for-bear assembly. She looked even smaller than on TV but just as nifty in another slinky silk outfit, her lips an even lusher shade of red, and her eyelashes like the tines of little rakes.

"Are you curious," she began, "about how Hitler could have killed six million Jews when there were only 600,000 Jews in Germany when he came to power in 1933?"

"Most of the Jews he killed were not in Germany," shouted a man in the audience, "They were in Poland and Russia and other countries he invaded during the war."

"I will take questions later," said Ms. Elm with a smile.

The man pressed on: "The Protocol of the Wannsee Conference in 1942 outlined Hitler's plan to annihilate not just six million but over eleven million Jews throughout the continent."

"But aren't you curious," Elm said, "about why in fact not a single document has ever been found with Hitler's signature ordering extermination of Jews?"

The woman sitting beside me called out:"Gestapo Chief Heinrich Mueller instructed *Einsatzgruppen* commanders to inform the *Führer* about their work on a continual basis."

"Excuse me," Elm interrupted her, "*Einsatzgruppen*? I don't speak German."

"They were the mobile killing squads active in Eastern Europe."

"Thank you."

"And the police in Riga," added someone up front, "were ordered to murder all Jews in their city as per Hitler's specific wish."

A young man, no more than a teen, piped: "SS Chief Heinrich Himmler told SS *Gruppenfuehrer* Gottlob Berger, and I quote—" The boy read from a slip of paper, his voice cracking: "'The occupied East will be freed of Jews. The *Führer* has placed the execution of this difficult order on my shoulders."

"Do *you* speak German?" Ms. Elm asked the fellow.

"No."

"Then how do you know what Herr Himmler really said?"

"This is a translation."

"By whom?"

"I don't know, I'll check."

"Don't bother. I know the translator and I know that he was once a member of the Jewish Defense League."

"So what?"

"Perhaps you are a member?"

"Uh, no."

"Perhaps at least you know that the Jewish Defense League's stated goal is to, and I quote, 'protect Jews from antisemitism by whatever means necessary,' and that those means have included bombing, kidnapping, and hijacking, and that accordingly the FBI considers the JDL a terrorist organization."

"Okay."

"Okay? That is *okay*?"

"I didn't know all that."

"Well, now you do." Elm cast cold eyes over the whole audience. "Now if I may, I'd like to continue."

A man in a Red Sox cap barked: "No, shut up!"

"Sir, I will entertain your suggestion after I complete my remarks, at which time I'll be glad to have a chat as I am signing your copy of my book."

The crowd hushed up enough to let Ms. Elm finish her presentation, though at five minutes it must have been a severely abridged version of it. Elm then stepped down from the lectern and strode to the table piled high with copies of *The Hell You Say!*

No one strode after her, though, and facing an emptying lecture space she sat her bantam body behind the wall of fat volumes and disappeared from view. Ben had gotten only half of what he'd come for, some loud beefs and rebukes but no fisticuffs. He turned to depart but some strange impulse made him turn back and approach Ms. Elm as she was putting on her coat. "You can sign my book," he said.

"Where is it?"

"Uh ... " Ben grabbed a book from the table. It occurred to him that a copy signed by such a notorious personage would be worth a lot of money at auction. Elm signed the book but her illegible zigzaggy scrawl made the book probably worthless on the open market. Ben dropped the book back on the table but realized he'd committed himself to paying for it by having the author deface it. In the cashier line the woman behind Ben tapped him on the shoulder. "I saw her sign your book," she said.

"Yeah, my mistake."

"Why did you ask her?"

"I shouldn't have."

"Do you agree with her views?"

"Hell no. Do you?"

"I don't know."

"What's not to know? She's a Jew-hater. Are you a Jew-hater?"

"Heavens no."

"Then you don't agree with her."

"Then I guess I don't."

Ben paid the cashier and headed toward the exit door. The woman he'd spoken with caught up to him. "Thank you," she said.

"For what?"

"For setting me straight."

"About what?"

"That Elm lady. She had me so confused, I didn't know what to think."

"You're welcome." Ben headed for his car.

"Hey, wait." The woman followed him. "Can I buy you a drink?"

"I don't drink."

Ten minutes later they were at a bar around the corner drinking.

By this point in Ben's spiel, we had killed the second champagne bottle. Luckily, he had a six-pack of Old Milwaukee in the fridge. "That's my beer," I said.

"No, it's mine."

"I mean I drink Old Milwaukee myself."

"Good, 'cause that's what I got."

We each cracked a can.

"I'm finished about Jasmine Elm," Ben said "Not much else to tell you."

"You've told me a lot."

"Unless you want to hear more about Faye Foxley."

"Who's Faye Foxley?"

"The woman I had drinks with."

I had no reason to hear anything about Faye Foxley but Ben's cottage was so cozy and warm compared to my bare, cold room at the motel that I wanted to stay put. "Tell all," I said.

A Girl Named Piggy

Faye Foxley was about Ben's age. Half of her mass of gray-flecked auburn hair was piled high on her head and the other half cascaded down below her shoulders. Her eyes were green. Her lips were russet. Ben normally didn't socialize with floozies but the girlish lilt in this one's obviously smoke-hoarsened voice was almost charming, and if she was buying the drinks, what the heck?

The Ballyvaughan Inn was Ben's first-choice watering hole but Ballyvaughan was fifty miles from this Barnes & Noble in Montpelier. Ben wouldn't bring Faye to the Ballyvaughan Inn anyway because Avital might get jealous which she had no right to do since Ben was married, though Avital wouldn't know this since Ben's wedding ring had slipped off in the shower recently and disappeared down the drain. So Ben squired Faye to the Gin Fizz Lounge around the corner from the Barnes & Noble.

"What'll it be?" said their server.

"I'll have a Gin Fizz," said Faye.

"Sir?"

"When in Rome."

He and Faye drained their first Gin Fizzes like they were ginger ale. They ordered seconds. "Who starts it off?" Faye asked Ben.

"Starts what off?"

"Telling their life story."

"Mine you don't want to know."

"Well, here's mine: I was born at Glenfarne General Hospital."

"Good for you."

"Actually, I was born at home on our ping-pong table. A midwife delivered me. She was my daddy's friend, his best friend. Actually, they were screwing."

Ben signaled for the tab. Already he'd heard enough from this woman.

"One more round," Faye said to the bar boy. "Where was I?"

"They were screwing."

"And my mother knew. She didn't care, she needed a midwife and this wench was good. More important, her services were free."

"You weren't well off?"

"We got by," Faye said. "Lottie—that was my mama's name—took in laundry and my daddy Hughie played the ponies by day and card sharped at night."

"When he wasn't screwing."

"Correct."

"I think I've heard enough about your parents."

"Good, because now I'll talk about me." Ben thus learned that Faye was her parents' only child, the only one they admitted to at any rate. "You're my favorite daughter," Hughie would tell little Faye as he tucked her into bed, implying one or multiple other siblings hidden somewhere. When Hughie handed Faye off to Lottie for a bedtime story Lottie would read *Cinderella*, substituting Faye's name for Cinderella's and thus giving the girl two possible wicked stepsisters to contemplate.

"If you tell me everything about your early childhood," Ben interrupted, "we'll be here all night."

"That wouldn't be so bad, would it?" Faye ordered a third Gin Fizz for Ben and herself. "Okay, we'll skip prepubescence and jump way ahead." She only jumped to middle school where she floundered and had to repeat eighth grade. "I got zero in everything," she said. "I couldn't finish my homework because of all my needlework." She claimed to mean embroidery, tapestry, quilting, and appliqué but the proto-hippie rebelliousness she exuded suggested to Ben that she was pricked, often, by a needle of a different sort. She buckled down in high school, though, where her latent genius earned her straight A's and nomination as the valedictory commencement speaker. The football captain who had ignored her to that point grabbed her after the ceremony and doinked her still in their gowns and mortar boards under the stadium grandstand. The stud didn't mind that she was seven months pregnant at the time, and was pleased in fact since he could never be named in a paternity suit.

Two months later Faye gave birth to her little bundle of joy who at nine pounds eight ounces was not so little relative to normal newborn weight. "Oh, she was a porker all right. Her nose was snout-like and she didn't wail and cry like all other babies, she grunted. The mailman saw her and called her a piglet. I pointed out that her hands weren't pig's trotters; they were leathery little baseball mitts, knobby knuckled as if she had arthritis already and with the two middle fingers sticking straight up like she was flipping off her mother. The mailman asked her name and I said Anastasia and he said that's a Communist name and I should just call her Piglet which sounded gross to me so I changed it to Piglette which is more feminine."

"The mailman was wrong," Ben said to Faye as their server brought either their fourth or fifth round of drinks. "Anastasia, if he was thinking of Grand Duchess Anastasia Nikolaevna of Russia, born June 5th, 1901, died July 17th, 1918, was the youngest daughter of Tsar Nicholas II, the last sovereign of Russia, and his wife Tsarina Alexandra Feodorovna. So Anastasia was not Communist, she was the antithesis of Communist." Ben was startled that he knew all that, but it just materialized in his brain. Maybe it was a repressed memory from his high school class in Russian and European history. It was an AP course and Ben was helpless in it, collecting enough F's on test and quizzes to flunk out of it halfway through. Yet all this time later he remembered that Imperial Russian factoid. It turned out that the school secretary had mistakenly placed him in that class, switching his name Ben Marble with the class brainiac's name Ben Markle whom she assigned to wood and metalworking shop which, classically unsuited to the manual arts as he was, he flunked.

"What did you just say?" Faye asked Ben.

Ben knew he'd said something historically significant but he couldn't remember what.

"Aaah, who gives a shit?" said Faye. "I didn't call her Anastasia anyway."

"You called her Piglette."

"Piggy for short."

On her eighteenth birthday Piggy announced that she wanted to go to college. Faye applauded her announcement. Then she took her daughter's hand and led her in a little mazurka.

Faye was so excited for the girl. At the same time, she was aggrieved knowing that once Piggy left for college she would never come home again and Faye would live the rest of her days in an empty nest. But Faye didn't cry. Does the robin cry when its fledgling takes wing? And just possibly Faye would not die alone after all. When her baby got her degree she would be too burdened with college loans to buy her own house, or even rent herself an apartment, and so she would fly back home to live with her mother again. Faye would die in her daughter's arms after all, warm, secure, and at peace with what awaited her in the afterlife. All's well that ends well, wasn't that the saying? This world was a funny old apple, and while its first bites were bitter, its aftertaste was sweet.

Unless Piggy received a full scholarship and thus had no loans to repay and would not need to live with her mother.

Or, God willing, Piggy would not be admitted to any college and she wouldn't leave home in the first place. On the other hand, God forbid that Faye should suffer the shame of her daughter being rejected by every school she applied to. But that shame looked inevitable because Piggy's high school grades were not impressive. She'd never earned as high as a B in her life. She was a brilliant student but she froze on quizzes and tests. As Faye told Piggy's high school principal Bill V. Pulck, her inclination to panic just showed her emotional hypersensitivity, not any lack of intelligence. Listen, Mrs. Foxley, said Pulck, your daughter could be a straight-A student and still no college would take her, not with her disciplinary record. What disciplinary record? Faye said. Pulck pulled out the record. It was a thick folder. At the top was the report of Piggy pulling a hunting knife on another girl in the lunchroom.

"That was not my daughter's knife," Faye said.

"Whose was it?"

"My late husband's. And the girl she pulled it on threatened her."

"With words," Pulck said, pointing to the record. "Which hardly merits having a knife held to your throat."

"It does if the other girl had a knife, too."

"Which she did not."

"But she *said* she did."

"No knife was found on her person, her book bag, or her purse. But your daughter actually did have a knife."

"For protection."

"Against whom?"

"The bullies."

"Who are the bullies?"

"Everyone."

Faye wasn't lying. Poor Piggy was bullied by her schoolmates unmercifully. She came home every afternoon with tears running down her cheeks and worse. Worse was scratch marks on her neck and crude words written in plum gloss lipstick on her forehead.

Faye knew what being bullied was like. She'd been bullied herself through middle school. She'd been told she had a learning disability but she pushed that diagnosis back in the experts' faces and rubbed their noses in it by finishing first in her high school graduating class and giving that valedictory address and then having intercourse with that jock which was not her first intercourse, it was her second but it was the best of her whole life to that point and would remain so forever after.

Piggy was never going to give a valedictory address but that didn't mean she couldn't go to college. Or for that matter, be schtupped by a

96

football captain. But Piggy had to find the right college, one which recognized her unique genius; one which looked past her disciplinary record and her mediocre grades and perceived the greatness of the particular talent she possessed which rendered moot aberrant social behavior and scholarly inaptitude.

Piggy's particular talent was acting. She was cast in every school play, albeit as Fourth Peasant or Horse's Hindquarters or the partridge in a pear tree in the Christmas pageant or Goose-a-Laying #6. But she was honing her gift in supporting roles and soon would be playing Blanche DuBois and Mary Poppins. Thus the perfect college for this budding drama queen had to have the world's best drama teacher on its faculty. It also had to have a president who would override his admissions committee which, like all admissions committees, would not admit applicants who brought weapons to school, flunked standardized tests, and were not already Olympians in three sports. Fortunately, there was a college that had both the best drama teacher and a president who surely would overlook academic and behavioral deficiencies and would fully appreciate singular artistic gifts. That college was Ballyvaughan College. For one thing, the renowned drama teacher Anton Wohlgemuth was a star professor there. For another thing, and by purest luck, Ballyvaughan's president Dr. Amos Loeb was a former friend of Faye's. She hadn't seen him in nearly two decades but he would have no trouble remembering her. Funny how he and she had grown apart but life is a superhighway with its crazy detours and on and off ramps. You're rolling along nose to tail then suddenly the other driver veers off without flipping his turn signal. Now you're the only car on the road in the middle of a black and fogbound night.

No problem. Roads have a way of reconverging and Faye now picked a route leading back to her old friend. While she eagerly awaited her reunion with Dr. Loeb for personal reasons, the trip's real purpose would be to introduce Piggy to him. Right in his office Piggy, holding a bloodied axe, would perform Clytemnestra's immortal soliloquy standing triumphantly and without shame over the body of Agamemnon whom she has hacked to death for killing Iphigenia their daughter and for sleeping with Cassandra whom Clytemnestra has just murdered also. Faye, taking the Chorus's part, would bemoan the curse of eternal violence that Clytemnestra's brutal deed had set upon Argos. Flipping them the bird, Clytemnestra would snap back, "I would remind you that extremism in the defense of liberty is no vice. And let me remind you also that moderation in the pursuit of justice is no virtue" which was Faye's own paraphrase in more modern language of what the ancient Greek dramatist had put in Clytemnestra's mouth.

Loeb would be so knocked out that he would grant Piggy admission to his college before she even finished her speech. If he didn't, Clytemnestra would have her axe to persuade him, except that Faye didn't own an axe so her late husband's hunting knife would have to do as Piggy's stage prop.

"So how did the audition go?" Ben asked Faye after ordering another two gin fizzes but being told the bar was now out of gin.

"It hasn't happened yet. We've got an appointment scheduled with Dr. Loeb at nine a.m. on November 1st."

"That's the day of the football rally."

"Perfect, eh?"

"Will you stick around for the big bonfire?"

"I've never missed a fire in my life."

We'd finished Ben's Old Milwaukee six-pack by now. I was laid out on the couch half asleep. "No axe, huh?" I mumbled.

"What?"

"Faye Foxley didn't have an axe for her daughter's big audition for Dr. Loeb so she brought a knife to the campus. Maybe she killed Loeb."

"Who did, the daughter?"

"The mother, the daughter, who knows?"

"The writer wants to play detective." Ben laughed derisively.

"Or *you* killed him."

"Yeah, right. Nice try, Nancy Drew."

"With your whittling knife."

"That thing's old and dull, wouldn't cut butter."

"It cuts wood."

"Wood's not butter. Hey, I know: *you* killed Loeb."

"You got me, lock me up."

"I'll do more than that." Ben pulled out his service revolver, aimed it at me, and said, "Pow."

"Missed me."

"I won't miss Tom Dunraven."

"You're going to shoot him, are you?"

"He deserves to be shot."

"You're kidding, right?" Considering Ben's record of lethal conduct in Boston, maybe he wasn't kidding.

"What'd you think I'd do, just write him a ticket?" Ben stood up, holstered his pistol, and put on his parka and ski cap.

"Don't leave yet, Ben."

"Can't wait any longer. Got to go nail that bastard."

"How can I reach you while you're away?"

"Why would you want to reach me?"

"I may have more questions."

"What about?"

"Dr. Loeb. Jasmine Elm, the Foxleys. You're my prime source. And don't worry, you'll get full credit in the book."

He named a motel in Connecticut. He wouldn't be in his room much, though, he said. Then he picked up his suitcase and went out the door.

I followed him out. "It's after midnight, Ben. Get some sleep and leave in the morning."

"I'm wide awake."

"You've been drinking."

"Doesn't affect me."

"Then how about one more for the road?"

"There is no more."

I pulled my secret flask of whiskey from my coat and unscrewed the cap.

"That's yours," Ben said, "you drink it."

And I did, all of it, as Ben fired up his car and burned rubber in the driveway tearing away.

Point Counterpoint

I did more digging on Jasmine Elm and learned that not long after her Barnes & Noble event, which Dr. Loeb attended, posters went up all over the Ballyvaughan campus announcing that she would be coming to the college to debate Loeb on the first day of October.

The college was not amused. Protests against Ms. Elm's appearance were launched from all quarters. Students called her a racist anti-Semite whose bullshit bigotry shouldn't be dignified or even acknowledged by an appearance on a college campus. Academic departments spit out their history-based, science-based, politics-based, philosophy-based, legally-based, sociology-based, spiritually-based, and even astrophysics-based reproofs. An English professor graded Elm's hypotheses thusly:

A for **A**sinine
B for **B**alderdash
C for **C**ontemptible
D for **D**egenerate
E for **E**vil but **E**legantly **E**xpressed
F for **F**ucked Up.

The Alumni Office polled graduates' opinions which ran three percent approve, eighteen percent disapprove, seventy-seven percent strongly disapprove, and two percent kill the bitch. The Phys Ed office withheld comment on Ms. Elm's opinions but said that anatomically she was quite a piece of work.

Glenfarne residents feared Ms. Elm's appearance would provoke street violence. Local petitions demanding her speech be cancelled sagged under the weight of so many signatures.

Ms. Elm's bookstore appearances had so far gone off without major incident, which is to say with no more than minor bruises and lost teeth suffered by the pro-Elm placard bearers greeting attendees as they filed out. But Elm knew from experience how combustive college audiences could be, and how rioting for the latest lost liberal cause was practically a sanctioned sport. Thus she asked Dr. Loeb if he could assure her safety on campus. His response to her, which he self-quoted in his daily column for the college newspaper *The Ballyhoo*, went as follows: "In the words of Voltaire, 'I disapprove of what you say but I will defend to the death your right to say it.'"

"Voltaire didn't say that," Elm said, "English biographer Evelyn Beatrice Hall did in 1906 describing Voltaire's defense of free speech."

"I was paraphrasing."

Ms. Elm remained concerned. For one thing, Loeb could not possibly approve of her views and would obviously relish her intellectual humiliation, if not a physical assault on her person.

"Approval or disapproval don't matter," Loeb replied. "What matters is the right of free expression under the First Amendment. Or, as Patrick Henry said: 'Give me liberty to speak freely or give me death.'"

"I could do without the last part."

"Again, paraphrasing."

"Does your vow to defend me imply that indeed there will be hell-bent factions to defend against? The First Amendment also gives the right of peaceable assembly. Do you guarantee a peaceable event?"

"On my honor."

"Will you be in personal attendance to guarantee this?"

"Yes, I swear."

To those at the college opposing Ms. Elm's appearance, which was just about everyone at the college, Dr. Loeb insisted that institutions of higher learning should listen to all sides of any issue before condemning the wrong side to perdition. They got his message: that he was going to hang Jasmine Elm out to dry; hoist her on her own petard, so to speak.

Of course I was avid to know how Elm had fared in her face-to-face clash with Dr. Loeb on that October 1st afternoon, so I asked the college about the event. They told me that rather than tell me about it I could watch the videotape they'd made of it. Luckily, I hadn't returned my player to the electronics store yet.

Unlike the splendiferous color palette of Dr. Loeb's sun-kissed travel videos, this tape was in black and white. It opened with a pan of the audience in the Founders' Hall auditorium. Despite calls to boycott Ms. Elm's presentation, the place was packed.

Two chairs had been placed onstage for the debaters, and between them was a moderator's lectern behind which stood Lou Pinto, the dean of the college. Raising his hands to quiet the excitedly jabbering crowd, he spoke into the microphone, but earsplitting feedback obscured his voice. A techie rushed out and fiddled with the microphone, made signals to the sound booth up behind the balcony, gave Pinto a thumbs-up, and departed. Pinto tried again. "This has been billed as a debate," he said loud and clear. "But Dr. Loeb has decided not to set himself and his guest as adversaries, but rather as interlocutors who have agreed to disagree in a mutual quest for, if not common ground, then at least a greater mutual understanding, which might be shared by those in attendance here today. Thus it is my ... " Pinto looked down at his notes. "... pleasure to welcome to Ballyvaughan College Ms. Jasmine Elm."

There was a smattering of courtesy hand-claps when Elm walked onstage, but most of the crowd Bronx cheered and hissed. "Hello, Ballyvaughan!" Ms. Elm called back to the crowd like a rock star on a 50-city tour opening her set. She had a rocker's look, in fact, in her high-top sneakers, gold hoop earrings, and silver lamé suit. When she was seated, Pinto introduced Dr. Loeb, then looked left, then right, expecting Loeb to appear, but Loeb did not appear. "Dr. Loeb? Are you here?" No Loeb. Instead, the techie returned and whispered into

Pinto's ear then left the stage. "I am told that Dr. Loeb has been delayed en route."

"En route?" piped Ms. Elm. "From where? His office? That's right across the street."

"I do not have details," said Pinto.

"We don't need any. Obviously, Amos Loeb has gotten cold feet!" Elm cackled at her own joke. Instead of laughing, the crowd responded with whistles and hoots. "Ah, good, I see that all my fans have showed up. But where is security?" Ben, standing at the back of the hall, raised his hand. "*You* are security?" she said in jeering disbelief. Ben was the only uniformed security officer in the auditorium. That amazed him, given that the tension around campus was at a boiling point. Why had Dr. Loeb not requested that Chief Roby be present? What was Ben alone going to do if things got out of hand here, spray tear gas and shoot up the joint? Honestly, with present day undergrads avenging poor grades by slashing their professors' car tires and demonstrating for animal rights by running various livestock for student senate and electing a sheep, there was no telling what these liberal young zealots might do tonight.

A paper airplane sailed toward the stage, on course for Ms. Elm. She reached out and grabbed it, unfolded it, snickered at what she saw, then displayed for the audience a drawing of herself goose-stepping, her right arm extended in a Hitler salute. "An excellent likeness, I commend the artist," she said. "But where's the mustache?" With a ballpoint she scribbled in a Hitler-style mustache then held up the enhanced image, actually earning a little applause and some genuine laughs.

Dr. Loeb had still not appeared and as minutes passed some in the audience got up to go to the bathroom, some ate the remains of their lunches which they'd brought wrapped in napkins, some huddled and murmured conspiratorially. When a half-hour had elapsed Ms. Elm snapped, "Fuck it, let's start."

"Obviously," said Dean Pinto, "we can't start without our host."

"Who needs him?" Elm fired back. "I talk to empty suits most of the time. An empty chair tonight is good enough."

"If you will excuse me for a moment," said Pinto. "I will go check on Dr. Loeb's whereabouts. I will be right back." He departed the stage, leaving Elm alone on it.

"I could sing some Schubert lieder while we're waiting," she proposed to the restless attendees.

"We'll do the singing," someone responded and promptly began vocalizing spiritedly in Hebrew. Of course I didn't understand the Hebrew words but I have since acquired a translation of "*Zog Nit Keyn Mol*," the famous World War II Jewish anthem that begins:

Never say this is the end of the road.
Wherever a drop of our blood falls, our courage will grow anew.
Our triumph will come and our resounding footsteps will proclaim:
We are here!

The solo voice is then joined by several others:

From the land of palm trees to the far-off land of snow,
we shall be coming with our torment and our woe.
And everywhere our blood has sunk into the earth,
our bravery and vigor will blossom forth!

By now the whole assembly was on its feet and in full voice:

We'll have the morning sun to set our days aglow.
Our evil yesterdays will vanish with the foe.
But if time is long before the sun appears,
let this song go like a signal through the years.

Up on the stage Jasmine Elm sat gazing vaguely at the ceiling as if she wasn't even hearing the ever-louder chorale. She looked back down when the crowd began leaving their seats and approaching the stage.

This song was written with our blood and not with lead.
It's not a song that summer birds sing overhead.
It was a people amidst burning barricades
that sang the song of ours with pistols and grenades.

Now the onrushers reached the stage and started clambering up upon it while Ben, too stunned by this uprising or simply too impressed to want to restrain it, remained at the back. Jasmine Elm stood and thrust out her hand in the manner of a policeman stopping Nuremburg rallygoer traffic with a Hitler salute. As the crowd pressed forward she cried, "Halt!" and then as they closed in around her she whimpered to the man who was not there: "Dr. Loeb! Help me!" and then when the mob was inches from her person she reached into her purse and pulled out a gleaming knife.

The House of Atreus

The next morning, Friday November 1, 1988, was an autumn classic, the sky that stunning Vermont deep royal blue, the air crisp as bacon just fried in a cast iron skillet on a wood stove burning piñon chips. Dr. Loeb sat in his office before a TV on which played the video of the previous night's Jasmine Elm fiasco in Founders' Hall. Loeb hunched close as on the screen Elm pulled her knife to defend against the maddened crowd and in the next instant a pistol-waving Ben Marble entered the frame commanding the students to stand back and firing a warning shot at the ceiling when they continued forward. With the crowd thus halted, Ben rushed to disarm Jasmine Elm who, before he reached her, fled into the wings still clutching her knife. And then the screen went black.

A knock on the office door prompted Loeb to pull the tape from the player and go and greet his two visitors. Minutes later he was weathering Piggy Foxley's Aeschylus routine, flinching reflexively each time she brandished her knife. Piggy's mother stood close by, prompting the girl when she forgot a line, which was often.

As Piggy declaimed, Loeb turned back toward the window through which he noted the ugly dead leaves all over the green which Buildings and Grounds had not swept up yet. "What a mess," he muttered, causing Piggy to halt mid-soliloquy.

"No good?" she said.

"What? No, very good. Great. I wish you luck."

"There's more."

"No more needed."

"So you'll take her?" Faye said.

"It's not up to me."

"You're the president."

"Exactly, just the president. I'm afraid admissions is not my bailiwick." He motioned the women toward the door. He said he had a busy day and was behind schedule. Hundreds if not thousands of alumni were on campus expecting to meet him personally and offer their congratulations on his good work. And then there would be the big bonfire rally tonight. Loeb needed to bone up on the twenty-five verses of the college anthem so he could lead the lead the crowd in singing it.

Faye understood. She would not take any more of the president's time if he answered two simple questions: One, after witnessing her daughter's brilliant performance did he not agree that she was prime Ballyvaughan material? And two, considering Faye's and Dr. Loeb's past relationship, might Loeb now find it in his heart to pre-empt his admissions committee and grant this artistically gifted child immediate admission to the college?

No, Loeb said, he could not find it in his heart to do either of those things.

"Well, to hell with you," Faye snapped. She grabbed the knife from Piggy and after mock-threatening Loeb with it, stashed it in her purse.

Dr. Loeb's wife Lucy entered at that moment with beef and her own knife. "Not now!" Amos roared and Lucy turned and fled. Faye and Piggy followed her out.

A Chosen One

Was I a writer playing detective, as Ben had snidely suggested? Not at all. I wasn't writing about a crime, I was writing about a community's reaction to a crime. Vibrant characters would drive my book, not some creaky murder mystery plot. As a nonpartisan observer I was rooting for neither Ben nor Roby to succeed in solving the Loeb murder. And I certainly had no stake in cracking the case myself. I viewed certain individuals as "persons of interest," but not as possible criminals, rather as colorful supporting characters in my story. I knew quite enough about Tom Dunraven and Charlie Cubbage to depict them fully and fairly. I knew more than enough about Jasmine Elm and Faye and Piggy Foxley, three oddballs who at worst would be feminine counterweights to the male actors in the drama, and at best would provide comic relief. Lucy Loeb was, dramatically speaking, a weightless presence, and would be a bit player for whom a line or two of dialogue would suffice.

Not so comic or weightless was Avital Mittelman about whom Ben Marble had told me a certain amount. Ben had boasted in fact about his relationship with her, which he implied was sexual, though he'd only described their first kiss. When I asked him for more information about her he buttoned his lip. That was vexing since without a fully researched and faithfully rendered accounting of this woman's life, or at least the parts of it relevant to the Loeb case, my portrait of her would be incomplete. Ben had mentioned that she worked at the Ballyvaughan Inn bar and that's where I caught her one night. I opened by complimenting her pretty Irish lass server's outfit and lauding her attentive service. Before pumping her for Loeb-related information I had to establish that I viewed her as a human being not just as a potential character in the book I was writing. I would lay out my literary mission only after she'd taken the bait.

And so I did, and the prospect of appearing in a book excited her. Looking back, I understand that I was smitten with her from the first instant, though I didn't admit it to myself at that moment. All I knew was that the prospect of spending extended time with this beauteous and no doubt fascinating woman thrilled me.

"Where to begin?" she said.

"At the beginning."

"Of what, my whole life?"

"Start at last summer."

"You don't care about my whole life?"

"We'll get to that. First tell me about your association with Dr. Loeb."

"I wouldn't call it an association."

"Your acquaintance with him."

"I met him last summer. I came to ask him for some information."

"About ... ?"

"His time at Auschwitz."

"You're a World War II buff?"

"This was more personal than that."

"Did he give you the information?"

"Yes, he did. He was very accommodating, completely candid, and basically just so nice."

"But not so nice to everyone."

"What do you mean?"

"Not so nice to those who wanted him dead."

"No, to them he was a prick."

"A very big one apparently."

"Very big."

"So perhaps the part of his body the assailant severed was symbolic?"

"Of what?"

"What his enemies thought of him. A prick, as you said."

"I can tell you're a writer."

"How?"

"Using words like that."

"Prick? That was your word."

"Maybe I could be a writer."

I cleared my throat to assert the end of this silly diversion from the main topic. "How well did you know Dr. Loeb, Avital?"

"I knew him very well."

"But you'd only met him last summer."

"You can know some people in one minute. Like I'll bet you knew me at first sight tonight."

"Hardly. Ben Marble mentioned you once or twice. That's how I knew you worked here."

"Ben Marble."

Her restatement of his name was affectless, suggesting indifference to the man rather than affection, which pleased me. But Ben wasn't my main interest here. "What did you know of Dr. Loeb before you met him?"

"What everybody knew from the magazine stories and all his books and awards. He was famous, a hero, God's gift to humanity."

"And when you met him he did not disappoint?"

"Not at all, he seemed like God's gift to *me*."

"You came for just one meeting with him, is that right?"

"That's right."

"And that was last summer but here we are in the New Year and you're still in Glenfarne. Why did you stay?"

"I liked it here. I still do."

"What do you like in particular?"

"What everyone likes, the exciting college atmosphere, the cute little town, the trees, the mountains. Everything."

"And you wanted to stay near Dr. Loeb?"

"Of course, he had what I needed."

"Information about Auschwitz, and more than you could get in one meeting."

Avital hesitated before answering. "Correct."

"What more did you hope to get?"

"Whatever he could give me."

"About ... ?"

"Auschwitz, like I said."

"What about Auschwitz in particular?"

"The people he might have met. Like my mother."

"Your mother was a prisoner at Auschwitz?"

"From 1942 to 1945."

"Oh, my goodness. Avi. That's what you meant when you said this was personal."

"Amos—Dr. Loeb—was there right when my mother was and I thought he might have met her. That was dumb of me."

"Why dumb?"

"You know how many Jews were sent to Auschwitz?"

"A million?"

"More than a million. So he couldn't have known my mother, I mean what were the chances?"

"And that's all you wanted to know, if he'd known your mother?"

"No, I wanted to know all about the camp, anything he could tell me, what it was like for him as a prisoner, and for the other prisoners, so I would know what it was like for my mother."

"She didn't tell you herself?"

"No."

"Why didn't she, do you think?"

"Why didn't she? Now *that's* a dumb question. She wanted to forget it. Obviously. She gave me a death stare each time I brought it up to her."

"So you did bring it up to her."

"A few times then I stopped. It was useless. No, worse, it was scary to see her freeze up like that."

"I can understand."

"Oh, really? Are you serious? You can understand what she went through? When you can't understand why she wouldn't want to remember it? I thought writers were smarter than that."

"I'll be more careful with my questions."

"And hey, don't writers only ask questions they already know the answers to?"

"That's lawyers in criminal court. We're the opposite."

She looked away. Was I losing her? It seemed that I was, so I turned to a blander subject. "Where are you living in Glenfarne?"

After apologizing for her little snit, Avital said she'd rented a cottage that was very nice and a step up from the unlovely County Mayo Motel, Glenfarne's cheapest hostelry, where she and her mother Esther Mittelman had checked in upon arriving in town a few months earlier. (I myself was currently residing at the County Mayo for economy reasons as I was writing my book not on commission from anyone nor with a publisher's advance, but on spec).

"Your mother is here with you?"

"She's a depressive and needs supervision. I couldn't leave her back home."

"Tell me more about your mother."

Avital said her mother had spent the first week at the motel propped up in bed with her bottle of sweet vermouth while Avital prepared for her meeting with Dr. Loeb. Esther was a drinker. Well, she had her reasons. It was surprising that Avital had not become alcoholic just by watching her mother souse herself every day. Avital relaxed by smoking the occasional joint. She wasn't proud to use an illegal substance but she wasn't ashamed to do so, either. As the singer said, whatever got you through the night. In short, Avital wasn't a sinner and she wasn't a saint. She didn't damn herself for her impure actions and she didn't congratulate herself on the purity of her thoughts.

Avital didn't smoke pot to reach a higher level of consciousness. She just needed help in loosening up. She was such a shy person. Shyness was her curse. When she arrived at a party everybody stopped talking. They stared at her as she slunk in. That was how she perceived it, anyway. She smiled, she waved, she flashed two thumbs up. She tried to shout out a friendly hello to this and that person but began stuttering the moment she opened her mouth. She was shy in other places, too. Her blood pressure jumped fifty points at the doctor's office. The supermarket cashier asked, "Cat got your tongue?" when she wouldn't divulge if she'd brought any discount coupons. "A penny for your thoughts," said her date when instead of mooning into his eyes she just stared off into the void. To make it up to her date she let him make love to her, and she extended the same courtesy to almost everyone else she spooked. She was promiscuous, yes, but with a purpose: to show the world she had a warm body, if not a warm heart.

Was no one else in the world shy besides herself? she wondered. Had everyone else been best friends since birth? It seemed that way sometimes, especially when you were Jewish. Which she was. Jewish. From old German Jewish stock. She wasn't shy about admitting that. Why be shy about being one of the Chosen People? Unless you were clothing shop owners Moshe and Esther Mittelman in Magdeburg, Germany in 1938. But it didn't matter if you were shy about admitting you were one of the Chosen People in Germany in 1938 because everyone knew already. That's why they made you wear a yellow badge in the form of the Star of David with *Jude* inscribed in faux Hebrew letters on it which made you known to all as a Jew whether you were shy about it admitting it or not. It was why a year earlier your shop window was shattered and your inventory destroyed on what, because the streets sparkled with glass fragments afterwards, was called *Kristallnacht.*

Avital's mother Esther told her teenage daughter how she and her husband Moshe were arrested and sent to Auschwitz-Birkenau on

October 21, 1944 where Moshe was immediately taken to the gas chamber and she was tattooed with her prisoner number and, since she was a clothier, was put to work in the tailoring studio mending the very fashionable apparel of the commandant's wife. SS guards overseeing the women's work were sometimes female but Esther's group was overseen by a male guard nicknamed Zänker by his SS supervisors. Zänker was a Jew himself and a prisoner here, one who had been assigned to oversee his fellow prisoners. These overseers were called kapos. Candidates for the kapo jobs had previous criminal records, or, like Zänker, just showed especially violent natures. The SS respected violent natures, especially in Jews where it was so unexpected. Jews were meek, they had observed, and only violent in their deviousness. Being Jewish didn't stop many kapos from treating their fellow Jews with notable cruelty. The harder they were on other prisoners, the better they were treated by the SS higher-ups. They got more food, warmer clothes, and they were not beaten. The kapos who worked prisoners to death the fastest would have their own lives spared, so they were told. Kapos lived a bit longer than other prisoners, but at a cruel price.

Esther told Avital that Zänker treated the seamstresses in his charge very harshly, but her less so. One time alone with her in a supply closet he said that he personally had spared her from immediate execution. Why? Because she reminded him of his mother who had died in this very camp the previous year. Esther might well survive the war if she worked well and made no trouble, Zänker said. *Arbeit Macht Frei*, he reminded her, and doing her kapo's personal bidding, would set her free also.

The Holocaust destroyed families and family histories so Esther was diligent in teaching her daughter the facts of her lineage. Thus Avital heard that she was conceived in Magdeburg just hours before Esther and Moshe were arrested there on October 21, 1944, and she was born a fatherless child on July 21, 1945. By that time Auschwitz had been liberated by the Soviet army and Esther, since Magdeburg had been mostly destroyed by Allied bombing, had been assigned to a displaced persons camp in northern Germany. Avital gained a stepfather when Esther, certain that Moshe had died at Auschwitz, married an American soldier stationed in Germany in 1950. She and Esther became American citizens when the little family then moved to the United States. Alas, Esther, guilt-ridden for betraying her wedding vows of eternal fidelity to Moshe—even though Moshe was presumed dead—divorced the American soldier.

Years after Avital heard this history from Esther orally, Avital found Esther's recollections of her wartime years, written in a notebook a few years after she left Auschwitz, and hidden since then in a locked steamer trunk which Avital found in the attic and pried open with a crowbar. Clearly, these private memoirs were not for public consumption but Avital was not the public, she was the memoirist's only child and as such could rightfully read whatever her mother wrote. She would have asked permission to read the notebook but her mother, severely depressed now for decades, could not have responded rationally.

The recollections were a revelation. Some incidents in the memoir were so bizarre and indeed shocking that Avital wondered if her mother had made them up. Some very significant events and calendar dates just did not compute. Unfortunately, Esther was too mentally unwell to clarify matters.

If Avital had been a World War II scholar or a Nazi hunter like Simon Wiesenthal she would have tracked down Auschwitz survivors and SS guards and gotten their reactions to her mother's diary, and more importantly would have learned who that Jewish kapo was who saved Esther's life. But by now those Auschwitz survivors and guards were probably all dead. There were not all that many survivors anyway to begin with. Between 1940 and 1945 over one million Jews were sent to Auschwitz. Most died in the camp and most of the rest were evacuated when the Red Army was nearing the gates. When Auschwitz-Birkenau was liberated there were only 7,000 prisoners remaining, left behind because they were too old or sick for a death march through Poland in the middle of winter.

Avital could have looked in archives for documents about the Nazi camps that might have shed light on her mother's recollections, but Avital had trouble reading massive amounts of printed material. She had trouble reading small amounts of material too. She was dyslexic. She was shy about her dyslexia at first but then it was a relief to explain to people why she couldn't read through a sentence with adverbs and adjectives in it. She had a condition, like some people have spina bifida. She didn't ask for this condition, she was born with it but the world doesn't care what you were born with, aortic stenosis or a club foot or a disease in your genes like vascular dementia that waits until you are older to show up. The world says you made your bed so damn it, sleep in it.

So Avital let the whole issue of her mother's notebook drop. She stopped being curious. She willed away her curiosity. It crept back frequently but she quashed it every time. And she forcibly forgot about finding and thanking that kapo to whom her mother owed her life, and by consequence to whom Avital owed her own life as well. He probably couldn't be found anyway. He had probably changed his name and been absorbed back into society. Or he was dead in which case the whole matter was moot.

But then on the cover of *Time Magazine* in the summer of 1988 Avital saw the face of someone who could help her in her search. The face belonged to Dr. Amos Loeb, the president of Ballyvaughan College. The article on Dr. Loeb said he had been a prisoner at Auschwitz-Birkenau and Avital realized he had been there at exactly the same time as her mother. "Do you recognize him, Ima?" Avital asked Esther, showing her the picture but not expecting a cogent verbal response since Esther was in was one of her darker funks at that moment and was not speaking. "Blink once for yes, two for no." Esther blinked several times which was inconclusive. But how could she recognize someone whom she had last seen forty-plus years ago if she had seen him at all? People change. "He might know who saved you at the concentration camp," said Avital. The desultory blinking continued. "I want to go meet him. Do you mind if I bring your notebook? Yes, I found your notebook and I've read it. I hope you don't mind." Esther's blinking stopped. Her eyes moistened. Avital realized they might be moistening at the thought of being left home alone in a helpless condition. "You'll come with me, of course."

Of course Esther would come with Avital. She couldn't be left home alone in her emotional state. In her darkest periods she didn't get out of bed. When her meds were working she lightened briefly and behaved like a toddler who opens every household cabinet that isn't locked and pulls out liquor bottles and power drills and roach killer and sewing kits. And she wandered, not just inside the house but all around the neighborhood and sometimes beyond the neighborhood. Once she was captured by the state police as she was ambling up the on ramp to the southbound Interstate. The other problem was her pyromania. She would light matches and watch the flames, transfixed, and would not flinch or even make a sound when they burned down and singed her fingertips. Avital caught her one day when she had piled up crumpled newspapers on the dining room table and was trying to ignite them with a Bic lighter which fortunately was out of butane.

Esther wasn't quite elderly but her catastrophic experiences had wrinkled her, whitened her hair, and caused her to walk with a stoop. Her depression was treatable in theory but ten vain years of psychiatry and psychotropics made it seem not so treatable in fact.

But Avital's own prospects were looking up. On the drive to Vermont she mused over her own good luck in coming across the magazine feature on Amos Loeb. What if she had not gone to the dentist that day and picked up that magazine in the waiting room? Her curiosity, now revived and more ravenous than ever, might never have been satisfied and her thirst to find out the man who was her mother's guardian angel and perhaps much more than that might never have been slaked.

The bar manager had clumped over to our table. "Is this guy bothering you?" he said to Avital, giving me a threatening look.

"I'm just a writer," I said.

"You could still bother somebody."

"He's no bother at all," Avital assured the manager.

It was after midnight. I thanked Avital for sharing so much about her mother with me.

"I'm just getting started," she said but before she could continue the manager, shaking his keys, said he was locking up. I told Avital she could tell me more tomorrow but she suggested doing so right now over coffee at the bus station which was open all night.

A Displaced Person

The coffee, dispensed from a vending machine, was steaming and almost bubbling hot. I burned my tongue on my first sip.

"Dr. Loeb's office is in the Ballyvaughan Administration Building," Avital said. quaffing her scalding brew without wincing. "You know the Administration Building?"

Of course I did. I'd explored Dr. Loeb's office. The edifice was a stolid, three-story mass of ivy-choked brick with a plantation-style columned front portico. Avital described walking right in and climbing right up the grand staircase to the executive offices and marching right to Dr. Loeb's office suite and knocking on the door. Nobody stopped her. In a later era there would be metal detectors and guards asking you to state your business, but society in 1988 was more free and open with minimal terrorist incidents compared to subsequent decades.

But really, why should anyone stop a pert and pretty 42 years-young woman walking to the college president's office, notepad in hand and purse over her shoulder, even in a paranoid social climate? She wouldn't fit the typical terrorist profile so why should she set off alarms? But then again many terrorists don't fit the terrorist profile either.

Dr. Loeb's secretary looked familiar to Avital. The Swiss-style braids, fair complexion, and sky-blue, slightly misaligned eyes recalled Avital's childhood nanny Gudrun, but Gudrun, an avid mushroom hunter, had eaten an *amanita virosa* mushroom and passed away ages ago. The familiar saying, "There are old mushroom hunters and there are bold mushroom hunters but there are no old, bold mushroom hunters" thus held true. "Recognizing Dr. Loeb's secretary here today is just my memory playing tricks," Avital told herself. "Good old *déjà vu.*"

The secretary let Avital in to see the president immediately, almost as if Avital had made an appointment. Avital was amazed by this casualness but then she remembered Dr. Loeb saying in the *Time* magazine article that in making Ballyvaughan coeducational he was granting women full and immediate access not just to the college's esteemed faculty but also to the president himself. "My door will always be open to you, ladies," he declared to the first group of entering females, "I am here for you day or night."

On the magazine cover Loeb had presented an irregularly featured but not uncomely face, with a scar on the right side as if closing a parenthesis around the noble, slightly skewed Roman nose. And those bedroom eyes! Avital was smitten immediately, not in a romantic way since Loeb had a wife, Lucy, who appeared in her own photo as a clearly camera-shy Swiss Miss-type. No, Avital was smitten with the realization that this man Loeb was someone who could fill in details about what her mother had written about Auschwitz, and more importantly, who might identify the kapo who saved her life.

A toilet flushed somewhere. A moment later Dr. Loeb appeared through a door in the back wall, tucking in his shirt and tightening his belt. "Do you like what you see?" he said to his visitor in his amiably *männlich* tone of voice as he then tightened the four-in-hand knot of his wine-dark necktie which a fashion innocent might take to be polyester but any Loeb intimate would know was pure silk.

"Excuse me?" said Avital.

"The college. Are we treating you girls all right?"

"Yes. That is, no." Avital cleared her throat. Loeb frowned. "That is, I'm not at the college."

"Ah, of course. It all still seems like a dream, I'll bet."

"I'm not a student at the college."

"No? Why not?"

"Should I be?"

"You look like a perfect fit."

"I'm too old."

"Never too late to learn, I say." He waved her into his enormous oak-paneled office with a stuffed elk's head high on one wall.

"My name is Avital Mittelman."

"Beautiful name."

Avital felt a tickle in her belly. "Thank you."

"I knew some Mittelmans once."

"It's a common Jewish name, I imagine you've known many."

"One or two in particular." He saw Avital staring at the elk's head. "I didn't shoot that."

"Pardon?"

"I'm not a hunter. That was here when I took over this office. I've been meaning to have it removed."

"You'd need a ladder to reach it."

"The workmen would bring that."

"Or you could throw a lasso and pull it down."

"Would you like a glass of iced tea?"

"No, thank you."

"It's not instant, I make it myself. I buy the green tea leaves direct from the grower in Ceylon. Er, Sri Lanka. I roast them in my oven. First I clean the oven to remove any residue of bread or meat. I lay paper towels in a baking pan and spread tea leaves on the towels to no more than point-five centimeters in height. I've preheated the oven to eighty degrees centigrade. That's, hm, one hundred seventy-six Fahrenheit, not very hot. Then I place the pan on the middle rack and I roast the leaves for ten minutes, tossing and stirring them frequently lest they burn."

"All right, I'll have some."

Loeb made no move to get the iced tea. "So you're here to check us out?"

"Well, not precisely."

"You want to get a feel for the place, chat with some current students, meet a few professors, sit in on a couple of lectures, press flesh with the kommisariat."

"I'm not applying for admission."

"I'm very sorry. Why not? Of course, you already have a college degree."

"Actually, no."

"You don't think you can afford college."

"It's not that."

"Many scholarships are available."

"It's my age."

"You're what, late twenties?"

"I'm forty-two years old."

"Nonsense."

"I'm almost forty-three."

"Compared to me you're a cub."

"I'm sure this is a fine college, but—"

"But it does not meet your expectations in some way?"

Avital had no expectations, none for going to college this late in life and none for Ballyvaughan College per se. Her expectations, or at least hopes, were simply for whatever Loeb could tell her about Auschwitz.

"We are not Yale or Harvard," Loeb said.

"Who wants to be Yale or Harvard?" Avital said.

"Bingo! Now I *know* you were made for Ballyvaughan."

In fact, Avital did feel made for Ballyvaughan. She was enchanted by its mix of Georgian and Greek revival architecture, its sylvan setting, and the picture-postcard village that surrounded it.

"Oh, you'd love it here," said Loeb, pressing his absurd point.

But Avital felt that indeed she would love it—to feel young again and thirsty for new knowledge, to be virginal and unfledged. She wasn't old, barely forty, yet she was ever more pessimistic about her personal prospects, given the dire straits of mother-care she was in.

Yes, feeding, washing, and clothing a woman as great as Esther Mittelman was a privilege and often a pleasure. But the added challenge of lifting her suicidal moods was becoming more than Avital could bear.

"Then I take it we don't meet your expectations," Loeb said.

"Honestly, Dr. Loeb—"

"Amos."

"I came here not knowing what to expect exactly."

"So there is hope!" The secretary entered holding a silver tray with two glasses of iced tea and a sugar bowl. "This is Lucy," Loeb said, "my wife."

Of course, his wife. That photo of her in *Time* magazine. "Hello, Mrs. Loeb," said Avital.

"We call her Lucy," Loeb said.

"Pleased to meet you," said Lucy in a near-whisper.

"Did you make this tea at home and bring it here?" Avital asked her. "How nice of you."

Lucy shook her head.

"You didn't make it at home?"

"She makes it right here," Loeb said. He explained that there was a small kitchen in the administration building, with stove, oven, fridge, and sink. "You could make Thanksgiving dinner in there," he said.

Lucy added in her whisper, "Once I did."

Loeb elaborated, "One Thanksgiving our power went out in the president's mansion so we came to this office of mine for our feast. My desk here became our banquet table. Fun. It felt like dining out. Who carved the bird, Lucy?"

"I did." Still whispering.

"She always carves. I'm hopeless, can never find the leg joint, I hack and hack and the bird ends up shredded. My wife knows where to slice. Are you hungry, Avital?" Avital shook her head. "Bring us a little something, will you, Lucy?" Lucy nodded and departed. With silver tongs Loeb picked a sugar cube from the bowl, held it to Avital. "One lump or two?"

"None, please."

"Ah, just like I take my whiskey, neat."

"Cubes don't dissolve in iced tea very quickly."

"No, they make you wait." Despite preferring unsweetened tea, Loeb dropped the cube into his glass and watched it begin to disintegrate. "Go ahead, drink yours. It'll get cold if you don't."

"It's already cold."

"That's the joke."

Avital took a sip. "Delicious."

Loeb continued watching his sugar cube until it was one with the liquid. Then he looked back at Avital who he realized was still standing. "Sit you down, sister, rest you." He rubbed the seat of the chair facing his desk as if to warm it up.

Lowering herself, Avital gazed through the window at the great whitewashed brick buildings of Ballyvaughan Row across the green. She had wandered their corridors yesterday in late afternoon, cheered by the scratching of chalk on chalkboards, beguiled by the lilting drone of tenured faculty as they lectured from their wisdom-worn, yellowed notes. The drone was not lulling, it was galvanizing, almost titillating in how it stroked the divinely sensitive tissue of the listener's intellect.

Loeb settled into his desk chair. "Have you had your admissions committee interview yet?"

"No."

"Shall I set one up for you?"

"Maybe later."

"*Carpe diem.*"

"Excuse me?"

"*Quam minimum credula postero.*"

"What does that mean?"

"You enroll here, you'll find out."

Avital felt very small all of a sudden, not because she was that much smaller than Dr. Loeb who probably didn't stand six feet (she was five-nine), but because the chair he had given her was so much lower than his, almost like the chairs in a kindergarten classroom that parents have to squat down to sit on when they come in for conferences with their kids' teacher. Avital was not a parent but she remembered her mom complaining that when she squatted down to face Avital's preschool teacher her knee joints cracked like pistol shots.

Loeb's chair was like a throne, black-upholstered, gold braid trimmed, overstuffed, and with a back rising higher than its occupant's head. It was on a swivel. As Loeb waited for Avital to declare her mission he swiveled around to gaze out the nearly floor-to-ceiling window at the green where in just two months the Autumn Inferno bonfire would be lit and would burn furiously for hours until it was a huge mound of smoldering ashes which the fire department would then drench in water so that it didn't spit sparks and ignite the trees surrounding the green.

"My parents were at Auschwitz-Birkenau," Avital said. Dr. Loeb continued gazing out the window. "Right when you were, I think."

Loeb swiveled back to Avital. From his throne he looked downward at her so she had to look up. To see the elk's head on the wall she had to look up even higher. Once back in grade school she'd pelted her worst enemy Marilee Reuven with a spitball and was sent to the principal's office where she sat in a small chair opposite the principal standing like a colossus behind his big steely desk. She felt tiny then like she did now, ant-like. The principal looked so tall that Avital thought he must be up on a pedestal. He had the bellicose mien of the war hero's statue in front of the DMV building where she was later issued her driver's license. "What's your name, Missy?" the colossal principal had said.

"Av-Av-Av- ," Avital had stuttered, her tongue stuck to the roof of her mouth. The principal didn't have an elk's head on the wall like

Dr. Loeb did, he had pictures of his gap-toothed kids and his stick-figure wife. He let Avital off with a one-hour detention. She had expected much, much worse. He was known to rap mischief-makers on the knuckles with his metal draftsman's ruler.

"Your parents were where?" said Dr. Loeb, not yet touching his iced tea.

"Auschwitz-Birk- ," answered Avital, tripping on the B-word as thoughts of the camp's horrors clenched her throat. She tried again: "Birk-Birk-Birk-," sounding like a clucking hen.

"At Auschwitz-Birkenau. And they died there?"

"My father did, Moshe Mittelman. My mother is still living, Esther Mittelman."

"Give her my fondest, will you?"

"You knew her?"

"Knew her? Oh, dear child, I knew no one there, it was not possible."

"Of course it wasn't."

"Yes, some faces became familiar but as for learning names—"

"Of course, I'm sorry, what am I thinking? There were thousands of you there."

"Tens of thousands."

"Tens of thousands, right."

"Hundreds of thousands."

"Please forgive me."

"No, dear child, forgive *me*!"

"For what?"

"I might say for surviving."

"I *congratulate* you for that."

"Please, that only makes it worse."

"Makes what worse?"

"The particular condition."

"What condition?"

"KZ syndrome, from the German term *Konzentrationslager.*"

"Survivor guilt."

"Your mother has it, no doubt, the anxiety, depression, nightmares, mood swings."

"She has all that."

"The lassitude persisting for weeks or even months, years sometimes."

"Tens of years so far with her. But now and then she lightens up and seems to forget what's depressing her."

"That would be nice sometimes."

"What?"

"To forget."

Lucy Loeb entered again, this time with a larger tray on which were napkins, utensils, two plates, a foot-long shiny knife, and a platter weighted with a great steaming block of roast beef.

"Have you had lunch?" Loeb asked Avital.

"I have a banana with me."

"That's not enough." Loeb took the knife and started slicing the meat, but with some difficulty. He addressed Lucy with seeming annoyance: "Not sharp enough."

From out of somewhere—a pocket in her apron? thin air?—Lucy drew a knife sharpener, took the knife, and started sharpening it. Avital watched mesmerized as the blade slid back and forth over the little discs that looked like nickels: *swish-swish, swish-swish*. Finally, Lucy returned the knife to her husband who eyeballed it as if scanning it microscopically for burrs and nicks. Lucy awaited his judgment, stolid as a defendant before her sentencing. Loeb then ran the blade across his forearm. The hairs lopped cleanly and fell like a miniscule clear-cut stand of oak, leaving a little bald patch above the wrist.

Avital watched quizzically, then got it. "Oh, I see. If the hairs don't cut easily then the knife's not sharp enough?"

"Don't try this at home," Loeb chuckled. He resumed carving the beef which was on the rare side so blood seeped out and pooled at the tray's perimeters.

"I thought Lucy did all the carving," said Avital.

"Just the birds," said Loeb. "I cut the beef."

When he finished carving Lucy took the tray, knife, and sharpener and vanished. Avital was on her first bite when Loeb said, "What did your mother tell you about Auschwitz?" After swallowing Avital replied that her mother had rarely spoken of her time there and now with her depression she was totally mum on the subject. "However," Avital added, "she did write down her recollections."

"Recollections?" said Loeb, hunching forward.

"Of her experiences at the camp."

"What did she recollect?"

"You can see for yourself, I have her memoir right here." Avital took a notebook from her purse and set it on Loeb's desk. He regarded it like it was ticking. "Open it, have a look." He did not open it. "I can summarize its contents. Or I can leave it here and you can read it at your leisure."

"Leisure! Me? Ha!"

"I want you to read it because I have a bunch of questions for you."

"About?"

"What she wrote."

"These are her recollections, not mine. Why ask me about what she wrote?"

"Because you were there at the exact same time she was."

"Was I?"

"My mother was imprisoned from October 21, 1944 to not long after January 27, 1945."

"The date that Auschwitz-Birkenau was liberated."

"Exactly."

Loeb gazed out the window. He was always gazing out that window. "Then yes, we did overlap."

"I understand you're very busy, Dr. Loeb. Me asking you to read my mother's notebook is presumptuous, I know that."

"You can read it."

"I've read it already."

"I mean read it to me. Not every line, just the key sections."

"Right now?"

"*Quam minimum credula postero.*"

"Wow, okay. *Carpe diem*, right?"

And so Avital walked Dr. Loeb through Esther's notebook of recollections, highlighting especially vivid descriptions while Loeb pointed out apparent inconsistencies and potential fabrications. "Some of this struck me as fanciful also," said Avital. "But then again she's not the type of person to make things up."

"She was addled in the camp, don't forget," Loeb said.

"Addled?"

"That's a gentle term for what I really mean."

"She wasn't crazy."

"We all were crazy." He explained the mental derangement suffered by prisoners of any type, and its extreme form in those in a concentration camp.

"You went crazy in the camp, Dr. Loeb?"

"Everyone did, I'll leave it at that."

"But you recovered."

Loeb stood up and walked toward one wall until he was standing directly under the elk's head. "Here's my point: You can't hold your mother's intimately personal account to the same standard of truth as you would an objective third-party report."

"What do you mean?"

"Because it is a subjective report."

"What do you mean?"

"I mean your mother is the subject and the reporter both."

"Well, yes, it's a memoir."

"It needs corroboration."

"That's why I came to you."

"I'm glad you did."

"Did you know my mother?"

"As I've said, I did not."

"And you would not have known my father." Loeb shook his head. "Did you know the kapos?"

"Ah, the kapos."

"Perhaps the one who saved my mother? The man she describes in what I just read to you? Who took a liking to her and told his supervisor what a good seamstress she was and thus saved her from being killed in the camp?"

"Well, he must have been my twin."

"How so?"

"Your mother describes him as she would have described me, had we met."

"Except for the sadism."

"Pardon me?"

"A Jewish prisoner beating fellow Jewish prisoners."

"That apart, I would hope."

"Though he didn't beat my mother."

"And that redeems him, do you think?"

"A little maybe. A tiny bit. I mean however monstrous he was, if he were, say, my father, there might be some redemption in that."

"Your father? What are you talking about?"

"Nothing, I hope. But look at what my mother writes, and pay attention to the dates."

Dr. Loeb did not look. Instead he remained under the elk's head.

"As I said, my mother does not concoct stories."

"And as I said, memory, especially tortured memory, plays tricks."

"I believe that my mother was raped."

Loeb transited to the window once more and stood there perfectly still and perfectly mute, staring out at the idyllic campus green and noble buildings that made Ballyvaughan the jewel of the Ivy League.

"And I believe I am the child of that encounter." No response. "Dr. Loeb?"

"You say you are what?"

"I believe I am the child—"

"Of rape?"

"By that Jewish prison guard, yes. That's my conclusion."

"Ho, ho, that's making quite a leap."

"You take that lightly?"

"I take it with several large crystals of kosher salt."

"No, come here, it's right in these pages, I've connected the dots."

"Connections can trace varying patterns."

"Mine are a straight line."

"At first glance, perhaps." Loeb remained at the window.

"Why are you skeptical?"

"I'm not skeptical." He turned and came to Avital. "I'm just cautious regarding that in which I put my faith."

"Like God?"

"Like premature conclusions."

"I'm not premature. If anything, I'm too late!"

"My point is look before you leap. A chasm can be as wide as it is deep."

"You say look. I have looked, word by word, date by date. And now you're looking with me."

"But forming conclusions will need far more study on my part."

"Well, you can start by studying this: " Avital read aloud from her mother's notebook. "September 21ˢᵗ, 1945. 10:30 a.m. I give birth to Avital.' Does that seem weird?"

"Delivering a child? "

"Delivering a child on *that date* in that place."

"What place?"

"Look!" Avital thumped the page where it named the displaced persons camp Esther was sent to after Auschwitz was liberated.

"What's your point, Miss Mittelman?"

"Go back nine months from there to December 21ˢᵗ, 1945. Where was she on *that date*?"

"In Magdeburg with your father."

"No. She was at Auschwitz-Birkenau. She'd been taken away from Magdeburg two months earlier."

"When she was arrested with your father."

"Arrested with the man she always *told* me was my father."

"She was arrested in October 1944."

"Yes, October 1944, *eleven* months before I was born. That's the last time she and my father could have had sex."

"And thereby conceived you."

"Yes."

"Which they did, on that date, according to what your mother always told you."

"If they did on that date, and Moshe Mittelman was really my father, then I'd have been born in the displaced persons camp on July 21ˢᵗ, 1945. But I wasn't! I was born on *September 21ˢᵗ*, 1945! She records it right here." Again, Avital thumped her mother's words on the page: *"September 21ˢᵗ, 1945. 10:30 a.m. I give birth to Avital.'* That's what she wrote. And why would she write it? So there would be a record of the truth."

"But as I've said, your mother must be considered a classic unreliable narrator of events."

"Unreliable about giving birth to a baby with my name? Specifying exact date, time, and location? About naming the nurse who helped her through her labor? About describing in detail the inside of the medical tent at the DP camp? And about specifically identifying the Jewish guard who had raped her nine months earlier?"

"Wait a minute, she knew the kapo's name?"

"His nickname, Zänker."

"That's of little use."

"And his prisoner's tattoo number."

"She saw it?"

"He showed it to her."

"Why would he do that?"

"To make her not afraid of him. To remind her that they shared the same fate because they shared the same faith."

"She told you this?"

"No! She told me nothing, she wrote it in her secret book."

"Why didn't she tell you in person?"

"Would you tell your child that she was the product of a rape?"

"I don't have a child."

"Would you want your child to know that a rapist was her father? Not to mention that he betrayed his race?"

"By which you mean—"

"Capitulated to his captors, brutalized his fellow Jews in a death camp."

"That is such a complex topic."

"It's *simple* if you examine my mother's book. Moshe Mittelman simply can't be my father. I repeat: my birth date is eleven months after the last date he and my mother could have conceived me."

"They never met in the camp?"

"They were separated immediately. He went to the gas chamber."

"Apparently not."

"What?"

"Look here." Loeb focused on another entry in the notebook. "She says two months later, in the camp, she and he happened to meet."

"For less than half a minute."

"So he was not gassed."

"He was gassed later. First he was put to work in the crematorium. But the prisoners working in the crematorium were killed eventually because they knew what the Nazis were doing in these death camps. They knew the Nazis' secret, and if the prisoners survived they might let the secret out. Why am I telling you? You know all that."

"Still, if Esther and Moshe encountered each other at Auschwitz, it's conceivable—"

"That they could have conceived me then? In fifteen seconds? In the midst of a thousand other prisoners? On open ground between the main guard house tower and the medical experiments barracks? In the howling wind and the sleet?"

"All I'm saying is that their meeting was nine months before you were born, as your mother records in her memoir. Granting the unlikelihood of your conception in that moment, at least the timing would have been right."

"You were in the camp, Dr. Loeb. Did prisoners have sex with each other?"

"Not often."

"Is that a joke?"

"It happened."

"How?"

"You'd be surprised."

"And they were not beaten to death by the SS guards? Or by their kapos at least?"

"As I said, it is a very complex issue."

"Sex in the camps?"

"The kapos."

"You care about the kapos?"

"As objects of study, yes."

"As war criminals."

"As human beings who were perverted by inhuman circumstances."

"That mitigate their guilt?"

"That explain it. Maybe. I don't know yet, I am examining it in my book."

"What book?"

"My dear, it is more than fortuitous that you arrived at my door today, and with your particular mission. Because I have been on a similar mission."

"I know all about your work, I read the magazine."

"I mean a very specific mission within my overall mission, upon which I have just embarked."

"What mission?"

"That of identifying the Jewish prisoners assigned to guard other Jewish prisoners. The kapos, the exact monsters about whom your mother wrote and about whom you today speak. I am writing a book about them."

"You are?"

"You'd rather I did not?" Dr. Loeb said.

"No! I mean, no ... a whole book? That's amazing."

"You seem nonplussed."

"No, I'm just amazed since this is exactly what I came here to talk to you about."

"So it seems we were fated to meet."

"I'll certainly want to read your book."

"Patience. I've barely made a start."

"Maybe I could help you with it."

"You've helped already by bringing me your mother's notebook."

"I could go to the library, assist you with your research."

"No need to assist me, my dear. I'm an academic, for good or worse. I have sources, back channels, secret methods of getting at the truth. You leave all this to me."

"I can at least type up your manuscript."

"My good wife does that. Now when are you leaving Glenfarne?"

"I'm not."

"Eh?"

"I like it here." Avital told him she'd taken a job in the area and that after a dismal stint at the County Mayo Motel she'd rented a little cottage for herself and her mother.

Loeb waved a fly away. "Your mother?"

"That motel was the pits, the toilet was backed up and the water from the faucet was rusty colored. Plus, the room was too small for two people."

"Your mother is here with you?"

"I couldn't leave her at home. As I said, she's depressed. Would you like to meet her?"

"Does she see people?"

"No, but she'd see you. So do you want to meet her?"

"It would be a great honor. Perhaps the greatest of my life."

"We're at 229 Cork Street. Drop by any time."

"Would tomorrow at three o'clock work?"

"Perfectly. You know, Dr. Loeb, the minute I saw you on that magazine cover I had the strangest feeling."

"My mug does that to people."

"A feeling that you could help me find the man who saved my mother's life."

"Identify him possibly. Find him, though? Alive? He is most probably dead. The war was a long time ago."

"Just forty or so years. He'd only be about sixty years old by this time."

"And if alive he may be living incognito, probably far from the place of his crimes."

"Like Israel maybe?"

"It could be anywhere."

"Wouldn't Israel be logical?"

"Well, in fact, many kapos were taken to Israel after the war."

"And forgiven?"

"Many were savagely beaten there by lynch mobs."

"Killed?"

"Let me just say that starting in 1950, kapos' cases were adjudicated by Israeli criminal courts. Those convicted were imprisoned."

"Not executed?"

"No."

"So say he served his term and then was released."

"Released. Exactly. Back into the big wide world."

"Where he could be traced."

"Or not."

"Now you're sounding pessimistic."

"Dear, do you know how many males there are in the world today?"

"A billion?"

"2.580 billion. And you think there is a good chance that you can find and arrange to meet this single one?"

"There's a better chance now that I've met you. Anyway, all I need is *some* chance, just a small one, that he'll turn up on some census record or something somewhere."

"Not everyone in the world appears on a census record."

"And not everyone is identified with a Nazi concentration camp tattoo number. So that narrows it down. And I know his tattoo number."

"I will keep you posted on how my work is progressing."

"You are going to help me, then?"

"Of course I'm going to help you."

"Oh, Dr. Loeb, Dr. Loeb, I feel like crying right now."

"Go ahead."

"I'm too overwhelmed at this moment, I'll cry tonight."

"As you see fit."

"I don't know how to thank you, sir."

"No thanks necessary."

"So I should leave the notebook with you?"

"Please do."

"You asked me to forgive you earlier."

"I ask many things of many people. Some say I ask too much."

"I could forgive you."

"I was joking."

"I know you were."

"You're an angel, you know that, Miss Mittelman?"

"I'm certainly not an angel."

"Let others judge of that."

"Yes, how can we judge ourselves after all?"

"We can't."

"I forgive you."

"You have ten seconds to take that back, Miss Mittelman."

"And after ten seconds?"

"It just may be too late."

That evening at the Ballyvaughan Inn Avital celebrated meeting Dr. Loeb with the first distilled spirit of her lifetime, a double Laphroaig. The bartender said on the rocks? She said what Loeb said when specifying his own preference, neat.

An hour into her shift she served a man with a Licensed Security Guard badge on his shirt. "I'm Ben Marble," the man said after ordering a margarita.

"I'm Avital."

"Pretty name. Your mother's?"

"My mother's name is Esther."

"Join me for a drink?"

"She's at home."

"No, you."

"I'm on duty."

"Me, too."

"You can drink on duty?"

"My shift'll be done by the time you get back."

"I'll be quick."

"Take your time, I've got three minutes left on the clock."

Avital went and returned with two margaritas. Ben said he'd been joking about his shift ending in three minutes. His shift never really ended because his job of guarding Dr. Loeb was continuous. When he wasn't with Loeb physically, Loeb could reach him by walkie-talkie if there was trouble. Then Ben asked Avital her name again and she said she'd already told him her name and he said, "Oh, yes, Esther," and Avital said no, Esther was her mother's name, her own name was Avital, and Ben said, "Avital What?" and Avital said, "Mittelman,

Avital Mittelman." Then she said she was sorry but now she had to get back to work.

"But what about your drink?" Ben saw that Avital hadn't touched the second one she'd brought.

"I brought that for you, Mr. Marble. Save me another trip."

In the bus station the snort of an arriving bus's brakes interrupted Avital's narrative. I looked at the bus through the window. No one was getting on or off. In fact, I saw no driver.

Avital looked at me curiously. "I thought you were a writer."

"I am."

"But you're not writing."

"The writing comes later."

"I mean you're not writing down what I say. You're not taking notes."

"I use a tape recorder."

"I don't see any tape recorder."

I tapped the tiny microphone clipped to my shirt collar.

"I thought those hidden mics were for spies."

"I guess I am a spy of sorts."

"*The Spy Who Loved Me.*"

"I beg your pardon?"

"By Ian Fleming, that James Bond book." Avital had finished her coffee. Mine was still too hot to drink. "Where was I?" she said.

"Shall I play you back the tape?"

"No, I know, I was serving Ben Marble. Well, he hung around until closing time and came to me as I was polishing glassware. He said he'd loved watching me serve customers, and how fetching I was in my Irish barmaid getup of white tights, lime green lace-up vest, and tutu-length forest green skirt. He asked my age. Then he said no wait, he'd guess: thirty-two. I said no, but thank you very much, I was over forty. He said no. I said yes. He said, 'Married?' I shook my head. He said I should be married. I asked him why I should be married. He

140

answered because I was almost past the age of having kids. I said why do I have to be married to have kids? He said he meant biologically past the age because babies of mothers past the age of forty often had deformities. I said I thought he'd meant a child born to an unmarried woman was illegitimate. He said that was also true."

A policeman who'd been patrolling the deserted bus station came up to Avital. "Is this guy bothering you?" he said.

"He's no bother at all," Avital answered. The cop didn't seem convinced but he left us in peace. I asked Avital how the meeting between her mother and Dr. Loeb went.

"It was incredible," she said.

"How so?"

"The way they looked at each other, it was electric. And he was such a gentleman. He even got her to talk."

"What did she say?"

"I don't mean they had a conversation. She actually only said one word, I think."

"What word was that?"

"Move along, you two," the policeman interrupted, shouting from the other end of the room.

"We're waiting for our bus," I shouted back.

"Which bus?"

"To Atlantic City," Avital said.

"There's no buses to Atlantic City."

"We go to New York and change there."

"The next bus to New York is five hours from now."

"No problem, we've got our coffee, we can wait."

The cop slouched away to catch some bigger criminals. I asked Avital again what word Esther Mittelman had uttered with Dr. Loeb.

"Out of context it wouldn't mean anything to you," she replied.

"Try me."

"Really, you'd need to know the whole story of that afternoon."

"I'm listening."

Book Burning

"Oh, my dear, dearest Mrs. Mittelman," Loeb greeted Esther that afternoon upon arriving at the women's cottage for kosher afternoon tea, bearing still-warm challah bread as a housewarming gift. Esther said nothing, regarding the visitor blankly and remaining blank during the ensuing half-hour during which Loeb and Avital chatted inconsequentially.

"Mother, I showed Dr. Loeb your notebook," Avital said once her conversation with Loeb had petered out.

"Indeed, yes, here it is," said Loeb, drawing the notebook from his valise. "I almost forgot. It is a brave and magnificent achievement, Mrs. Mittelman. I salute you, I congratulate you, I thank you from the depths of my heart." He dabbed his eyes with a handkerchief. "Forgive me, your courage has touched my soul, your strength has made me weak."

"Zänker."

"Say that again, Mother?" Esther had broken her silence. Now we're getting somewhere, thought Avital. But Esther didn't repeat the word.

"Ah, Zänker," said Loeb. "Alas, for both good and ill he is in our presence here today, is he not? So to speak." He and Avital waited in vain for Esther's response to that statement. Loeb whispered to Avital, "Does she know that you think that the prison guard is your father?"

Avital shook her head.

"But she knows you read what she wrote in her notebook."

"I haven't told her that I read the notebook."

"Zänker," Esther now repeated.

"Who is Zänker, Mother?"

Esther didn't answer and took a bite of the bread.

"Mother, who is Zänker?"

"She doesn't remember," Loeb said. "Or she won't, she has suppressed the memory. She has KZ syndrome, don't forget." He held the notebook to Esther. "I return this with profoundest gratitude, madame." Esther accepted it. "And so I must be going." He pulled on his black leather gloves.

"No," said Esther.

"People to go, places to see."

"No." Esther repeated.

"No? No, what?"

Avital answered: "She means it's *places* to go, *people* to see."

"You're sharp, Mrs. Mittelman. Sharp—" He took Esther's hands and kissed them. "—as a tack."

Avital followed Loeb outdoors. "Thank you for coming. It meant a lot to her."

"Perhaps."

"And to me."

"Good."

"How's the book coming?"

"Book?"

"On Auschwitz, on the kapos."

"Ah. I've so many books. I'm usually writing two or three at a time."

"What have you found out?"

"Regarding?"

"The kapos. Or the kapo who is my father."

"I have some possible names, possibly."

"You do? Great. When can I see them?"

"They are most likely all of them dead."

"All I need is a name. Then I'll be happy."

"Will you?"

"To know who my father was, of course I will."

"And what will you do when you know who is your father?"

"If he's dead, nothing."

143

"And if he's not dead?"

"Go meet him."

"And do what?"

"I'll know what to do."

"Hug him? Kiss him?"

"Possibly."

"After what he did to your mother?"

"Hug him, kiss him, then shoot him dead." Avital laughed, sort of.

"You own a firearm?"

"Or cut his prick off, that would be more appropriate."

"Figuratively."

"Literally."

"If I do find the name—"

"Don't say *if*, say *when*."

"I may withhold it from you."

"No! You can't withhold it. Why?"

"Because it may do you no good."

"Who says it won't?"

"I do."

"For what reason?"

"Your own best interests."

"I think I can decide my own best interests."

"Too late, your mother already did."

"When?"

"When she put her notebook under lock and key."

"For me to jimmy open."

"She never dreamed you would."

"She didn't withhold the guard's name, though."

"I don't recall his name being in her notebook."

"His nickname, she put his stupid nickname Zänker. She didn't know his real name, which left finding it up to me."

"Which she didn't want you to do."

"If she didn't she'd have burned the evidence. Wouldn't you have burned it? I mean if all that had happened to you?"

"We are hypothesizing now which is very dangerous."

Loeb's gaze slipped by Avital to something beyond. Avital turned to see Esther in the doorway, the notebook in one hand and a lighted match in the other. "No, Mother!" Avital shouted but all she could do was watch the pages ignite.

I drove Avital home from the bus station. I told her I'd love to see her again, not just for further information, but because I'd enjoyed her company. She said she'd enjoyed mine. I hugged her and she hugged me back. I was tempted to kiss her, just on the cheek, but held back. Did she anticipate a kiss? Did she hope for it? I couldn't tell by her face, it was too dark. "So when can I see you again?" I asked her.

She said, "You know where I work."

A Man of the Theatre

Just as the real estate agent says "Location! Location! Location!" to sell a house, so the good writer says "Characters! Characters! Characters!" to sell a book, while the lesser writer says merely, "Plot."

And so I widened my search for local color, wangling invitations to cocktail parties, crashing weddings and bar mitzvahs, and bumming comp seats to amateur theatricals in town and college sporting events. There were no currently running college theatrical productions as the winter production of *West Side Story* had been cancelled for some reason having to do with the indisposition of its director, the legendary Professor Anton Wohlgemuth.

Wohlgemuth's legend, which I gleaned from his self-written profile in the Ballyvaughan course catalogue and later substantiated with theatre department records and colleagues' accounts, derived from his being not just a director but also a lighting, sound, and costume designer. He even helped paint scenery. In his spare time he wrote the odd play or two. Like Shakespeare and Molière before him, and like his countrymen Goethe and Schiller to no small degree, Herr Professor Doktor Anton Wohlgemuth was an *homme de théâtre* to the marrow, or a *Mann des Theaters* as this *stolzer deutscher künstler* would rather have you state.

Folks called Wohlgemuth a jack-of-all-theatre-trades but they didn't say master of none of those trades. "You can have your real life," he liked to proclaim, "you can have your dream life, your social and political life—and take your sex life, too!—but the play's the thing for me." He said it first in German then translated as he did with most of his utterances.

In addition to practicing the dramatic arts, Dr. Wohlgemuth taught them brilliantly to Ballyvaughan Drama Department students. When

Dr. Loeb hired him as an adjunct professor in 1972 that department was in a shambles. The then-chair was found to have falsified his Ph.D. credentials. The theatre building had been condemned by the fire department after the burning of Atlanta scene in a production of *Gone With The Wind* flared out of control. The once-famous, now-disgraced playwriting instructor, during the New York run of his contemporary domestic tragedy *Joe Casta*, was found to have plagiarized, albeit radically updated, Lodovico Dolce's 1549 play *Giocasta*. The instructor was not technically guilty of copyright infringement since Dolce's work was in the public domain, but that didn't excuse his failing to admit his dramatic source, thus setting a poor example to students who might be tempted to submit their own ostensibly original writing which they themselves had cribbed from Ibsen or Arthur Miller or The Bard himself. A script entitled *Mack & Beth* does not hide its true source. Nor does *Street Carnal Desire* disguise a Tennessee Williams wannabe's work.

The shameless Ballyvaughan instructor claimed he had merely exercised his poetic license but the college declared his poetic license expired and booted him. With all these calamities, the drama department was a campus laughingstock and the butt of faculty cocktail party sick jokes. The number of students declaring themselves drama majors dropped from sixty-five to a semester average of five-point-two. And then Anton Wohlgemuth arrived to set things right again in what had become Ballyvaughan's academic backwater, its house of academic, dramatic, and quasi-criminal ill-repute.

He set to work immediately. Knowing the importance of spirit in any organization he had one of those foam fingers made, the kind you see at football games, with the index finger raised and **#1** printed on the finger. Under the finger he put:

Ballyvaughan Department of Drama
HERR DOKTOR PROFESSOR ANTON WOHLGEMUTH
Abteilungsleiter

He ordered five hundred of the fingers and gave one to every member of the Ballyvaughan faculty and also to the football team to wear during pre-game introductions. He gave the finger to any student who took a theatre course (two to those who signed on as drama majors). ROTC took a gross. A creative freshman removed the index digit and set it upon the adjoining knuckle for a middle finger salute. The leftovers went to the Save the Children Federation and the Maryknoll Sisters.

The foam fingers were an immediate hit and remained so for years as professors and students in all departments and even the frat boys who thought every drama student was gay (Ben thought that, too) proudly waved their mutant-sized digits not just at football games but during classes, while studying in the library, and in chapel services. In the gym locker room the fingers were available to sweaty athletes, as they made efficient scrubbers of hard-to-reach areas when showering.

In 1988 Wohlgemuth wore his own double-sized finger to the Autumn Inferno bonfire but got too close to the flames and the foam melted into scalding goo causing second degree burns on his right hand and forearm. The next day he dismissed his personal pain as nothing compared to what Amos Loeb had suffered at the hands of a mystery assailant later that same night. As he told the *New York Times* reporter who phoned him for comment: "*Niemand verdient es, dass ihm seine Männlichkeit genommen wird, am allerwenigsten ein Mann so männlich wie Amos Loeb und so gut und wahr.*" ("No man deserves his manhood to be taken from him, least of all a man as manly as Amos Loeb, and as good and true.")

The reflections of such an admirer of Dr. Loeb would be gold for my book so I sought Anton Wohlgemuth out. When I got to his office, though, all of his books and papers and other belongings had been removed. A passing student informed me that Wohlgemuth had left his job and moved out of Glenfarne.

"Oh, my God," I said. "When?"

"End of October."

"He resigned just like that?"

"He was fired, I heard."

"Why was he fired?"

"I'll never know."

"Who does know?"

"Dr. Loeb."

"Dr. Loeb is dead."

"That's why I'll never know."

The student turned to go. I grabbed her. "Wait, he was fired at the end of October?"

"The day before Dr. Loeb was attacked."

"That's kind of weird."

"I know."

Magic Fingers

In order to see Avital Mittelman daily I became a regular at the Ballyvaughan Inn bar. Oddly, though, after being so incredibly forthcoming about Dr. Loeb and her mother during our first meeting, Avital was notably reserved in subsequent days. Either she had little else to tell me or she regretted having told me so much.

It was just as well probably. I felt real affection for Avital but I was a journalist and she was one of my subjects and the journalist-subject relationship should be all business, certainly nothing even approaching a matter of the heart. So there was just one way for me to react when she said, "Your place or mine?" out of the blue one starlit night.

Actually, there were two ways, the second being expressing preference for one venue or the other, assuming that her query meant what I thought it meant, which it turns out it did.

"Your place," I said, to prevent her seeing the underwear I'd left soaking in my motel bathroom sink.

My car was in the shop so she drove. When we arrived at her cottage she wouldn't get out of the car, though. "I left it a mess in there, I can't let you see it." I told her I was used to messes and had made quite a few of my own but she wouldn't budge. "How about we go to your place?" she said.

"My place is a motel room."

"I love motel rooms."

"Why?"

"The Magic Fingers."

"I don't think they have those anymore."

"Some places still do. Maybe yours does, let's go check."

At the County Mayo Avital tempered her disappointment over my bed's lack of Magic Fingers by sniffing my bright, white bath towel. She loved the smell of chlorine, she said. In a germ-laden world it made her feel safe.

"Well?" I said, wondering who would make the first amorous move.

"Well, what?"

"Here we are."

"Say, is this room 102?"

"It is."

"Then it's the same room my mother and I stayed in when we arrived in town last summer."

"What a coincidence."

"It's tiny."

"I'm just one person."

"We were two, that's why we moved out. Plus, the toilet didn't work."

"It works now."

"What's this here in the wash basin?"

"Just some things." I lifted out the underpants and pulled the plug.

"Are those boxers or briefs?"

If Avital had had a romantic tryst with me in mind she seemed to have had second thoughts about it. "Briefs."

She advised that tough stains wouldn't soak away with just soap, I had to use bleach. I thanked her for the tip. Then for at least a full minute she stood there staring into the draining sink while I stared at her reflection in the mirror doing so. The last of the water glugged out. "What's up, Avital?"

"What do you mean?"

"You asked to come here."

"So I did."

"But now you're standoffish again."

"Again?"

"Like you've been since our first time together."

"Things have been happening."

"Like what?"

"My mother had a breakdown, she's in the hospital."

"I'm very sorry. What else?"

"That's not enough?"

"What else, Avital?"

"You don't want to know."

"I do. Tell me."

"You'll be angry."

"How could I possibly be angry? I couldn't be angry with you."

"I can't risk your being angry."

"Risk it. Tell me, damn it. What the hell is going on with you?"

She seemed about to cry. I reached to her but she batted me away.

"It's me, isn't it?" I said.

She shook her head.

"I'm the problem, aren't I? I've been too aggressive with you, asking you all these questions. You need a break."

"That's not it." She didn't say what "it" was.

I told her I'd been thinking about our relationship and how it was improper for someone in my position to have personal feelings for a person in her position.

"What's my position?" she said.

"You're my subject."

"So you're my king?"

"Excuse me?"

"Like a royal subject is ruled by a king?"

"I'm no king, just a poor writer."

"And I'm just a character in your book."

"You're more than that, Avital. Much more."

"Do I get a percentage of your royalties?"

"That's not how royalties work."

"How do they work?"

"Whatever price a book sells for I get ten percent."

"What about your characters? Or subjects or whatever you call them."

"I cite them in the acknowledgments section."

"Do they get paid?"

"No."

"Then why do they talk to you?"

"Why do *you* talk to me? You don't have to, you know."

"Will you use what I've already told you?"

"If you permit me."

"How could I stop you?"

"By not signing a release."

She seemed to mull that option. "What if I sign it and I don't like what you write?"

"Then don't buy the book."

"What if I think you've distorted what I said? What's my recourse legally?"

"You can sue me."

"I couldn't afford a lawyer."

"Then I guess you're up a creek." I meant that to be funny but my funniness caused her to weep. But when I reached to her this time she didn't repel me. "I won't distort what you say to me, Avital." She regarded the two of us in the mirror. "Please believe that. You believe it, don't you?"

"I don't know."

"You have my word."

"Because you're a writer? Because that's all we get from a writer: his word?"

"It's all I've got."

Surprisingly, Avital now surrounded me with her arms and held me as tightly as I was holding her. Would she kiss me? Should I kiss her? "I have something to tell you," she said.

"What?"

"I shouldn't tell you. I don't really want to."

"Tell me."

She loosened her arms, drew away from me, and left the bathroom.

"Tell me!" I followed her.

She stood before the bed. "I can't, I'm too exhausted, I need to sleep."

"Lie down then."

She lay down. She shut her eyes tight. She opened them. "I can't sleep."

"This'll do the trick." From my suitcase I took a bottle of Canadian Club and poured some into one of my bathroom cups.

"Aren't you drinking?" she said.

"I can't, I'm on duty."

"On duty? You're a writer."

"My duty is to write."

"When does your shift end?"

I checked my watch. "Just did." I poured another cup for myself. "Skol, Avi."

She smiled weakly. Her tears were now dry rivulets on her cheeks. "Skol."

We each took a swallow and winced the wince you wince when something's so good it hurts.

"Who do you think killed Dr. Loeb?" she said suddenly.

"No idea."

"Oh, come on."

"Those two old grads maybe."

"The ones that idiot Ben Marble is chasing?"

"I thought you liked Ben Marble."

"I do but he's an idiot."

"He is, I agree." I didn't agree but I feared Avital had been sleeping with Ben, thus her recent coolness to me. I couldn't be kind to a rival.

"Maybe *I* killed Loeb," she said.

"Of cour se you killed him. It's so obvious."

"Don' turn me in."

"I'll have to."

"I'm teasing."

"Well, that's good."

"I didn't kill Amos but if you knew the truth about him you'd wish I had killed him."

"What's the truth about him?"

"You'd hate me if you knew."

"I could never hate you, Avital."

"Oh, yes you could."

"Never."

"Never say never."

"How could I hate you? I love you."

That was a conversation stopper. Neither of us spoke for a long a while.

"Where the hell did that come from?" I said finally. It was a rhetorical question needing no answer. "I'm sorry, I'll take you home now, Avital."

She held up her empty cup. "One more for the road?"

I refilled her cup then mine.

She said, "I certainly don't love *you.*"

"No. Of course not. I really must apologize. What I said just slipped out. Whiskey does that to me."

"Don't worry." She took another swallow. "I *like* you, though." She held out her cup for a third splash. "You know why I like you?"

I couldn't imagine why. I was a snooping scribe who preyed upon traumatized strangers for material for the bestselling book I'd been trying to write all my life. I was the literary version of an ambulance-chasing lawyer. I barely liked myself.

"I like you," Avital said, "because you're sweet."

"You wouldn't say that if you really knew me, Avital."

"What I know so far I like."

"There's plenty more that's not so pretty."

"Then I don't want to know it."

"For example—"

"Stop."

"I lied about not being married."

"I don't care."

"I mean I'm married but we're separated."

"Shut up!" I shut up then she said, "I lied, too."

"About what?"

"Liking you. I mean I do like you. But maybe I love you, too."

"You don't. Or you shouldn't."

"Why shouldn't I?"

"What I said before."

"About writer and subject?"

"More than that."

"What more?" Avital looked genuinely puzzled. Then she said, "Oh, I know: You think because the last man I loved was murdered that I'm bad luck."

"What last man?"

"Dr. Loeb of course."

"You and he were lovers?"

"Well, not quite."

"What does that mean?"

"Nothing."

"You were lovers or you weren't."

"Why not both?"

"Who started it?"

"Oh, it doesn't matter."

"Did he seduce you?"

"Who cares? Yes, you do, for your book. Well, as your royal subject I'll tell you: He phoned me, invited me over. He said his wife was out. Classic, right? So I drove over. He offered me wine. We drank a bottle."

"Each?"

"It was French wine, a Beaujolais. Yes, each. And then I kissed him." She paused, clearly reliving the moment. "And then I kissed him."

"I got that."

"Again, and again. I kissed him many times, so many times, and then he—"

"He kissed you."

"No. He didn't."

"Well, of course he did."

"He pushed me away."

"Yeah, sure."

"I thought he was playing. So I grabbed him, grabbed his belt buckle, started unbuckling—"

"Okay, stop." Was I jealous? Of a dead man?

"He didn't stop me."

"Who would?"

"Not physically. He just said no. I said, 'No as in yes?' He didn't answer. So I continued. I got his fly down, his boxers. He was ready. What a sight. Gorgeous. He stood there before me. Me facing him. I kneeled down." Avi paused, touched my chin. "Are you crying?"

I shook my head.

"So I went for it, went all in. He sighed, he shivered, held me there by my hair, both his hands on my hair, tugging, yanking my hair, hard, yanking down then up, tilting back my head so I caught him on my teeth, and he yelped, and I looked up and he was shaking his head, his face was wet, I thought he was sweating but it was tears from his eyes, then he said stop."

"And you stopped."

"So I kept going."

"But he said stop."

"And then he hit me."

"Oh, no."

"He said he was sorry. He said, 'Forgive me.'"

"I've heard enough."

"He pulled his pants up, turned his back. He turned his damn back! But I forgave him."

"Avi, stop." I really was jealous.

"'I can't do this,' he said. 'You're doing fine, Amos,' I said. He told me I was a lovely person, beautiful and smart, and he loved me. I said, 'And I love *you*!' He said, 'But I can't love you this way.' I said, 'What way?' He said, 'Like a lover.' 'What way *can* you love me?' I asked him. His answer was, 'Like a father to his kid.' 'I'm no kid,' I said. 'I'm a middle-aged woman and you're a middle-aged man.' 'I'm an *old* man,' he said. 'Oh, Amos,' I said, 'you're a stud.' 'That's true,' he said, 'I am. And that's all I am.' And I said, 'No, that's ridiculous, you're so much more than that. Ask anyone.' He said, 'Ask your mother.' I said, 'She thinks so, too.' 'Ask your mother,' he repeated. Then he rolled up his sleeve and showed me his Auschwitz prisoner's tattoo. 'Ask her if she remembers this number.' When I got home I did ask her, and she nodded, but I realized she didn't need a tattooed number to tell her that Amos Loeb was my true father because I could see in her eyes that she already knew. And now I did, too."

We finished that bottle of Canadian Club over the next several minutes during which both of us were completely silent.

"You think I'm making this up," Avital said at last.

"You're telling me Dr. Loeb was that Jewish prison guard who raped your mother at Auschwitz."

"Yes, and how would you feel about a man who raped your mother?"

I refused to even imagine what she was suggesting so I didn't answer.

"Would you want revenge?" Avi proceeded. "How would you get it? What would you do?"

"I don't know."

"Would you kill that man?"

"No."

"You'd let him run free?"

"No."

"You'd hurt him."

"Yes."

"With a knife maybe."

"With words. In the press. I'd expose him. I'd tell the world the truth of what he did."

"You'd tell them that this man who raped your mother was thus your father, too?"

"If it was true."

"They wouldn't believe you so you wouldn't have your revenge. You'd have to get it another way."

"What way?"

"You tell me."

"I really don't have a clue."

"So you'd do nothing."

"I'd move on."

"Move on? But he raped your mother. What kind of son are you?"

"Revenge achieves nothing. It wastes our time."

"You mean life's too short."

"Exactly."

"You wouldn't kill your mother's rapist because you had better things to do."

"That's not what I said."

"Or would you not kill him because he was also your father? Is that the real reason?"

"The reason is that killing is a sin."

"In your religion."

"I'm an atheist."

"That's what I mean."

"I wish I had a religion. I wish I were like you."

"You do? What do I get from my religion? What did my father get? What did my mother get?"

"I can't answer those questions."

"What do you get for being an atheist?"

"I don't know."

"Think hard."

"Freedom?"

"You're asking?"

"I don't know what I get."

"What do you *want?*"

"I want you."

"Why?"

"Because I love you. And you said you loved me."

"I said maybe."

"Maybe is no good."

"How's this then?"' She kissed me. Then she said, "I've got to go."

"Don't go."

She tried to get up from the bed. I held her down.

"Am I your prisoner?" she said.

"My subject, remember?"

"And what does my king want from his subject?"

"For her to stay."

"Can a subject refuse her king?"

I shook my head. "Not today."

Avital's screams woke me up.

"You're under arrest," Grayson Roby said as he handcuffed her.

She shouted, "No!"

"What the fuck, Roby?" I yelled at him, hoping I was dreaming but knowing I wasn't.

"Fun's over," said Roby to Avital. "Let's go." He yanked her out of the bed. She was naked. She pulled the covers with her, exposing my own nakedness. She was screaming like a banshee. The clock on the night table said ten past two.

"What's she done?" I yelled at Roby. "Let her go!"

Avital fought Roby despite her now-shackled wrists. I grabbed one of her arms but he yanked her from my grasp and pushed her out the door.

I followed them. A winter storm had blown through overnight and while Roby shoved Avital into his patrol car my bare feet stung under several inches of new snow. They went numb as the car sped away.

PART THREE

Jailhouse Rock

The next morning I went to see Avital at the police station but Roby blocked me from the cell area. Avital was on the can, he said. I told him I'd wait until she was off the can. He said have a seat. I stayed standing. "That was a hell of a thing breaking into our room," I said.

"Had to be done."

"You had a warrant?"

He waved a sheet of paper at me. "Read it and weep."

"Who signed it? What judge?"

"Friend of mine."

I reached for the sheet but he stashed it in a desk drawer. "What did you arrest her for?"

"For what she said."

"When?"

"In your motel room just before you went at it."

"What did she say?"

"She said she killed Loeb."

"Bullshit."

"Maybe I heard it wrong." He punched PLAY on a cassette machine on his desk. "*Maybe I killed Loeb,*" said Avital on the tape.

Roby paused the tape. "Nope, I got it right."

"How did you make that recording?"

"I didn't make it. You did."

"Hell I did."

"Very fine quality, too. How much did you pay for that thing?"

"What thing?"

He pointed to the tiny microphone still clipped to my shirt collar.

162

"How did you get the tape?"

"I swung by and picked it up this morning."

"From where?"

"Your motel room. It was in your suitcase."

"How did you get into the room?"

"Same way I did last night. But I knocked this time out of courtesy. You seemed to have vacated the premises, though, so I let myself in."

"With another warrant?"

"Of course, I go by the book."

"Are you going to keep the recording?"

"Got to, for the prosecutor to play in court. Turns out I didn't need it for myself, though. I have total recall so I remembered every word I heard with my own ears last night. The tape just confirmed my memory."

"You were at the motel?"

"My regular nightly patrol. There's often trouble there. That's a rough place."

"You were listening outside my door."

"I heard suspicious sounds, talk of killing someone."

"She said maybe she killed Dr. Loeb. *Maybe.* And for Christ's sake, she was joking."

"So why did you believe her?"

"I didn't."

Roby pressed PLAY again. We both now heard me say to Avital: "*Of course you killed him. It's so obvious.*"

"What I meant by that—"

"Quiet, there's more:"

Avital again: "*Don't turn me in.*"

Me again: "*I'll have to.*"

Roby stopped the machine.

I said, "Keep it rolling. Then she says she's teasing."

Roby pressed REWIND. "No, I want to play you the best part where she calls Ben Marble an idiot. She sure was right about that.

Oh, and earlier her babble about going down on her father. Sickening. What was that all about?"

"You're a bastard, Roby."

"My mom and dad never married, so you're right. Both of them teenagers, they couldn't drink or vote."

"That little bit of tape won't convict Avital."

"You're putting the cart before the horse. Conviction is for later. First thing is locking her up for probable cause."

"Probable on what evidence?"

"You just heard the evidence."

"Hard evidence. Fingerprints, witness testimony."

"I've got her own testimony."

"That crap she said to me?"

"No, what she said to *me*."

"When?"

"Last night after she calmed down."

"What did she say?"

"She confessed."

"I don't believe you."

"Believe this:" He showed me another sheet of paper. "See, she signed it right there in ink."

I didn't bother to look. "I want to talk to her."

"I'm not sure she's finished back there."

"Well, go check."

With a mock-obeisant nod he went off to the cell area. Now I sat down on the only chair in the visitor area. There were some magazines on a side table, with *Guns & Ammo* on the top. I checked the stack for something more appealing but saw that all the rest were *Guns & Ammo* too.

Roby returned. "She doesn't want to see you."

"Of course she does."

"She says come back tomorrow."

"She can tell me that herself." I started toward the cell area. Roby held me back. "She's cramping. Cramping, get it? Full moon tonight. She's at the age so have a heart."

I turned to leave, I seemed to have no choice.

"Oh, one thing more," Roby added. "She asked if you'd do her a favor."

"What favor?"

"Go see her mother in the hospital."

"Why?"

"To tell her that her daughter is in jail."

"Why doesn't she phone her?"

"All that screaming at me last night, she's lost her voice."

Miss Popularity

I dreaded meeting Esther Mittelman. Yes, she could be a grand character for my book but she was a depressive and I've always kept my distance from that ilk. It's silly but I feel like I'll catch what they've got, almost as if I would become depressed if they sneezed in my face. Depression isn't communicable like the common cold, of course, but the fear of depression is communicable. I'm proof.

The hospital was in a larger town several miles away. I took ten deep breaths before entering.

"You're late," said the nurse in Mrs. Mittelman's room.

"Sorry." I hadn't alerted the facility to my arrival so there was no way I could have been late, or early for that matter. In fact, there was no way the hospital could have been expecting me at all unless Avital forewarned them and Roby said Avital couldn't talk. Not that I believed Roby.

"What's your name?"

I gave her my name. "Madeline Vlasic, RN" read the name plate on her blue scrub top.

"Who's here?" said Mrs. Mittelman from the bed.

"Your second visitor in two days," the nurse told her. "Aren't you Miss Popularity."

I suspected Grayson Roby had been yesterday's visitor, grubbing for dirt on Mrs. Mittelman's daughter, the better to justify his detaining her.

"Ten minutes," Nurse Vlasic said to me, and left.

"Did you bring the cat?" Mrs. Mittelman asked me.

"What cat?" I said.

"Hadrian's Tomb."

"Who's Hadrian's Tomb?"

166

"My cat. Did you bring him?"

I improvised: "I forgot."

Despite her snowy white hair, liver-spotted hands, and stress-marked face, Mrs. Mittelman was, as Avital had said, not an old person but a middle-aged one who had aged prematurely. It was easy to imagine the ravishingly beautiful woman she had certainly once been.

"I'm a friend of your daughter," I informed her. "She may have mentioned me."

"You're a famous writer."

"Then she has mentioned me."

"No, I dreamed I would meet a famous writer."

"Actually, I'm not famous. Yet."

"What's your name?"

I said my name.

"Sorry, I'm a little deaf."

I handed her my business card which she examined minutely as if it were a forgery. Then she ripped the card in two. "What the hell are you doing?" I said, regretting the vulgarity.

"Do you have another?"

I gave her another. This one she eyed like a jeweler, one eye open and one shut.

"Your daughter sent me with a message," I said.

"She's in jail?"

"How did you know?"

"I dreamed it."

"Well, you're right."

"What did she do?"

"Nothing."

"Good."

"So she'll be out of jail soon, once I hire her a good lawyer."

"Hire me one, too."

"What for?"

"Get me out of this place."

The depressives I've known, albeit from afar, all ultimately lapsed into morose silence. I was startled by this woman's volubility, especially since, according to Avital, she'd been essentially mute in her meeting with Dr. Loeb.

"I'll see her again at the jail tomorrow, Mrs. Mittelman. Is there anything you'd like me to tell her from your end of things?"

"She's not in jail really."

"I'm afraid she is, but she'll be out once I hire her a good lawyer."

"You said that already."

"I wasn't sure you heard me."

"I'm not deaf." She coughed and continued coughing.

"Mrs. Mittelman, are you all right?"

"Fill this back up for me." She handed me a paper cup.

"What was in it?"

"Chateau Haut-Brion 1958."

I filled the cup with water at the sink and brought it back to her. "I hear you had a visitor yesterday."

"Yes, my husband."

Her depression had made her delusional obviously. She must have mistaken Chief Roby for her long-deceased spouse and Roby, to tease out information about her daughter, had not corrected her mistake. It wasn't my place to correct her, either.

"Well, it's been a pleasure meeting you, Mrs. Mittelman."

"You're going?"

"I must."

"Why? You have something to write?"

"I do."

"What are you writing?"

"A book."

"What about?"

"This town, the college."

"Boring."

"No, quite interesting, really."

"Write about my daughter."

"She's one of my characters, in fact."

"She's a character, all right. Who else?"

"I can't tell you."

"Why not?"

"I would need their permission."

"What if they don't give you permission?"

"Then they won't be in the book."

"They can choose to stay out of it?"

"If that's what they want."

"Why would they want to stay out of it?"

"If they revealed to me something embarrassing."

"Like what?"

"Some indiscretion."

"Like what?"

"Say an infidelity."

"I thought you meant something serious."

"Some things they divulge are more serious."

"Like what?"

"Maybe a crime."

"Murder?"

"Sure, why not?"

"So you're a crime writer?"

"Sometimes."

"What else do you write?"

"This and that."

"Published?"

"On occasion."

"Random House?"

"Small presses."

"Have I heard of you?"

"Apparently not."

"Why not?"

"Probably because I haven't had a bestseller yet."

"You want a bestseller?"

"It's on my bucket list."

"You'll need a great story."

"I'm always looking."

"I've got a great story for you."

"What story is that?"

"My husband's story."

"I know your husband's story."

"We were in Auschwitz together."

"So your daughter told me."

"What did she tell you?"

"That the two of you were separated there, and that he died."

"I thought he died, too."

"You don't have to talk about it."

"But I want to. I want to very much."

"Why?"

"For your bestseller."

"That's good of you but reliving the loss of your husband would certainly cause you great pain."

"But I didn't lose him it turns out."

"I'm sure he's still alive and well inside your heart."

"He was alive yesterday right where you're sitting."

"You thought your visitor yesterday was your husband?"

"He was my husband."

"That was Police Chief Grayson Roby."

"Who's he?"

Mrs. Mittelman was off her hinges, way beyond depressed. Clearly, Roby had been merciless in messing up her head. I told her I knew the pain of losing a life partner, without mentioning that in my case it was by a mutually agreed upon separation, not a tragic death.

She ignored my expression of sympathy. "Of course, I was surprised to see my husband, I'd long thought he was dead."

"You thought right." It was time to square with her, cut off her mental meandering, and make my getaway.

"You see, I thought he had died at Auschwitz, "

"He did."

You know Auschwitz?"

"Not personally."

"He and I were both taken to Auschwitz on October 21st, 1944."

She wouldn't drop the subject. I yearned for the nurse to return and say my time was up. I wanted out of here, this whole hospital was giving me the creeps. It was like a penitentiary. There was a uniformed guard at the front gate. Out Mrs. Mittelman's window I could see a weed-choked exercise yard bordered by a chain link fence. An underfed dog of indeterminate breed lay inert on a bed of broken glass or crockery, I couldn't tell which. I prayed I'd never be sick enough to land in such a place. I'd kill myself first.

Since the nurse wasn't coming I decided to leave on my own. "Goodbye, Mrs. Mittelman," I said and marched to the door. It was locked. Esther told me the door locked on the inside so patients couldn't get out. The nurse, she said, would release me.

"Where is she?" I said.

"Probably getting her hair done."

I rapped on the door to get someone's attention.

"Or her nails. Or both."

"How do I call her?"

"There's a button by my bed."

I returned to the bed and looked for the nurse's call button.

"Where was I?" Esther said. "Oh, yes, immediately when we arrived at Auschwitz my husband was taken from me and sent to the gas chamber. Or so I thought."

171

I found a button and pressed it. It was the button for raising the bed and Mrs. Mittelman was lifted to a straight-up sitting position. She didn't seem to notice.

"Are you listening?" she said.

"He was sent to the gas chamber."

"At the time that's what I thought."

"Where's the frigging call button?"

"But he came back."

"No one comes back from a gas chamber, Mrs. Mittelman."

"But he wasn't taken there it turns out."

I pressed a new button and all the lights went out. Mrs. Mittelman didn't notice this either. The death of her husband was obviously the root of her depression so she was doing what anyone would be doing: denying it to herself. But I can't tolerate denial and never could. At a point, though, it's useless setting deniers straight. Had I reached that point with Mrs. Mittelman? I made one more try at making her admit the truth. "Who exactly told you that he came back from the gas chamber, Mrs. Mittelman?"

"He told me himself, right here in this room yesterday. Now I want you to tell my daughter."

"Why?"

"Just do."

"Why not tell her yourself?"

"She won't believe me."

"Why would she believe *me*?"

"You're a writer. Everyone trusts writers."

"She can read it in my book."

"But then she'll have to *buy* your book."

"I'll give her a free copy."

"Don't do that; you're a failed writer, you need all the money you can get."

"I didn't say I was failed. I'm not *failed*."

"You have no bestsellers yet."

Though I'd kept on pressing buttons we were still in the dark. Then the next one kicked the TV to life. Its ghostly glow brought forth the underlying exquisiteness of Mrs. Mittelman's face.

"Do you want to die without one bestseller, sir?"

I couldn't answer such a piercing question.

"Come now, tell me: Do you want a bestseller or not?"

I nodded.

"Well, do you?"

In the dimness she hadn't seen me nodding. "Yes, I do."

"How much?"

"With all my heart." I'd never used that expression before with anyone for anything.

"Then you'll have to listen to my husband's story just as he told it to me yesterday. Will you do that?"

"I'll take a general outline."

"You need all the details. Are you ready for the details?"

What was to lose? "All right."

"Good. Because details you are going to get."

The *Sonderkommando*

"My husband Moshe Mittelman," Esther began, "was born in 1915 in Magdeburg, Germany. I was born five years later in the same city. We married in 1938 and opened up a little women's clothing shop. Aren't you going to take notes?"

"Of course." I pretended my left palm was a notepad and my right index finger was a writing implement. I mimed scribbling.

"You can't fool me, sir."

"Why do you think I'm fooling you?"

"Your pen is out of ink. Never mind. If you can't keep what I say in your head then you don't deserve to hear it."

"What kind of shop was it?"

"A clothing shop, I told you that."

"What kind of clothing?"

"Women's clothing. Pay attention."

"I'm paying attention." I flicked the switch on my hidden mic.

"What did you just do?"

"I had an itch."

"Did you turn on a tape recorder?"

"No, I had an itch. I scratched it."

"Tape recorders are not permitted in this place."

"They make allowances for writers."

"Not true."

"Okay, I'll turn it off." I pretended to turn it off.

"Where was I?"

"At the shop."

"I made skirts, dresses, gloves, undergarments. My mother was a seamstress, she taught me well."

"Hats?"

"Why do you ask?"

"For the record."

"Yes, I made hats also."

"What did your husband do?"

"The business. He took care of the business. And the business was very good from the very start. But it quickly fell apart."

"A risky business."

"Pardon?"

"Clothing is a risky business. Fashions change, it's hard to stay in step."

"This was not to do with changing fashions, sir. This was Germany and we were Jewish. We had to wear yellow Stars of David on our coats. On the stars was inscribed *Jude* in faux Hebrew letters. One night our shop window was shattered and our inventory destroyed. That was *Kristallnacht*. Such a pretty name for such a horrendous event, like some fairy ballet name."

"Like *Swan Lake*."

"You are a balletomane."

"You bet."

"Life was terrible after that. In 1944 we were arrested and sent to the camp at Auschwitz. We were dragged from our house naked. Dragged from our bed. Naked. We stood in the street, this was late October, there was an early snow, our feet froze, our whole bodies froze, waiting for the truck to take us to the railroad. We were making love."

"Love?"

"When the *Schutzstaffel* came my husband and I were having sexual relations."

"I don't need to know that."

"Making love."

"Yes, yes."

"Naked."

"I get it."

"Such a beautiful morning that turned into the worst day of our lives. Except for all the ones that followed."

"So you were taken to Auschwitz ... "

"In a first-class sleeping car. Joking. In a cattle train, in freezing, snowing weather, a four-day trip. And well, you know the rest."

"Do I?"

"My daughter told you."

"She left out a lot."

"Soon after arriving most prisoners were taken to the gas chambers."

"But not you."

"Some, like me, with useful skills, were tattooed with identification numbers and assigned to work at various jobs. "

"And your husband?"

"We were separated, my husband and I. You did know that."

"I did."

"All the men were separated from all the women. I assumed my husband was gassed until I saw him two months later. Instead of being killed he too had been put to work."

"What kind of work?"

"In a *Sonderkommando* unit. You know the term?"

"Vaguely."

"Those were the prisoners assigned to the crematorium. They disposed of the bodies, removed all jewelry and precious metal dental work, and then ground the bones for fertilizer. They had to be able-bodied for that work so they were better fed than other prisoners. But the *Sonderkommandos* didn't last long, three months at most. You can surmise why."

"The food made them sick?"

"No, they were *Geheimnisträger.*"

"I don't speak German."

"It means secret-bearers. They knew the Nazis' secret."

"Troop movements?"

"No, the Nazis' secret plan to exterminate all Jews. These prisoners were eyewitnesses, they saw the plan being carried out, and if they survived they could tell the world about it. So they were doomed. Thus after their short period of usefulness they were gassed and replaced by new arrivals. I did not know then that this was the camp's policy but I surmised it and thus I was sure that within a month after I saw my husband he would be dead."

"Did he know that would be his fate?"

"He pretended not to know but I am sure he did. But that's moot. He didn't care about his fate, he cared about mine."

"And how did yours look?"

"As if I could decide. As if I could do anything to influence my fate."

"You could continue to do good work. Then they couldn't replace you."

"Couldn't replace me! Ha! Ha!! Anyone could be replaced. One-point-three million people went to Auschwitz. Do you think none of them could sew on a button as well as I could? Everyone was replaced except those about to be replaced when the camp was liberated."

"Replaced meaning killed."

"Killed."

"You were not killed."

"By purest luck."

"What made you lucky?"

"Nothing I myself did, I'll tell you that."

"Someone protected you."

"If protected means being brutally attacked. If being raped is good luck." Mrs. Mittelman described the brutality of several Jewish kapos against their fellow Jewish prisoners, affirming what Avital had told me she'd learned in her mother's notebook. Esther now stated that one kapo nicknamed Zänker took a liking to her and treated her with relative kindness. He promised to spare her from execution if she did his personal bidding. What bidding would that be? Esther asked him.

At which point he kissed her. At which point she tried to get away. At which point he pulled off her striped prisoner's smock and raped her standing up. "You're nodding as if you know all this, sir."

"Your daughter told me, though not in such detail."

"I never wanted her to know."

"Why not?"

"It would shatter her, obviously, to learn that the man she'd thought was their father all her life wasn't her father after all. And that her real father was ... who he was."

"Children should know who their real parents are, that's their right."

"When they're the spawn of the devil?"

"If it's true."

"Do you have children, sir?"

"No."

"If you did would you tell them if you had been raped?"

"The question isn't relevant."

"Would you at least write down an account of your rape?"

"I haven't had that experience personally so I don't know."

"But you're a writer."

"And the writer's rule is write what you know."

"That doesn't leave much to write about."

"What do you mean?"

"There's so much you can't possibly know."

"Then don't write about it."

"You could make it up."

"That's called fiction. I don't write fiction."

"You only write what's true. How boring."

"Very boring. So I give it a spin. "

"What kind of spin?"

"A lyrical spin."

"You mean you fudge the facts."

"I make them entertaining."

"Like a novel."

"Exactly."

"Which is fiction."

"There's a difference between making something up and calling it fiction, and reporting what actually happened using fictional techniques."

"Is that what you do?"

"In my writing, yes. In my speaking, too. We all do."

"I don't."

"I'll bet you do."

"Have you read my notebook?"

"About Auschwitz? No."

"But you know about my notebook."

"From you daughter, yes, I do."

"I didn't spin anything in that notebook."

"Of course you didn't."

"I didn't use any fictional techniques."

"You didn't have to."

"Why do *you* have to?"

"To engage my readers."

"To make a bestseller."

"Just to get published."

"To make a bestseller, to sell a million copies, to option it for the movies. Come on, admit it, it's true."

"I seek as wide an audience as possible, *that's* true."

"And that's the difference between me and you."

"What is?"

"You write to make a killing with a bestseller, but I didn't write my notebook to be a bestseller, I wrote it just for myself."

"Why did you write it at all?"

"So there would be a record of what that man did to me."

"Did you think you might forget?"

"I thought if there were no record then he'd have gotten away with it."

"But he did get away with it."

"Did he?"

"His whole life, no one ever knew. Except you, and now your daughter whom you hoped would never know."

"And now you know, too. It's hard to keep a secret, isn't it?"

"But why did you hide your secret where your daughter might come along and discover it? Because that's what you wanted her to do? You could have put it in a safe deposit box at a bank, or burned it."

"I did burn it."

"I know, just recently. But by that time your daughter had already read it. Why burn it then?"

"Because why keep a secret that my daughter now knew?"

"And she has survived knowing it. So have you, like you survived the death camp."

"No thanks to Mr. Zänker."

"With all thanks to him, I'd say. He did protect you right through the liberation, didn't he?"

"He didn't protect me. He couldn't have even if he had wanted to. He wouldn't have had that power."

"Well, at least your lovely daughter came out of your encounter with him. And if you had no help in surviving then your survival is all the more tribute to your own fortitude. You were irreplaceable in the garment shop after all."

"You're saying that the damnable lie above the camp gate, *Arbeit Macht Frei*, was really true?"

"It was a lie for your husband but not for you."

"Why a lie for my husband?"

"Because he died in the camp. You said he was a *Sonderkommando* so he'd have been gassed within three months."

"That was his likely fate."

"I'm so sorry for your terrible loss, Mrs. Mittelman."

"Why be sorry?"

"Right, you get over it."

"You get over nothing when there's nothing to get over."

"I don't follow."

"When you didn't lose what you'd thought you had lost."

"You lost your husband."

"So I thought. But yesterday he came back."

"In your dreams, Mrs. Mittelman. Only in your dreams."

"When I awoke this morning that is what I thought, too. But then the sun coming through the window reminded me of him coming through that door, and I remembered him sitting right where you are sitting, and I remembered all the things he said to me, such as that he had come to America and was living in Colorado where he had married another woman, for which he apologized, since it meant he had broken his vow of eternal faithfulness to me his beloved first wife. I forgave him. After all, I myself had remarried."

Here is where Mrs. Mittelman drifted into an even more fantastical realm, her afflicted brain confusing what she wished had happened with what had happened in fact, her glaucomatous eyes seeing her long-deceased husband in the stubbled mug of a little village's chief cop. Thus I will set the remainder of Esther's story apart and in italics to distinguish her fantasia from my own fact-based narrative which precedes and follows it in this book.

Escape

It is April 1945. My husband weighs forty kilos. Not that there is any scale to stand on but the abscessed, frostbitten skeleton he has become could not weigh more than that.

He awakes one morning to SS guards shouting and dogs barking and guns blasting. Guards enter the block and drag the prisoners outside where hundreds of other prisoners are being kicked and shoved toward the main gates where "Arbeit Macht Frei" reads backwards to everyone on the inside, but now everyone is being herded out. Out! Is this possible? The gates are open! Is this a dream? Let it not be a dream, my husband thinks. If it is a dream, let me continue dreaming until I am beyond the gates and Auschwitz disappears behind me like a nightmare that someday I may be able to forget.

He passes through the gates. Is he free now? He stops, puts out his tongue to taste what freedom tastes like. A guard bashes his jaw with his rifle butt. This freedom tastes of blood.

Esther scanned my face for a reaction. I gave her none.

Now he is in a cattle wagon, peeking out through the slats. The locomotive's belching smoke grays the falling snow. The train plods and grunts. Sometimes its whistle shrieks. Time passes, impossible to know how much. The smoke smell is joined by feces stench. Someone has defecated. Now someone is vomiting. The train stops. The doors open. The SS pull the prisoners out.

"What is that look on your face, sir? You are bored. You have heard all this already from my daughter."

"Continue, this is all new."

The men are made to march. There are hundreds of men. Thousands. They march through the falling snow until the snow is smothered by the black night. They go on marching. But some cannot march any more. They stumble, they stop. They are prodded by SS rifle butts. They are stabbed with bayonets. Some resume marching. Those who do not are shot.

"You understand, sir, that the Nazis, knowing the Russians are advancing in Poland, are burning records and emptying the death camps. The remaining prisoners at Auschwitz are being driven toward other camps in Austria."

I said nothing.

"You are not listening, sir."

"Yes, I am."

"Your eyes have closed. You have fallen asleep."

"My eyes close when I am spellbound."

I opened my eyes. Mrs. Mittelman was staring out the window, no longer speaking, which was a relief since I couldn't bear to hear any more. I was about to tell her she needn't continue when out of my mouth came, "Don't stop."

Night becomes day. A day with no sun, only snow. The day passes. The snow deepens ...

"Halt!" The prisoners continue marching, dead to sound, numb to cold, blind to fate. "Halt!!" Shots are fired. Prisoners who are hit fall. My husband, though he is not hit, falls. Those not fallen are pushed into wagons of a new train standing at a siding taking coal and water. The fallen are left for dead and the train departs.

"And that's how he escaped? By playing dead?"

He makes his way to his home city of Magdeburg in Germany.

"On foot?"

"No, by chauffeured limousine."

"Sorry. Go on."

"He finds Magdeburg almost totally destroyed by Allied bombing. People are wandering around like blind people, stepping in bomb craters, tripping over uprooted trolley tracks.

"Esther Mittelman?" he asks these people. "Have you seen Esther Mittelman?" They do not know Esther Mittelman. "But she and I lived right on this street. We owned this shop." He points to what is now a heap of bricks and plaster. A woman tells him that if Esther Mittelman survived the war—it is early summer now and Germany has surrendered—the Red Cross may know her whereabouts. "Where is the Red Cross?" my husband asks her. She points in one direction, then the other, then admits she has not seen them since they were here assigning homeless former residents to displaced persons camps in other parts of the country. My husband takes the woman's hand and kisses it. "Thank you," he says, "for giving me hope."

I raised my hand like a schoolchild with a question for the teacher. "You said *Sonderkommandos* lived only three months, Mrs. Mittelman."

"Yes, I did."

"So by the time Auschwitz was liberated your husband would have been dead."

"Presumably."

"So he could not have been marched out of Auschwitz. He could not have returned to Germany to look for you."

"Then how did he find me?"

"He never did."

"He did yesterday."

"And how did he do that?"

"It wasn't easy. It took years. He went through Red Cross records, consulted with the new German government, scanned newspapers. He even wrote to the United Nations to see if they could help. The United Nations suggested he query the embassies and consulates of various nations, and he did so but they did not have any information. Finally, in desperation, he went to a detective agency, one with international connections that specialized in finding missing persons, and guess what?"

"What?"

"They poked around, wrote him a report, and the report said that in 1950 Esther Mittelman had married an American soldier stationed in Germany and had moved with him and her daughter to the United States. The report even had my new address. So my husband—my first husband Moshe Mittelman—sailed to America."

"To find you and reunite."

"Not to reunite."

"Then why did he come?"

"To be closer to me."

"But not see you?"

"Not even talk to me. He did not want to bother me. He did not want to disrupt and perhaps destroy the happiness of my new life. No, he would not do that. Any kind of personal contact, he thought, just would not be right. He would meet me only if I sought him out, but I would not seek him, of course, since I was no longer his wife, I was someone else's wife and I was the mother of someone's else's child and he had nothing to do with any of that, and he knew that I believed he was dead in any case, so he decided he would stay dead for my sake."

"But he didn't stay dead, he came to you yesterday. Why?"

"Ask him."

"He didn't tell you?"

"He did tell me but he made me promise not to tell anyone else."

"So he has stayed in America."

"Yes."

"Where has he settled?"

"Out west somewhere."

"In what state?" By pressing her for specifics she couldn't supply I would embarrass her into admitting her yarn was bogus.

"Colorado, Wyoming, one of those," she said.

"You're not sure. In fact, you have no idea."

"Colorado. Yes, Colorado."

"Not Kansas? Not North Dakota? Not Utah maybe?"

"No, Colorado, such a lovely state. I've never been there but he said he loved the clear air and sunshine and happy smiles, so different from the mud and freezing rain and gas chambers of the German death camps. But even here in America he was afraid that as a Jew he would be found out and taken to another camp and though the guards would all be smiling and the sun was warm and bright he would this time not be put to work and thus survive but would be killed outright. Therefore to avoid that fate which he was sure that as a Jew he would always meet in any corner of the earth he changed his name from Moshe Mittelman to something more blonde-haired, blue-eyed sounding, something you would never hear along a rubbled ghetto street."

"What was his new name?"

"I forget."

"He was here yesterday, you said. He didn't tell you his new name when he was here?"

"With me he didn't need a new name, just his old name, Moshe Mittelman, since I was Esther Mittelman, his old wife."

"And he didn't tell you where he was living?"

"In Colorado, as I said."

"Where in Colorado?"

"Why do you want to know? Will you interview him for your book?"

I almost said I didn't interview dead people but I stopped myself. "Sure, I'd love to. Can you set up a meeting?"

"You can meet him right here."

"When?"

"Today. He comes every afternoon."

"From Colorado."

"Yes, and he'll be here very shortly. He comes every afternoon at three o'clock."

My watch showed five minutes to three right now. I imagined myself shaking hands with a ghost. The nurse returned. "My time's up?" I said, hopefully.

"Afraid so." She stood in the doorway, holding the door open with her foot.

I took Mrs. Mittelman's hand and kissed it.

"Wait, there's more," she said.

"The man's time's up," the nurse told her. Then to me she said, "Was she telling you about her husband visiting her?" I nodded. "She's told it to me about a hundred times. It's the first thing I hear when I wake her up in the morning. I've got it memorized by now. I believe I could tell that story now as well as she could."

"It's a wild story."

"Dreams are like that. Especially the recurring ones."

"You think she dreamed all that?"

"Well, her husband has never been in here, I'll tell you that much."

"Who visited her yesterday?"

"That ugly cop."

I started toward the door.

"Wait!" Mrs. Mittelman said. "My husband didn't visit me after all."

"Of course not," I said.

"He wrote me a letter."

"Goodbye, Mrs. Mittelman."

"I have it right here." She rummaged in her bedclothes and drew forth an envelope. "I mean, how could he travel here from Colorado every day? Tell me that."

"It would be expensive."

"No, I mean the time it would take."

"Exactly."

"Everything I told you about him is in this letter he wrote to me."

"I'm sure it is."

"You're not sure at all. You don't believe me."

"I've got to go, I'm running late."

"Look here, it's postmarked from Colorado." She tapped where I could see a cancelled stamp.

"Give him my regards when you write back to him," I said.

"I will and I'll ask him when he'd be free to speak with you."

"You needn't do that."

"But you must speak with him for your book."

"I think you've told me enough, Mrs. Mittelman."

"But not the best part. I left out the best part."

"Really, I'm fine with what I've got."

"Fine to do what?"

"To write a very good book."

"A bestseller?"

"Let us hope."

"Why just hope? Why not guarantee it?"

"There are no guarantees."

"What my husband will tell you is your guarantee."

"He can drop me a line."

"He must tell you in person."

"Well, I'm not flying all the way to Colorado."

"Excuse me, sir, but do you want a bestseller or not?"

"All right, what will he tell me?"

"He'll tell you what I left out."

"Why did you leave it out?"

"Because you wouldn't believe it."

"I'll believe anything at this point." That was a lie, of course.

"Plus, he would be in big trouble if it were known."

"I don't think there's anything to be known because I think you've made all this up."

"He killed Dr. Loeb."

For a moment neither of us spoke, as if what she'd just said might be true, which of course it wasn't. I didn't call out Mrs. Mittelman on her lunacy, though, I didn't have the heart. "Noted," I said.

"Don't tell him I told you."

"Don't worry, I won't."

"Of course you don't believe my husband killed Dr. Loeb. You shouldn't. So go and hear it from the horse's mouth."

"It's not that I don't believe he killed Loeb, Mrs. Mittelman. It's that my readers won't believe it if I put it in my book."

"That's their problem."

"It's a big problem."

"Not if they know the specific reason he did it. Then it will all make sense to them. They'll see that he did what he had to do because they would do it, too."

"So what's the reason he did it?"

"I definitely can't tell you *that*."

"Was it that Loeb had raped his wife?"

"You knew. My daughter told you. So now all secrets are out. But for a good cause, right? Your bestselling book."

Without responding to this remark I made for the door. Nurse Vlasic caught my arm when I was half out. "So you write books?"

"When I have the time."

"Are you writing one about Mrs. Mittelman?"

"She may be in it, yes."

"Can I be in it?"

"What's your story?"

"Got a minute?"

My watch showed ten seconds to three, the hour of Mrs. Mittelman's husband's daily appearance. I felt a ghostly chill. But Mrs. Mittelman had corrected herself, he didn't come here in person, he wrote letters from Colorado about surviving gas chambers and murdering college presidents. How could I doubt such a story? Look at this envelope! See the Colorado postmark over the stamp! Why deny such incontrovertible proof?

I removed the nurse's hand from my sleeve. "Another time," I said.

I didn't want to report Mrs. Mittelman's ripping yarn to Avital, but the poor old woman had asked me to so I did, a half hour later, in Avital's kitchen.

"Who was it who said that our dreams are wish fulfillments?" Avital said.

"Jung."

"No, Freud. My mother dreamed her husband had come back."

"And then murdered someone."

"What do you mean?"

"She said he killed Dr. Loeb."

"Really? That's a new one, but in the same pattern of fulfilling wishes."

"Yes, wishing for justice for the rape of his wife."

"Not justice. Revenge."

"Was your father a vengeful person?"

"Which father? The one my mother told me was my father, or the American soldier who raised me, or the one who's my true father by blood?"

"The first."

"No. Moshe Mittelman was the least vengeful person imaginable, according to Ima."

"But he killed someone vengefully."

"In her dream."

"Yes, in her dream."

"Which only means she wishes he did."

The Boy From Kappa Kappa Nu

Your prime suspect in any murder case is the last person who saw the victim alive. And who was that in Dr. Loeb's case? Ben Marble, who was sitting bedside when Loeb breathed his last breath. Sure, everyone's a suspect until they're not, and Ben had a gun, but Loeb wasn't killed with a gun. Plus, Ben already had a very prime suspect in his sights.

So stepping back, who was the last person who saw Loeb just before the assault happened? The attacker, of course, but also hundreds of other friends, associates, and Autumn Inferno rally attendees in his immediate vicinity, all of whom could add depth and color to my book. I would probably never be able to identify all these people but I could certainly pursue certain individuals who I knew were in close contact with Dr. Loeb on the day of the crime. I chose Faye Foxley first. Why? Wrong question. A writer asks why not.

I caught her at her home in the suburbs of Glenfarne. One could call it a suburban home if one wanted, but I called it a flat-tired single-wide in a scrubby trailer park. I knocked on the door but no one answered so I just went in. Faye Foxley was in front of a small TV, watching news film of Dr. Loeb's funeral. I started in easy. "Hello, Mrs. Foxley."

"Sshh!" She hunched closer to the TV as Loeb's casket was lowered into the ground.

"Crazy world," I said. Faye turned off the TV and looked at me for the first time. She didn't seem alarmed that I had appeared out of nowhere. "Nice to finally meet you, Mrs. Foxley."

"Want a drink?"

"No, thank you."

"Then what do you want?"

"I'm a friend of Ben Marble."

"So what?"

"He mentioned you to me in passing. You sounded like such a fascinating person that I wanted to know more about you."

"Why'd he mention me?"

"He's helping me write a book."

"What about?"

"This place."

"This place?" She looked around her humble abode, not with any apparent shame but in seeming wonderment that her crappy digs would be the setting for a work of literature.

"I mean I'm writing about the town and the college."

"Boring." This echoed Esther Mittelman's reaction. Mrs. Foxley poured at least four fingers of gin into a beer stein and said, "Here's your drink."

I'd earlier refused a drink but I didn't remind her of that because now I didn't want to refuse it.

"I'm out of fizz," she said.

"You're not drinking, Mrs. Foxley?"

She upended the gin bottle and one last drop emitted. "All gone." She opened a window behind her and tossed the bottle out. "You're lying," she then said.

"Excuse me?"

"You're not writing about the town and the college, you're writing about the murder."

"I'm writing about how the murder is affecting the town and the college."

"You mean how it's affecting me."

"Today, yes, I'm talking to you. This is good gin."

"There's more where that came from."

"I thought it was gone."

"Just that bottle. I've got an extra case. Need a refill?"

I'd only taken one sip. "Not yet. Tell me about your relationship with Dr. Loeb."

"Great guy, swell guy, what a guy."

"You attended his Halloween party."

"What a party."

"You had a knife with you."

"For my daughter." Faye explained about the girl's acting audition for Dr. Loeb, the whole Clytemnestra bit. I already knew all about this from Ben but I wanted Mrs. Foxley's own account in case it varied from his.

"So your daughter is an actress."

"You should see her act."

"I'd love to meet her someday."

"Piggy!" Mrs. Foxley shouted in no particular direction. "Her birth name is Anastasia."

"Really? Why the name change?"

"It's a long story."

"Tell it to me."

"Why? You've heard it from Ben, I'll bet."

"He hardly told me anything."

"What did he leave out?"

"Well, for example, details of your relationship with Dr. Loeb."

"Who says we had a relationship?"

"Did you have one?"

"If I tell you will it be in your book?"

"Only with your permission."

"How much money will I get?"

"You will be cited as a prime source. And I will furnish you with a complimentary signed copy."

"No money."

"I'm afraid not."

"Amos gave me money."

"Amos?"

"Dr. Loeb."

"You call him Amos?"

"That's his name."

"He's Dr. Loeb to the world."

"Not to me."

"Because he was your friend?"

"Not my friend."

"But you knew him."

"Briefly."

"And you took your daughter to meet him in hopes he would admit her to the college."

"More fool me."

"What gave you those hopes?"

"Because he opened up the college to females. He said parents' daughters should come here, not just their sons. It was personal with him, or so I thought."

"Personal?"

"He could sympathize with those parents."

"Why?"

"Or empathize. Which is it?"

"You tell me."

"The one that means relate."

"Why could he relate?"

"For a writer you're not too quick, are you."

"He could relate to being a parent? A parent to a daughter?"

"So could you if you had one."

"I do have one." I lied to keep Faye talking.

"Then you and he are alike."

"He has a daughter?"

"Last time I looked."

"Where did you look?"

"Piggy!"

A toilet flushed. Then the bathroom door opened and an ample-figured, blonde-haired young woman walked out. "This is Piggy," Faye said. "Piggy, this is Mr. ... "

I said my name.

The girl curtsied. "I know you," she said.

"You do?"

"I've read your book."

"Which one?" There was only one.

"I forgot the title. Your picture was on the back. You had more hair then."

The book had been published some time ago. I offered to sign Piggy's copy but she said she'd donated it to Goodwill. I told her she had a very pretty name.

"First or last?" she said.

"First."

"Piggy?"

"Anastasia."

"That's not my name."

'Your last name's pretty, too."

Piggy's face went blank, as if she didn't recall her last name.

"Foxley," I said, helpfully.

"Your last name is pretty, too."

I'd never thought of my last name as pretty, or not pretty for that matter, but I thanked her for the compliment.

"How's it spelled?"

I spelled it.

"What's that, German?"

"Flemish."

"Never heard of it."

"Flemish," said Faye, "is the language of Flanders."

"Flanders is a country? I don't think so."

Piggy was right, Flanders had never existed as a truly independent country.

"I have to go to the bathroom," said Piggy to her mother.

"You just went to the bathroom."

"So?"

"Fine, go."

Piggy ran back to the bathroom. Frankly, I was just as glad to miss her Clytemnestra, especially with a lethal prop.

"You were talking about Dr. Loeb, Mrs. Foxley."

"*Ms.*"

"What?"

"I'm *Ms.* Foxley. I'm not married."

"Since how long?"

"What do you mean?"

"You have a daughter here so you were married. How long since your marriage ended?"

"It didn't end, and to be upfront with you, it never started."

"You're still married, then."

"No, I'm not *still* married because I've never *been* married."

"So your daughter was born out of wedlock."

"You make it sound illegal. Is it illegal?"

The toilet flushed once more in the bathroom. "I don't think so."

"Tell me yes or no."

"I don't know."

Piggy returned to us and Faye took her in her arms. "Come on, I have a bastard child, am I a criminal or not?"

"Not for being a mother per se."

"Then for what?"

I had a weird urge to say for the murder of Dr. Amos Loeb, just to shake her up and see how she reacted, but that would frighten young Piggy, no doubt. Plus, although Piggy's paternity was probably unrelated to Dr. Loeb's murder, I was too curious about it to let it drop. What appears unrelated to a writer's prime topic often turns out to be the most apropos. Sometimes it's the skeleton key that opens the frozen lock. I put it bluntly: "Who's your daddy, Piggy?"

"I demur to my mother on that."

"You *defer*, darling."

"Well?" I said to Piggy's mother. "Who is he?"

"Was."

"Eh?"

"He's out of the picture."

"Who was he?"

"I can't tell you."

"Why not?"

"The paper I signed."

"What paper?"

"The agreement."

"What agreement?"

"I forget what it's called."

Piggy remembered: "Non-disclosure agreement."

"I'd like to see it."

"I lost it."

"I know where it is, Mother."

"No, you don't."

"It's in the freezer." Piggy went to the refrigerator, opened the freezer compartment, took out a sheet of paper, and brought it to her mother.

I held out my hand. "Can I see it, Ms. Foxley?"

"You'll put it in your book."

"Only with your permission."

"I'm not giving you permission."

"Then just tell me who made you sign this."

"He didn't make me."

"Who offered it to you to sign?"

"The girl's father."

"And his name was ... ?"

"You'll be shocked."

"Shock me."

"This needs a little background."

"I'm listening."

"It's a long story."

"Tell it to me."

"Actually, it's short."

And so I learned that in the fall of 1968 Faye, a 17 year-old senior at Glenfarne High, disdaining her crude and callow male classmates, had cruised the Ballyvaughan campus every evening, chatting up witty, wise, and for the most part wealthy college boys in hopes of engaging one of them in a romantic relationship leading to marriage and a life of both luxury and high purpose, or hoping at least to lose her virginity which in the dawning of the Age of Aquarius hung albatross-like around her neck. This was before Ballyvaughan went coed so a woman on an all-male campus was as *rara* an *avis* as a Spix's Macaw at a birder's convention. And so one November night, amidst the wassailing brothers in the basement of Kappa Kappa Nu, Faye was spotted by Tom Dunraven just as he was suffering yet one more glorious beer-ponging defeat. "Come here often?" he slurred.

"Almost every night."

"I don't remember seeing you."

"Because you're always blind drunk."

"Ha-ha."

"Ha-ha."

A minute later they were on an ale-soaked sofa making out. A week later Tom was at the 1968 bonfire rally with Faye as his date. After the rally Tom took Faye to a party at the home of his European history professor Amos Loeb. All of Loeb's students were there including Tom's roommate Charlie Cubbage, plus several other faculty members. Of the students only those over twenty-one, thus the seniors, could legally serve themselves from the bar table groaning beneath bottles of wine, cordials, and hard spirits, even though at fraternities the minimum drinking age was conveniently overlooked. The faculty members, well over minimum age of course, took good advantage of their seniority and by the time Faye and Tom arrived they and their host were several sheets windward.

"Welcome Tim," Loeb said.

"Tom."

"Welcome Trixie."

"Her name's Faye."

"I'd've named her Trixie."

"You can call me Trixie if you want."

"Thank you, Faye, I will." Loeb poured her and Tom drinks from a glass beaker clearly swiped from the chem lab. "Vassar?"

"Huh?" Faye said.

"You're up from Vassar? You look like Vassar material."

"What's Vassar?"

"Smith? Holyoke?"

Tom broke in: "She's—"

"—Radcliffe, right?"

Loeb's wife Lucy sidled by with a tray of assorted canapés. "These aren't store-bought," said Loeb. "I make them myself, the little biscuits and the toppings all right from scratch."

"What are the toppings?" said Faye.

"Well, we have dill mousse, balsamic onion jam, beetroot, goat cheese, pea vol au vent."

"What's this fish?"

"Try it, you'll love it."

Faye bit into the anchovy. Loeb watched her like an expectant father. "Well?"

"Ick."

"First time, eh?"

Faye pulled it from her mouth, unswallowed.

"It's an acquired taste for some people. You'll get used to it and then you'll come to love it."

Faye purged her palate with her drink then sniffed her emptied tumbler. "What's in this?" she said.

"That's for me to know and—"

"—and for me to find out?"

Loeb poured her another. "How old are you, Faye?"

"How old should I be?"

"Tell me you're twenty-one at the least."

"I'm twenty-one."

"At the least?"

"The *very* least."

Funny, Loeb didn't care what age Tom was and he still let him drink. "Might I ask where you live, dear?" he asked Faye.

"She lives here," Tom answered.

"*Here*?" Loeb gestured to the room like an emperor then stomped the floor like he was landing on Plymouth Rock. "*I* live *here*."

Faye gazed about the room. "It's a beautiful home, Mr. Loeb. I love what you've done with it."

"I haven't done anything. I got it furnished."

"Well, I love the furnishings."

"There's more where these came from. Care to see them?"

"Where are they?"

"Upstairs, downstairs, I'll give you a tour." And off he took her, leaving Tom with his empty glass which he now refilled then refilled several times more in the twenty-seven minutes that Faye and Dr. Loeb were sightseeing.

Four weeks later Faye missed her period. Nothing to worry about, she'd missed one or two before. A month after that she missed another period and saw her doctor. "You're going to be a mother," the doctor said.

"No, I'm not."

"The test is positive."

"And I'm not going to be a mother, I'm positive of that."

Faye was not contesting the pregnancy test result, she was contesting that she would abide by it. She asked how she might terminate her pregnancy. The doctor, a charter member of the

National Right to Life Committee, would not tell her. "So I'm on my own?" Faye said.

"The child's father will support you, I would hope."

The child's father. It wasn't Tom Dunraven because despite the nightly necking and the tumescence of Tom's ardor, they hadn't had intercourse to this point. As eager as Faye had been to surrender her maidenhood, she'd been equally reluctant to relinquish it, having read that virgins attracted the best husbands. Sex before marriage, her pro-life doctor had told her, made you a slut. Well, Faye wasn't married and eight weeks ago she'd had sex with Amos Loeb on a pile of dirty sheets and towels in the laundry room of his house. You couldn't get much sluttier than that. On the other hand, Faye was pretty proud of her achievement. Kissy-facing a wet-eared sophomore was pleasant enough but had run its course. Screwing a college professor was a big step up. The slut with her little slingshot had bagged a 12-point buck, and on her first shot. Now if the buck divorced his wife and offered her marriage which under the circumstances he was certainly honor bound to do, or if he at least paid for an abortion, her slut status would be diminished, or at least covered up.

"Abortion is murder," said Faye's mother to whom Faye had entrusted her guilty secret.

"Who says it is?"

"Ask Father Ambrose."

"Abortion is murder," Father Ambrose said.

As a good Catholic, Faye had studied her ecclesiastical history. "How much for an Indulgence, Father?"

"Say again?"

"One of those chits for remission of a sin, how much does one cost? What's the going rate?"

"That item has been discontinued," the priest informed her, and shut the confessional window.

Faye was not scared of dying a sinner, just scared of the hellfire that awaited sinners after death. Sex before marriage was bad enough, you did hard time in Purgatory before ascending to Heaven, but baby killers were stuck in hell for life. Only by carrying her fetus to term then welcoming it into the world would she bypass that fate.

"Here's a thousand," said Dr. Loeb, writing a check in his office. "That should cover it."

"I'm not getting an abortion," Faye said. She did wonder if a grand might cover an Indulgence if they were ever back in stock.

"You should not have slept with that boy Tim," Loeb told her.

"His name is Tom and I never slept with him."

"Oh, you were the Virgin Mary, were you?"

"Not after what you and I did."

"But I withdrew, remember?"

"I guess too late."

"Listen to me, young woman."

"My name is Faye. Faye Foxley."

"I can't possibly be your child's father. I will swear to that on a Bible."

"But you're Jewish."

"On a Hebrew Bible."

"Lying is a sin."

"I'm not lying."

"*Abortion* is a sin."

"So is fornication."

"Two to tango, Amos."

"Look, why do you think my wife has never become pregnant?"

"She hates children?"

"Because of my low sperm count!"

"Well, it can't be zero."

"It's damn near that."

Lucy Loeb entered the office with a tray of roast beef and a carving knife. Dr. Loeb said he wasn't hungry. "I am," said Faye, grabbing the knife. She cut a fat slice and with the meat in one bare hand and Loeb's check in the other she stomped out the door.

Faye considered ripping up the check but then cashed it. Yes, the money was tainted but it was still legal tender. She dated a few other Ballyvaughan boys after that but none seemed good marriage bait so she asked Tom if he would take her back but by that time Tom had met Svetlana who waved him on to third base mere moments after first making out.

Faye didn't use Dr. Loeb's money for an abortion which would be a mortal sin. But what else was new? Faye was a sinner for having sex before marriage and she would be a sinner for aborting the result so she was damned either way. Sex on dirty towels was a guilty pleasure but in the modern economy where the wages of sin were $1,000 per maculate conception, it paid very well. The embryo it engendered was like a lavish tip.

That was Faye Foxley's story of Dr. Loeb's dastardly cunning, related to me with aching sincerity. But I along with the rest of the world knew Dr. Loeb to be an honorable man so I didn't believe a word of what she said.

Gang Violence

Getting anyone at Ballyvaughan to talk in detail about Herr Doktor Wohlgemuth was like pulling impacted teeth. His name had become toxic since his abrupt firing and departure from Glenfarne. Finally, I cajoled one of his former drama students to spill a few beans.

This chap said that Wohlgemuth had thought the best way to revive the college's spirits after Dr. Loeb's death would be to mount an uplifting spectacle. He'd originally planned on staging that dreary old Norse warhorse *Miss Julie* where the heroine ends by going off to slit her wrists, but he replaced it with the beloved *West Side Story* with its frisky street rumble where the gangs with different accents settle scores with switchblades while crooning pop melodies to full orchestra accompaniment as subways thunder overhead and fake steam made from dry ice blasts from manhole covers. The lead babe sings *I Feel Pretty* then her guy ends up pretty dead which is pretty ironic but that's the soul of wit.

The other problem with *Miss Julie* was that it only had three characters, two of them women, and Doktor Wohlgemuth wanted a cast of thousands, figuratively anyway, and most of the players to be male. Anton loved men. Not the way one might think. He was a manful man, quite the beefcake, who, according to his course catalogue bio, went hunting with a crossbow in the Burmese rain forest and speargun fishing in places like Baffin Bay and Great Slave Lake.

He leaned toward stage dramas with weapons in them, the kind that explode, the louder the better, or that thrust and cut silently and kill you before you know you're dead. For *West Side Story* he gave knives not just to the mortal foes Ice and Bernardo, he had every character wielding one, even Maria and her bridal shop coterie. He pasted mirror shards on all the blades so when they were brandished they reflected the stage lights out at audience members, blinding them momentarily and creating a planetarium effect within their heads.

"*Du nennst das erstechen*?!" Anton said to the young actor playing Tony as the boy nudged his stiletto tentatively at Bernardo.

"I'm sorry, sir, I don't speak German," Tony said.

"You call that stabbing?!" Anton translated. "I'd call it offering him a stick of gum."

"I didn't want to hurt him."

Anton said the blade was retractable. "No, it's not," said Tony and proved this by jabbing the blade two inches deep into a subway platform stanchion made of wood.

"Give me that thing," said Anton. Tony tried to free the knife but couldn't. Anton slipped it out like a straw from a smoothie. "Now watch and learn." He reared back then thrust the knife toward lower down on Bernardo's anatomy.

"Hey, back off my junk!" yelled Bernardo.

"Go for the gold, see, Tony?" Anton said.

Bernardo quit the production that afternoon. "Who wants to replace him?" Anton asked the other male actors. No hands were raised. "Come on, who's got balls enough?" A freckle-faced freshman boy finally volunteered on condition he could wear a cup. It was this freckled fellow who related all this to me, in fact. What follows below I learned from Wohlgemuth himself when I reached him many weeks later at the Yale Drama School where he'd been hired right after he left Ballyvaughan.

Loeb summoned Wohlgemuth to his office after the knife incident. Wohlgemuth had been wearing a track suit and jazz shoes during the day, better than civilian attire for a strenuous rehearsal in which he demonstrated all of Jerome Robbins's leaping, sliding, kicking choreography himself, including all moves for the women. For the meeting with Loeb he slipped into a copper lamé shirt unbuttoned to the bottom rib exposing a russet chestal thatch, under a teal faux-polyester matching jacket and pants which, if it were not 1988 and disco fashion had not died its unlamented death, one could call the leisure-suited offspring of a Sonny Crockett pastel t-shirt and rolled-sleeve white linen Armani suit. Wohlgemuth had never been married and didn't seem to date but, "Every girl crazy about a sharp dressed man," he was almost daily given to state, albeit in German.

"I've had a report," Dr. Loeb began.

"I know, from Bernardo."

"The name signed here is—"

"*Der junge spielt die rolle von Bernardo.*"

"We are in America, Anton."

"It's from the boy playing Bernardo, Rocky Lurtsema, sophomore, fragile soul, he complained about my choreography."

"Which involved a knife."

"A misunderstanding. We worked it out."

"He says you threatened him with it."

"He's thin-skinned, bruises with the slightest rebuke. He won't go far on Broadway, not because he lacks talent but because he can't take the rejection which is every actor's daily lot."

"He said you pointed the knife at his privates."

"Pointed. *Pointed.*" Wohlgemuth illustrated the motion, his index finger extended forward toward Loeb's privates, his whole body tensed like a shorthair retriever poised to shag a duck. "*Sie würden denken, ich hätte seinen Penis abgeschnitten!*"

"He did think that in fact, Anton."

"Well, of course he did, it's in the script."

"It is not. Tony does not castrate Bernardo in the play, he stabs him in the heart."

"And that's a symbolic castration."

"How so?"

"Heart, love. Love, sex. Sex, manhood. Manhood, dick. I just made it literal."

"You're trembling, Anton."

"I haven't eaten."

"Would you like something?"

"No, that's all right."

"I have some leftover roast, still warm."

"Still warm?"

"Lucy just brought it, I'm eating at my desk tonight, so much work."

"Okay, I'll have some."

"Or would you rather just have a drink?" Loeb opened the liquor cabinet.

"Sure, I'll drink."

From a bottle missing a label Loeb poured Wohlgemuth a shot of something mildew-colored, then poured one for himself. "*Prost!*"

"*Zum Wohl!*"

They clinked glasses. Amos delayed drinking until Anton had slugged his own beverage. "Another?" Amos said. Anton nodded. Amos obliged.

"What is this stuff?" Anton asked him.

"That's for me to know."

"And for me to find out?"

The men chuckled collegially. Amos poured Anton a third shot. He himself had stopped at one.

"*Genieße das Leben ständig! Eh, Amos?*" Wohlgemuth said.

"*Carpe diem,*" Loeb proposed.

"*Quam minimum credula postero.*"

"You speak Latin, Herr Doktor?"

"Was that Latin?" Anton held out for another shot.

"Three's the limit, my friend."

"Ah, that's the most unkindest cut."

"Oh, hell, here." Loeb handed Wohlgemuth the bottle. "Have all you want."

Anton refilled his glass. "You are the noblest Roman of them all, sir."

"*Et tu Brute?*"

"Fall Caesar!" Wohlgemuth made the same knife-thrusting move, again at Loeb, this time thrusting closer.

"But in all seriousness, Anton."

"You got more?" The bottle was now empty.

"In all seriousness I am forced to suspend you from your faculty position."

"Uh ... what?"

"Effective Monday morning."

"What are you talking about?"

"Which gives you two days to clear out."

"Is this a joke?"

"You've crossed a line, Anton. Many lines on many occasions, in fact. But this particular incident is the worst, and when news of it gets out—"

"Which it won't."

"Master Lurtsema has alerted the press to what occurred."

"The press will consider the source."

"The boy's parents will back him up."

"I will issue a denial."

"The press will consider the source of that denial."

"But I will be the source. Why would the press doubt me?"

"Your reputation."

"For teaching excellence?"

"For violent confrontation."

"Onstage! Between actors! Spouting made-up words while wearing silly costumes on a painted set. This is theatre, Amos, not real life."

"The knife was real."

"Real*istic*. It couldn't cut butter, it was a prop."

"That's not what this report says."

"The report is shit. Who wrote it? A teenage actor so muddled I wrote his lines on cue cards because he couldn't keep them in his head. A drama student? He should switch to pre-med."

"If this goes national—"

"It won't go national, it won't go local, it won't go past the end the block."

"It will go worldwide and there will be repercussions."

"For whom?"

"For both the college and for you."

"Why the college?"

"Alumni contributions will be affected."

"They're already affected."

"Oh, are they? By what?"

"Look, I respect what you've done here, Amos."

"What have I done?"

"Your reforms and all that."

"My reforms have affected contributions?"

"We all know they have but you did what you had to do."

"You'd have done differently?"

"I'm not the college president."

"Would you like to be?"

"Please, I'm a poor, modest man of the theatre, I would never presume—"

"So why did you say what you said?"

"What did I say?"

"You don't remember?"

"My mind's fuzzy, I think I've had too much to drink."

"You've hardly had a drop."

"I had a drop or two at home before I came here."

"I thought I smelled it on you."

"I say the darndest things when I drink."

"Then why drink?"

"Why does anyone drink? Why do you drink?"

"To loosen up."

"Exactly!"

"Well, Anton, I advise that before you talk to the press you sober up."

"I'm just fuzzy, I didn't say I was drunk. I'm never drunk."

"But you have been on many occasions."

"What occasions?"

"I will read to you from certain reports."

"Fuck the reports."

"We can be civil, Anton."

"If you're firing me? Then fuck civil."

"I guess so."

"And fuck you, Amos."

"Ah, now we're getting down to it."

"Getting down to what?"

"Why you don't like me."

"What are you talking about?"

"You hardly know me, Herr Doktor, how can you hate me so much?"

"I love you! Or I *did.*"

"I know why you hate me."

"Do you? I don't."

"I know why you wish I was dead."

"Spill it, then."

"Because you are German."

"*You* are German, Herr Loeb. We both are. So what?"

"There's a difference between us."

"*Wir nehmen das Schicksal der Nation in die Hände!* Agree? So there's no difference. We are kinsmen!"

"But you were in the Hitler Youth."

"What?! No. No! How could I be in the Hitler Youth? I was too young!"

"You joined in 1944 at age 14."

"I was four years old in 1944."

"Not according to my research."

"I was born in 1940."

"You were born in 1930, I looked it up."

"Where?"

"I have my sources."

"I will show you my birth certificate."

"It's a fake."

"So I'm a Nazi who hates all Jews and so I hate you?"

"If the jackboot fits."

Wohlgemuth shot a fist at Loeb's jaw that Loeb parried with his left forearm before staggering Wohlgemuth with a crushing right. The professor stumbled backward until he hit the far wall where he buckled and slid to the floor beneath the glass-eyed elk.

"This will not go unanswered," burbled Anton through a mouthful of blood.

"Answer it right now," said Loeb. "Or don't you have your knife?"

The college's official press release said Wohlgemuth departed for personal reasons, specifically to spend more time with his family. But as far as anyone knew he didn't have a family. His students found a "CLASS CANCELLED" sign on the rehearsal room door the following Monday. Another sign reading "COURSE CANCELLED" was taped over it an hour later.

A Lucky Guess

Kandy Roby paid a visit to Avital in jail. "Cold in here." she said. "How can you stand it?"

"Nothing I can do."

"Grayson!" Kandy hollered toward her husband's office. "Grayson, get this woman some heat!" She turned back to Avital.

"I'm his wife."

"I know."

"He told you?"

"No."

"Then how do you know?"

"Everybody knows."

"And everybody told you?"

"No."

"Then *he* told you."

"He didn't tell me anything."

"Not even that he had wife?"

"Why would he tell me that?"

"In case you had scruples about sleeping with a married man."

"What are you talking about?"

"You and my husband."

"Excuse me?"

"He confessed to me, don't play dumb."

Avital fell silent.

"Tell me, Miss Mittelman, why are you here?"

"In Glenfarne?"

"In jail."

"I have no idea."

"You must have done something. I mean in addition to what you did with my husband for which, by the way, I can sue you for alienation of affection. If he showed you any affection, which I doubt."

"Okay, I'm sorry, I'm very sorry. It was one night only."

"Which night?"

"Does it matter?"

"It matters very much, to me at least, whether I was in the house at the time or somewhere far away."

"I assumed you were away."

"Why did you assume that? Wait, I know: because you stayed all night and as far as you could tell there wasn't a third party in the bed, and if there was, which there is occasionally, it wasn't me."

"What's the difference where you were?"

"The difference is between my humiliation if I was on the premises while being cheated upon, and at least some remaining dignity if I was not present and was therefore unaware of the goings-on."

"You're right, I did something awful. I told you I'm sorry."

"Sorry for yourself or for me?"

"Both of us, I guess."

"Why for me?"

"What you said. About dignity."

"Is that pity? Are you pitying me?"

"I take that back. I shouldn't have said it."

"No, I'm glad you did. Get things out in the open. Like you did with that writer at the motel."

"What writer?"

"You know, what's-his-name."

"I *don't* know."

Kandy called to her husband: "Grayson, who was that writer?"

Grayson shouted back my name.

"Ring a bell, Miss Mittelman? Here's a hint: You told him you'd killed Dr. Loeb."

"I did not."

"You did not kill Dr. Loeb or you did not tell the writer that you did?"

"Neither."

"It's on tape, Miss Mittelman."

"What tape?"

"The writer's tape, that Grayson confiscated."

"Okay, yes, but what I told the writer was part of a whole conversation and if you heard the whole conversation you'd see I didn't mean what I said."

"I have heard the whole conversation."

"So why do you believe I was confessing to murder?"

"I don't. Grayson took your remark out of context. Shame on Grayson. He knew you hadn't murdered anyone. Anyway, you loved Amos. Why would you ever kill him?"

"How do you know I loved Amos?"

"Everybody knows. So why would you kill him?"

"I wouldn't."

"Why would you sign a confession?"

"I didn't."

"Grayson says you did."

"He's lying, believe me."

"I do believe you."

"You do?"

"And so does he." Kandy pointed in her husband's direction.

"But he arrested me and locked me up."

"Not for murder."

"Then for what?"

"For sleeping with that writer."

"That's ridiculous."

"That's jealousy. Grayson is a jealous man. When lovers cheat on him he goes a little batty."

"And charges them with murder? He has no right!"

"He knows that but jealousy makes him forget. It boils his blood, he starts to think he's Thor. And the Dexedrine doesn't help."

"He's a cop and he takes drugs?"

"Forget I said that."

"And then makes false arrests? That's illegal."

"He's well aware."

"He could lose his job for that. He *should* lose his job."

"And that scares him."

"Well, it should."

"And it scares *me* because then we'd have no money, which is why I'm here right now, to make things right."

"How?"

"By getting you released. I mean your so-called confession wouldn't have held up anyway. After hearing the whole tape the judge would have thrown it out. Plus, there was no physical evidence of your guilt. And just between you and me ... " Kandy leaned close to Avital and whispered: "I know who killed Amos Loeb."

"Who?"

Kandy nodded in the direction of Roby's office.

"Your husband?"

"Sshh!!"

"Why would he kill him?"

Kandy explained that her husband had found her in an intimate embrace with Loeb and had threatened to cut Loeb's dick off. "And a week later at the football rally he did."

"You had an affair with Dr. Loeb?"

"Oh, come on, you knew."

"No."

"Everybody knew. I'll bet you balled him, too."

"Me? Never."

"You can't fool me. I know you loved him, and he loved you."

"We just worked together."

"Nice work if you can get it, wouldn't you say? I would. So you and I have a lot in common, Avital. In a sense we're sisters. Oh, come on, you're not surprised. And don't worry, Amos just fooled around with me. But he truly loved you."

"Did you love him?"

"I don't love anybody."

"You had sex with him."

"Sex, not love. Which is what I told my husband but he was jealous anyway. Crazy wild jealous. 'I'll kill that bastard,' he said."

"Does your husband threaten to kill all your sex partners?"

"Every single one, so you're lucky I never hit on you."

"Not funny."

"Not meant to be."

"Apparently your husband never makes good on his threats."

"All bark, no bite. Perfect example: One day Amos threatened Grayson and Grayson turned the other cheek."

"How did Amos threaten him?"

Kandy called to her husband: "How did he threaten you?"

"Who?" Roby called back.

"Amos Loeb."

"With a knife."

Kandy turned back to Avital. "With a knife."

"Amos meant to kill him?"

"Since a knife is a deadly weapon, I'd say yes."

"Why would Amos Loeb kill your husband? Because he wanted you all for himself?"

"That was it partly. But mainly it was because my husband had something on him."

"What?"

"Well, for one thing, that Amos was cheating on his own wife Lucy. That would tarnish Amos's name if it got out."

"He could be blackmailed."

"Yes, but that wasn't the big thing Grayson had on him."

"What was the big thing?"

"It was information that would expose Amos for what he really was."

"An adulterer."

"Worse than an adulterer. Much worse."

"A Jewish Nazi collaborator."

"A kapo at Auschwitz, exactly. You knew. Did Grayson tell you?"

"No."

"How did you know, then?"

"Lucky guess."

"Grayson!" Kandy yelled. "Release this woman right away."

Grayson answered, "No can do."

"Stay there, Avital." Kandy left the cell area. Less than a minute later she was back with her husband who unlocked Avital's cell.

"Checkout time," he said. "Stay one more minute and I'll charge you an extra night."

Knives Out

I would love right now to report that Ben Marble returned to Glenfarne with Tom Dunraven chained hand and foot, but in fact Ben hadn't been heard from since he departed on his freelance mission to capture him. I didn't question Ben's focus on this single suspect but I couldn't ignore that certain other persons were linked with knives of a type likely used in the Loeb attack, to wit:

• Faye and Piggy Foxley with the knife Piggy used in her audition for Dr. Loeb;

• Jasmine Elm with the knife she'd brandished at her student assailants in Founders' Hall;

• Herr Doktor Anton Wohlgemuth with the knives he used as stage props;

• Lucy Loeb with the knife she used to carve roasted meat.

Grayson Roby hadn't brandished any knives in public, but Kandy Roby's revelation that he had threatened to castrate Loeb for cuckolding him put Grayson smack within the potentially guilty group.

Avital Mittelman, falsely detained by Grayson for Loeb's murder, was in the clear, and her mother had no connection to any knife. Those of you who suppose that Amos Loeb castrated himself should see my post on eBay for a bridge in Brooklyn. (Cheap.)

Were these links with knives coincidental? Maybe or maybe not, depending on which links one was talking about and which person or persons were thusly linked. That's the approach I take in all my professional researching, and for that matter in solving all of life's mysteries, suspecting everyone, suspecting no one, keeping all options open and calling no spade a spade until it's not. Which makes me sound more like a detective than a writer, I admit. But aren't writers detectives of a sort, just without search warrants? Imagine if every time we wanted to interview someone we had to get permission from a judge. And imagine if we could be sued every time we wrote something that our interview subjects didn't like. Well, we can be sued but most subjects can't afford the money, time, and trouble of hauling us to court. Those that can afford it soon find juries favoring writers' Constitutional rights of free speech.

That said, a writer has a conscience, even oftentimes a heart. A writer worries, just as does a criminal prosecutor, that an innocent interviewee will be fingered by another interviewee with a grudge, and thus the poor sap will be railroaded through a literary show trial ending in a guilty verdict in the court of public opinion and a sentence of a ruined reputation and an inability to ever again find work. There are plenty of innocent interviewees in this book of mine, the great majority, though most don't smell so innocent to start with. But who among us smells honeysuckle fresh at first whiff, come to think? Who, to lower his tax bracket on his IRS return, doesn't hedge a bit? One may hold these truths to be self-evident but don't go on Jeopardy unless you can name our country's twenty-seventh president and his secretary of agriculture. Likewise in reading this book the truth will out as one by one and sometimes in pairs the innocent souls drop off the radar and the true culprit reveals himself by the victim's blood under his nails and his own guilty stink. That's the moment of joy for an ex-detective like Ben Marble who wants back in the game. My joy is reporting and writing about that moment and all that led up to it. Your joy is reading what I wrote.

So who is our stinker? That's for me from my retrospective perch to know, and you, still *in media res*, to find out.

And oh, yes, how did Ben survive his dunking in the river? Only by a stroke of freakish good luck, but I'll leave that for later. For now, let me reveal to you a new piece of critical evidence in the Loeb case that I, despite not being a licensed detective, craftily turned up.

First, step back in time to my champagne-and-beer soirée with Ben Marble preceding his departure to apprehend Dunraven and Cubbage. After Ben drove away and after I finished off my own flask of whiskey, I scoured Ben's house for more hooch. He'd said he was clean out but I found a quarter-full bottle of sherry under the kitchen sink. It was cooking sherry but serviceable, in the way that a twig can be a toothbrush in a pinch.

Then, as I was about to turn out the lights and shove off for home my eyes fell upon four milk crates stacked between the stove and the refrigerator. I assumed their contents to be milk bottles but found they were full of mail, all of which seemed not to be addressed to Ben but to Dr. Loeb. Well, of course this was the trove of poison pen letters Ben had found in Loeb's office and took home with him, as I related in an earlier chapter. What a treasure chest of titillating material for my book. But while sorely tempted to read the letters, I did not. In a contest between a journalist's need to know and a subject's right to privacy, privacy must win out.

But whose privacy would it be in this case? Not Ben's since this wasn't his mail, it was Dr. Loeb's, and Dr. Loeb, being dead, didn't need privacy. This logic compelled me to return to Ben's place and read the letters. One of them, I hoped, would yield the clue to who, while the football rally bonfire roared on that cold November night, had wielded the fatal knife.

I was not disappointed. Halfway through the third crate I came upon an unsigned typed sheet in an envelope with no return address. While the author omitted his name, he didn't stint on his flamethrowing rhetoric. I was afraid the page in my hands might at any moment ignite. Compared to the mere glowing embers of resentment in all the other letters, this one burned white-hot.

Oddly, though, its grievances were not specifically college-related. They were more pointedly personal, and they pointed specifically to Dr. Loeb having recently had sex in Aspen, Colorado with the letter writer's wife, and more specifically to the sex act at issue being rape.

Revenge of a kind appropriate to the offense would be exacted, promised the letter writer, on an appropriate date at an appropriate place which Loeb might amuse himself by trying to anticipate.

Immediately I recalled Esther Mittelman's wacky claim that her first husband had survived Auschwitz, had settled in Colorado, and had killed Dr. Loeb to avenge Loeb's raping Esther at the death camp. Was Esther's first husband alive after all, and was he the sender of this murderous threat to Dr. Loeb? Had Mittelman remarried in Colorado and had Loeb, in addition to having defiled Esther at Auschwitz, now also raped Moshe's new wife? If so, Esther's story of Moshe's survival and eventual move to Colorado would not be Freudian flapdoodle, it would be the truth. If it were the truth then Tom Dunraven wasn't the man Ben Marble should be chasing, it was Moshe Mittelman.

All of which still struck me as complete nonsense until I noticed the Elk's Rest, Colorado postmark on the envelope, dated October 25, 1988, exactly one week before the attack on Dr. Loeb. If you've ever had a jolting "eureka" moment, you know how I felt.

But how to share this moment with Ben and call him off his pursuit of Tom Dunraven? This was before cell phones and emails so I couldn't speak with Ben until he phoned in a progress report. In the meantime I had to hope he didn't provoke a lawsuit from Tom for false arrest. It was comical to picture Ben clamping Tom in irons and giving him the rubber hose treatment to make him confess to a crime he hadn't committed. But Ben and Tom were reasonable men and I was sure they'd resolve the snafu peacefully. I eagerly awaited Ben's call so I could redirect him to Colorado to nail Dr. Loeb's killer there. As I was waiting, though, I had another thought. Why let Ben have all the fun? I'd go to Colorado and confront the man myself.

This impulse wasn't just wannabe-detective whimsy on my part. Colorado had breathtaking mountain scenery but I wasn't driven by mere wanderlust. My motive was purely literary: i.e. to produce literature that would, in the opinion of my literary agent and my eventual publisher, rake in a mountain of loot.

Indeed, the prospective monetary reward had become the carrot that kept me lunging toward the end of my current project's long stick. Its nonstop drama was exhausting me. The psychopathy of too many of its characters, intriguing initially, was now creeping me out. I'd have quit the whole business but with no other income than from writing I didn't have that option. Writing was still a joy for me but you can't take joy to the bank. Unfortunately, I had too long labored under the romantic illusion that you could, with the result that I'd lived just a tad above subsistence level to this point in my life. That had to stop. My body weight was dropping as my blood pressure was shooting up. I struggled mightily against the urge to resume smoking cigarettes, not that I could afford more than a dozen or so packs a week. I dreamed of affording a dozen cartons when one of my works earned a fat publisher's advance. (In this wishful dream of mine I added a case of Chivas to my shopping cart.)

The publisher paying the fat advance had to see my book as a sure-fire bestseller, of course. They weren't going to give me six figures (I'd accept five) for a title that would be remaindered after a month or two. Not to mention that my literary agent Bebe Spinoza would drop me altogether if this time around I didn't deliver the red-hot mass-appeal goods.

I'd conceded to sending Bebe chapter drafts as I wrote them and was unsure if her saying they didn't put her to sleep was encouragement or not. Her flinging out suggestions for improvement seemed to mean my work so far had strong promise. Bebe advised, for instance, that I cut the bone-dry cops-and-robbers police procedural crap which I should leave to law enforcement's own official incident reports. I said I wasn't writing a straight procedural, I was writing what Truman Capote called a nonfiction novel where procedure was the mere skeleton of the story and the community's responses to the tragedy were the flesh.

"But what's *your* response to the tragedy?" Bebe challenged me.

I replied that my response was irrelevant since I wasn't a member of the community.

"Well, *be* a member. Break bread with them, worship with them, hunt and fish with them, fight with them, fuck with them."

I said that I'd done some of what she was mentioning.

"*Some?* Do it all. Go whole hog, for Christ's sake. And take your readers with you. Listen, people today want immersive experiences, not by-the-numbers chronicles. They want to feel the bullet in the backbone, the knife in the chest, the garrote around the neck."

"I agree but a journalist must retain a certain objectivity."

"Objectivity these days is a myth. Modern writers don't just gather facts, they strip down and join their characters in the muck. Hunter S. Thompson isn't an objective third-person narrator; he's a first-person clown prince."

I said that while I hadn't sent in any clowns, my book was in the first person at least.

"But the first person can't be a wimp," Bebe shot back. "He has to be a stud. He's skydiving with the 82nd Airborne, he's scuba diving with Cousteau in the shark-infested deeps."

I steered clear of sharks, I informed her.

"Why? If you get torn to pieces, all the better for your book."

I said I would emerge from this project all in one piece, thank you very much.

"What's the matter, you scared of a little success? You want the fat advance? Go gonzo. Let it rip."

Now I was piqued. "Hell, I slept with one of my subjects. Is that gonzo enough?"

"Man or woman?"

"Excuse me?"

"You slept with a man or a woman?"

"What do you think?"

"Major or minor character?"

"She's the daughter of a Nazi war criminal, how's that for major?"

"Is she a Nazi herself?"

"You think I'd have slept with a Nazi?"

"You slept with me."

"She's not a Nazi, she's Jewish, actually."

"But her father—"

"—wasn't a Nazi, he was a prisoner of the Nazis. I misspoke"

"So he's not a war criminal."

"That's not clear-cut."

"You don't know what you're talking about or writing about. *That's* clear-cut."

"I know who killed Dr. Loeb."

"Good. Can you prove it?"

"I'm interviewing my prime suspect this week."

"Interviewing him? You mean having a little chat? To hell with chat. Drill a confession out of him."

"I just might."

"Over tea? After you light his filter-tipped cigarette? No, you've got to get down and dirty with these scumbags, go pub crawling with them, do some whoring together, share a line of coke. You want to be Joe McGinniss or not?"

"McGinniss has been sued for fraud and breach of contract."

"Truman Capote's a better fit?"

"Yes, except that I don't stray from the facts. He made some things up."

"Who gives a shit? He got his confessions and his book was a hit."

"*In Cold Blood* doesn't end with the confessions. It waits until the men are executed."

"Then let's execute your sonofabitch."

"I'll leave that for the authorities."

"Hell no, do it yourself. Bang, bang. Get your own life sentence, finish your book in solitary. *Notes From the Hole* we'll call it."

"Very funny."

"All right, don't kill him. But you get that confession and I'll get you a five-figure advance within a week."

"How about six?"

"Now *you're* being funny."

"I don't hear you laughing."

"Five figures and a deal for the sequel."

"Now that I can take to the bank."

Last Dollar

Do you know the Last Dollar ski trail at Aspen? It's a double-black diamond and until now I had never mastered it. In fact, it had broken my right leg in three places, thus my present slight limp. Stick to the blues, friends advised me. I said screw the blues, next time I'll conquer this double-diamond sonofabitch. And the day after I arrived in Colorado to meet Moshe Mittelman, and despite my right leg being a half-inch shorter than the left, I did.

I'd landed in Denver tense and exhausted from my recent exertions in Vermont so, after renting a car, I granted myself a snow day before my interview with the assassin. I purchased an all-day lift pass at Aspen Mountain the next morning and brought old Last Dollar to heel on my first descent. And that was it. Without taking another run I returned my skis to the rental shop. I was king of the mountain now so I quit while I was ahead. Confronting a killer would be easy compared to what I'd just accomplished.

Of course first I had to find the killer. His postmark placed him in Elk's Rest but his letter didn't give his name or street address. So the next day I visited the Elk's Rest postmaster who took a look at the hand-addressed envelope and said he recognized the girlish script as being that of a certain man in town whose wife came in daily to pick up his mail. I asked if the man was Jewish. The postmaster asked why I asked that question. "Just curious," I said.

"Well, his name's not Jewish."

"What's his name?"

"I can't tell you."

"Why not?"

"Rules."

"Whose rules?"

"U.S. Postal Service."

"But I'm a reporter." I showed him my press pass. After squinting at it for several moments he said the photograph on the pass wasn't me. I told him I had more hair then but he didn't relent. Then I told him if he gave me the name I wanted I'd put him in the book I was writing.

"Will I be paid?" he asked me.

"No, but you'll be famous."

He mulled the offer. "Sorry," he finally said.

"Okay, you'll be paid."

"When?"

"Right now." I handed him a two tens.

He eyed them dubiously. "But if I'm in your book they'll know I broke the Postal Service rules."

I handed him a fifty.

"Alvin Bagwell," he said.

So in America Moshe Mittelman had changed his name. Still afraid of anti-Semitism, even in the U.S., he'd taken a white-bread moniker for cover. I wondered how else he might have obscured his Jewish roots.

The Bagwell house on Peerless Street was a single-story brick ranch. No car was in the driveway so my hopes were low of finding Mr. Bagwell aka Moshe Mittelman at home. The woman answering my knock on the front door confirmed that Bagwell was out until evening. She was red-haired and fair-complexioned and she spoke with an Irish lilt. When I remained standing before her she asked what I wanted to see her husband about.

"Can I come in?" I asked her.

She said no and repeated no at the sight of my press pass but said yes when I said I'd make her famous.

Mrs. Bagwell brewed a pot of tea and while it steeped I showed her the letter her husband had sent Dr. Loeb threatening to avenge Loeb's rape of his wife.

Mrs. Bagwell burst out laughing. "Good heavens, it wasn't rape," she said, and continued laughing.

"What was it?"

"The most wonderful fifteen seconds of my life." Juiced by the memory as well as by the stiff shot of bourbon with which she "diluted" her tea (leaving me, by the way, to drink mine straight), Mrs. Bagwell told of meeting Loeb at the Aspen ski resort a year previously and being immediately smitten by him.

"So you're a skier?" I said, pleased by an apparent common passion.

"Goodness, no, I have poor circulation in my extremities. Winter weather freezes my fingers and feet."

"What were you doing in Aspen then?"

"Cleaning Dr. Loeb's hotel room."

I presumed she meant tidying up after their torrid lovemaking had laid the room to waste. "Let me guess how you and he met: You shared a chair lift ride and he invited you up to his room that night?"

"He didn't invite me, I was already in his room working."

A "working girl." I got it. And Loeb was paying an hourly rate. "Nice work if you can get it," I said without irony so she wouldn't think I disrespected prostitution.

She snorted. "You want to be a hotel chambermaid, you go right ahead."

I noticed the immaculateness of the room we were sitting in. Mrs. Bagwell's professional training clearly transferred to the domestic realm. "Well, we all have to make a living one way or another," I said empathetically.

"Cleaning hotel rooms isn't a living. You know what they paid me an hour?"

"Yes, but I imagine illustrious guests like Dr. Loeb left you big tips."

"That bastard didn't leave a cent."

"You call him a bastard? Really? But you were smitten with him."

"At the start."

"Meaning ... "

"He was different at the end than at the start."

"But you allowed it to start. Right? The sex was consensual, it wasn't rape."

"I consented at the start."

"Which would be for the fifteen seconds you mentioned?"

"Right, then it bombed after that."

I didn't press for details. I was more interested in Alvin Bagwell's reaction when he learned of his wife's indiscretion. "How did your husband find out about all this?"

"He saw it."

"He was there in the room with you?" Good God, a threesome.

Mrs. Bagwell clarified: Alvin Bagwell was the hotel's handyman and had arrived at the room to fix a leaking faucet. (So Mittelman had taken a low-grade, anonymous job to fly under the social radar. Crafty.)

Beholding the pertinacious conclusion of the escapade on the bed, he inferred it was rape and shouted for it to stop, brandishing the knife he always carried with him to accentuate his point. Loeb disentangled from Mrs. Bagwell, departed the bed, and with a hockey player's deftness, deked Alvin and escaped. "I'll have your dick on a plate!" Alvin hollered after the naked fugitive. "Your husband used those exact same words in his letter to Dr. Loeb," I pointed out.

"That letter was a joke."

"Some joke."

"Alvin is a stitch when he wants to be."

"Threatening someone with bodily harm isn't very funny."

"You had to be there."

"Why didn't your husband sign the letter?"

"Didn't he?"

I showed the blank space below the text on the sheet.

"Well, obviously he didn't need to sign his name because Dr. Loeb would know who wrote the letter by what the letter writer was talking about. How did *you* know Alvin wrote the letter?"

I ignored the woman's question and noted instead that Amos Loeb had his penis severed by an unknown assailant soon after her husband sent his letter threatening penile revenge.

"Dr. Loeb's assailant is unknown?" she said in mock surprise. "You mean you haven't caught him yet?"

"My job isn't catching criminals, Mrs. Bagwell. Mine is writing about them, and to do so I need more information. For example, where was your husband on November 1, 1988?"

"Right here."

"Are you sure? He wasn't traveling?"

"Let me check." She went and got an engagement calendar and flipped to November of the previous year. "Oh, yes, he was away."

"Away where?"

"He didn't tell me where he was going. He never tells me. He likes going solo, he doesn't have to argue with anybody about where to stay or where to eat. The only time he argues is with the airline when they forget to give him his free first-class seat."

"Why is it free?"

"Well, the war, of course. It's for what he suffered in the war." Mrs. Bagwell ticked the calendar page with her finger. "Ah, yes, he did go to Vermont, I forgot."

"When?"

"Just when you said, last November."

"Why did he go?"

"To see the foliage."

"The foliage is gone in Vermont by November."

"That's what he said when he got there. He was very disappointed."

"So you did know where he'd gone to."

"When he phoned me from there, yes."

"Why did he phone you?"

"So I'd know he'd arrived safely. Traveling is hazardous for him in his condition. I always fear he'll fall off a train platform or get stuck in an airplane lavatory and not be found until that plane has flown three times around the earth."

"He's disabled?"

"The war disabled them all, didn't it, if not in the body then in the head."

"Where did he phone you from on that trip?"

"I told you, Vermont."

"Where in Vermont?"

"No idea."

"Glenfarne?"

"That was it."

"You said your husband always carries a knife with him."

"It's from the war years."

"The war's over. Why does he still carry it?"

"He says the world is still a dangerous place, there's nowhere safe."

"He feels in danger?"

"Well, of course."

"Why?"

"Because of the prejudice, obviously."

"What prejudice?"

"Against people of his heritage."

"He's Jewish?"

"He doesn't talk about his religion."

"But he is Jewish."

"I can't answer that."

"Is he circumcised?"

"Goodness, what an absolutely bizarre question."

"I'm sorry but I have to ask you that for my book."

"What does circumcised mean?"

I told her and she said yes, he was circumcised but the book should leave that out.

"Bagwell isn't a Jewish name," I said.

"Oh, Bagwell isn't his real name. He had another name when he was born."

"Why did he change it?"

"He told me it was changed for him when he was adopted. He was orphaned very early."

"What was his birth name?"

"He never told me."

"Mittelman?"

"Could be."

"Was his original first name Moshe?"

"Sure, why not?"

"Was your husband married before he married you?"

"That's a sad story."

"What's the story?"

"His first wife was taken from him."

"By whom?"

"Very evil people."

"What made them evil?"

"The kinds of things they did."

"By any chance like what Dr. Loeb did to you?"

"Yes, but I let myself in for that one with Dr. Loeb. It was half my fault."

"Who was your husband's first wife?"

"He's never told me her name but he calls her the most wonderful woman in the world. He gets very sad when he mentions her. He even cries. I fear that I will never live up to her in his mind, and that makes me cry."

"Is this woman still living?"

"So my husband says."

"Does he have any contact with her?"

"No, and I hope he never does."

"Why is that?"

"Because I'd lose him to her, He'd want to stay with her; he still loves her so much."

"Did she bear him any children?"

"There was a daughter but he's never met her."

"Why hasn't he met her?"

"I asked him but he wouldn't tell me. Just as well. I'd rather not think about him having a child with another woman when I can't give him one."

"One more question, Mrs. Bagwell, it may seem a silly one. Does your husband speak with any kind of accent?"

"Oh, yes, a strong one."

"Why kind of accent?"

"Of his people, of course."

"He's not American?"

"Not going way back."

"Who are his people?"

"You'd guess if you heard him talk."

"I'd love to hear him talk. Could I come back to meet him this evening?"

"Do you like schnapps?"

"I love schnapps."

"So does my husband, he has one each night at six. Come and join him."

"Schnapps is a German spirit. I'll bet he likes German beers and wines, too."

"Loves them."

"Well, then, *auf wiedersehen*, Mrs. Bagwell. Or should I say *Lehitra'ot?*"

"What do those words mean?"

"Ask your husband, he'll know."

Ten minutes later I was on the phone to Chief Grayson Roby. "Great news, Chief, we've got our man."

""Who is 'we?'" he said.

"Me. I got him. Maybe I shouldn't have, it's not my job, I'm not a detective, that's your job. I wasn't trying to go behind your back, Chief, or over your head, I just stumbled on the guy."

"What guy?"

"Dr. Loeb's killer."

"Dr. Loeb's killer is dead."

"Not at all, he's alive and well in Colorado, I'm meeting him tonight. I could make a citizen's arrest or I could get the local constable. Which do you think?"

"What the hell are you talking about?"

"The Amos Loeb murder case is solved, I solved it."

"Ben Marble solved it."

"Due respect, Chief, Ben's lead was no good. And since when are you a Ben Marble booster? You shit on him every chance you get. Mind you, Ben's a good man, a thorough professional, but sometimes you can be too professional and get lost in a huge forest of evidence and miss that one guilty little tree."

"That tree is in Connecticut."

"No, Chief."

"In Southport, Connecticut."

"That's where Tom Dunraven lives."

"Lived."

"What?"

"Lived. He doesn't live there anymore."

"Why not?"

"Because he's dead."

"I'm sorry to hear that. No, I'm not, he was an asshole."

"He was a murderer."

"He wanted to be but he chickened out. The murderer's here in Colorado."

"That's not what Ben thinks."

"I'll call Ben when we hang up, I'll set him straight."

"You know where to reach him?"

"At home, if he's back."

"He's not back."

"Then at his motel in Connecticut."

"He checked out."

"He'll probably call me pretty soon."

"When he does, find out where he's calling from."

"It'll be somewhere between Connecticut and Vermont."

"Make him be specific. But don't tell him why you want to know."

"Why do *you* want to know?"

"The police wherever he is will want to know."

"Why?"

"So they can arrest him."

"For what?"

"Murder."

"Yeah, sure. So what is it really? Has he gone missing?"

"Big-time. He's a fugitive from justice at this moment."

"What are you talking about?"

"There's an APB out for his arrest."

"What did he do?"

"As if you didn't know."

"I don't know anything. He murdered someone? Who?"

"Tom Dunraven. ... You still there?"

"Oh, good God."

"And you know what he used to murder him with? A knife."

"Oh, good God, good God, this is terrible."

"And you know where on Dunraven he used that knife? At the place where Dunraven used his own knife on Loeb. Get the picture? Ben left a note, too. It said *I killed Tom Dunraven because Amos Loeb told me to.*"

"This is a disaster."

"It is for Dunraven. And for Ben who when he's caught'll be facing twenty to life. Poor bastard, he had the right man but he should've let the law take its course. A suspect is legally innocent until he's not. Ben knew Dunraven killed Loeb but he hadn't proved it yet. Ben played judge, jury, and executioner. Classic cart before the horse."

"Wait a minute. You believe Dunraven killed Dr. Loeb?"

"Got a better idea?"

"It's just that there's no physical evidence against Dunraven. Did the police search his house?"

"I assume so."

"Did they find a big knife?"

"Probably, but there's big knives in every house."

"So you assume Dunraven killed Loeb just because Ben said he overheard him saying he wanted to?""

"Cubbage confirmed Dunraven saying it."

"The police have talked to Cubbage?"

"Right, and Cubbage sang like a starling. He said Tom was schizophrenic, didn't take his meds, talked about killing Loeb all the way back in college."

"Did Cubbage actually see Dunraven attack Loeb at the rally last fall?"

"He says he did. Funny that a guy can act so chummy with somebody he now says he hates. You ask me, Cubbage should be charged as an accomplice for not stopping Dunraven doing what he did."

"But Dunraven didn't do it."

"Tell it to the judge."

"Ben killed an innocent man, Grayson."

"I don't think so. Ben's smarter than I thought. He had Dunraven pegged as the killer from the start. He just jumped the gun on the punishment and now he'll pay the price."

"This is my fault."

"What's your fault? Skipping out to the Rockies? How's the skiing?"

"If I'd only reached Ben earlier."

"How could you reach him? He wasn't home."

"I knew his motel."

"You were too busy to call him; you were shredding moguls. How's that bum leg holding up?"

"I could have stopped him."

"There's no stopping Ben when he sets his course."

"When did Ben kill Dunraven?"

"Around seven o'clock last night."

"I could have called and headed him off yesterday afternoon. I mean if I'd known then what I know now, but I didn't know because I waited a day to find out."

"Who cares, it's too late."

"It's too late because I went skiing. An innocent man is dead and a good cop will take a murder rap because I hit the slopes!"

"If you'd called Ben he'd have hung up on you. He'd decided who was guilty. His mind was made up."

"What'll I do now?"

"About what?"

"About the man out here who I know damn well is the real killer."

"Give him my best. And make sure you get Ben's location when he calls you. And act like you don't know anything. That shouldn't be too hard, right?"

No, I wasn't a detective so no, I had no formal responsibility to solve the Loeb murder case. But having stuck my oar into this sordid affair I had a responsibility to proceed with all due diligence. Instead, I'd dawdled and thus allowed an otherwise competent law enforcement professional to make a fatal mistake. I couldn't commute Ben Marble's probable life sentence and I couldn't bring the innocent Tom Dunraven back to life, but nabbing Dr. Loeb's killer would make amends for my delinquency in some small way. That Loeb's killer happened to be Esther Mittelman's beloved first husband would make his apprehension bittersweet. That he'd been Avital's reputed father for most of her life would make his arrest for murder very hard for her to take. But his being the murderer of her mother's rapist would, I hoped, mitigate the shock.

Attempting to make a citizen's arrest of a well-armed and dangerous Alvin Bagwell aka Moshe Mittelman would be foolhardy so I got the local police chief Ron Rust to accompany me to do the honors, and to provide backup in case things got ugly. Ron said he knew the Bagwells very well and frankly couldn't imagine Alvin as a killer. I told him to watch out for a knife.

Mrs. Bagwell opened the door on my first knock. She greeted me with a warm smile and then to my surprise a warm hug. "What are you doing here, Ron?" she asked my companion.

"This fellow wants to meet your husband," Rust said.

"What's Alvin done now? Jaywalked across Main Street?"

Rust burst out laughing at Mrs. Bagwell's apparently sidesplitting joke. "Good one, jaywalked."

"Well, come in, gentleman. Alvin's in the kitchen, I'm just feeding him."

Ron hesitated in the doorway. "If this is a bad time, Ruby, we'll come back."

"Any time is a bad time with Alvin," Mrs. Bagwell replied with a wink, bringing more guffaws from Rust. "Kidding."

Ron said, "No, you're not." It was Mrs. Bagwell who cracked up this time.

My first view of Alvin Bagwell was from the back. He was smaller than I'd anticipated. But I'd never seen a photo of the man so what had I anticipated? Moshe Mittelman was German-Jewish but what does a typical German-Jewish man look like? Far be it from me to assume an individual's appearance by a Teutonic-slash-Hebraic stereotype. Still, this dwarfish, hunched figure seemed as far from a cold-blooded cut-and-run assassin as you could get. I was sure, though, that when he turned to me I would see both the death camp survivor and death-dealing slasher in the lines of his face. Since he wasn't turning, though, I moved around him for a frontal view. As I did, Mrs. Bagwell lifted a forkful from what I saw was a candle-studded birthday cake to her husband's lips and commanded him to eat. Half of the candles were still burning, their wax pooling and hardening on the purple icing. An empty bottle of schnapps stood beside the cake.

"Turning forty today, are you, Alvin?" said Chief Rust.

"He's forty-one," Mrs. Bagwell corrected.

What? Forty-one? Moshe Mittelman should be over seventy years old by now. For all I knew Moshe Mittelman could be legless and wheelchair-bound as this man before me was but Moshe Mittelman would not be an American Vietnam veteran as Chief Rust now informed me Alvin Bagwell was, and he sure as hell wouldn't be, as the man seated before me was, black.

Chief Rust perceived my shock. "Old Alvin might be handicapped but he still gets around. Did Ruby tell you he flies first class for nothing?"

I turned to Mrs. Bagwell. "You said he was a hotel handyman. How is that possible?"

"He's so handy with his hands that he doesn't need legs and feet." She fed her husband another piece of cake. He chewed and swallowed it. He hadn't uttered a word yet. Maybe the horrors of war had rendered him mute. My own horror was having presumed this decorated hero to be a murderer. I literally shuddered with the realization that it was I who had fingered the wrong killer, not Ben Marble.

"So what was it you wanted to see Alvin about?" Mrs. Bagwell asked me sweetly.

"Never mind," I said.

The Voice

"I did what I had to do," was the first thing Ben said when he called me.

"What did you do?"

"Guess."

"Where are you calling from?"

"Can't tell you."

"Are you in jail?"

"Not yet." Ben said he was proud to have avenged the death of Dr. Loeb his savior, mentor, and all-time best friend. "Justice has been served," he said.

"In this case frontier justice." But with Ben what else was new? His vigilantism had gotten him fired in Boston and would now put him behind bars for twenty years minimum, once he was caught. But hadn't I myself been a bit of a vigilante in my freelance junket to serve justice in Colorado? Ben, though, should have learned from his prior mistakes. "Why didn't you just arrest Tom Dunraven, Ben? Now he'd be locked up, instead of you facing a life sentence."

"I did what I had to do."

"Why did you have to?"

"Because Amos told me to."

"When did he tell you?"

"On my drive to Connecticut. He talked to me."

"What do you mean, he talked to you?"

"He rode along with me. He said he'd take the wheel if I got sleepy."

"Are you sure you didn't get sleepy and pull over for a nap and this was just a dream you had?"

"No, I stayed awake."

"And you saw Dr. Loeb sitting next to you?"

"I didn't see him, he wasn't there, not his body anyway. But I heard his voice inside my head."

I thought of Mark David Chapman hearing voices commanding him to murder John Lennon. I hadn't realized Ben was so delusional. I asked him again where he was calling from.

"The Great Beyond," he said.

"Beyond what?"

"Beyond feeling like shit for letting Amos die."

"Congratulations. Now turn yourself in."

"Maybe later."

"Why not now?"

"I want to enjoy this for a while."

"You enjoy being a hunted fugitive?"

"It's great, you should try it." He didn't sound like he meant that.

"Why are you calling me? You don't think I can trace this number?"

"Go right ahead."

Of course Ben wouldn't stay at this number, he'd be shoving off for parts unknown to anyone but him. He asked me if his note at the crime scene had been read and understood.

"You mean about Dr. Loeb telling you to kill Tom Dunraven?"

"I didn't plan to kill him, just cuff him and turn him in. But Amos said that wasn't enough for someone who'd committed a genital crime, much less a capital one. You understand what I'm saying?"

"Ben, it's hard to understand your committing a murder on the orders of someone who was himself dead."

"It's unusual."

"It's insane."

"What's insane about an eye for an eye?"

"Or a dick for a dick, apparently."

"That was Amos's idea. You remember the night you and me had champagne at my house and I told you Dunraven deserved to be shot?"

How could I forget Ben saying that? But I'd thought it was the Veuve Clicquot talking.

"Well, Amos said in the car that shooting was a bad idea, too noisy, the neighbors would hear the shot and call the police. Better to kill him with a knife. And I shouldn't just stab him in the neck or the heart. I should get him right where he got Amos, that'd serve him right. A dick for a dick, like you said. This wouldn't be just for Amos's benefit. Amos knew I felt responsible for his being castrated and so he said by returning the favor to Dunraven I'd get rid of my guilt."

I suspected the car radio had been on while Ben drove drowsily in the wee hours of the night and he'd mistaken an announcer's voice for Dr. Loeb's as he zoned in and out. It occurred to me that if Ben was clinically delusional then his rooted notion that Tom Dunraven had killed Dr. Loeb faced serious questioning. I myself was questioning it at this moment, though not aloud to Ben. If in fact Dunraven wasn't Dr. Loeb's killer then Ben had just murdered an innocent man and the real killer was still on the loose. God forbid he should remain so forever. That would kill my book. Again, I urged Ben to turn himself in.

"In good time," he said.

"I'll have to tell Roby you called me, you know."

"Be my guest."

"Well, goodbye, Ben, and good luck."

"Wait. You're writing a whodunit, right?"

"I'd call it a bit more than a whodunit."

"Call it what you want, just tell me who done it."

"Who done it? *You* done it."

"Not who did it to Dunraven, I did that. Who killed Loeb is my question."

"According to you it was Tom Dunraven."

"Forget me. Who's your pick?"

"I don't have a pick."

"So you don't know."

"I thought I knew, I thought it was Dunraven."

"Why?"

"Because *you* thought it was Dunraven."

"You trusted me."

"Yes."

"But now you don't."

"I don't know who to trust anymore. I can't even trust myself."

"Good. Nobody should trust himself."

"Why?"

"Because there's too much that nobody knows."

"Exactly."

"But don't you want to know it?"

"Know what?"

"What nobody knows."

"Like who killed Dr. Loeb? Of course I want to know."

"And don't you *need* to know? I mean for your book."

"What do you know about what I need to know for my book?"

"I know you need an ending."

"That's not your problem."

"It's not my problem, it's your problem and if you trust me that Dunraven killed Loeb then your problem is fixed."

"Trusting you that Tom Dunraven killed Dr. Loeb doesn't mean he did kill him."

"Having no idea who killed Dr. Loeb is worse. Ignorance ain't bliss."

"Ignorance is better than a false conclusion."

"Speak for yourself on that one."

"I do," I said, and hung up.

Ben's discourse on the craft of writing eerily echoed my agent's badgering me for a socko ending to my book. Unfortunately, Bebe's badgering hadn't stopped. Every day she called to see how my ending was shaping up. I told her I couldn't just make up an ending before the real events of the story played themselves out.

"But they're not playing out, they're just meandering."

"Exactly, like life itself." I reaffirmed my commitment to actuality every chance I got.

"Well, give events a nudge."

"How?"

"Tell people where they're obviously heading and kick them in that direction."

"I wouldn't know what direction to kick."

"Toward the truth."

"There is no truth yet."

"Somebody killed that college president. That's truth. Just because those yokels up there can't find the true killer doesn't mean he doesn't exist."

"Those yokels are highly esteemed professors and undergraduates who scored in the top five percent on their SAT tests."

"That marbles-for-brains rent-a-cop is no genius."

"Ben Marble is street smart."

"And the town chief sounds like a real piece of work."

"He's pigheaded, I admit."

"Your floozy, though, takes the cake."

"Excuse me but Miss Mittelman is probably the smartest person up here."

"Smart enough to get away with murder?"

"What are you talking about?"

"Maybe she killed the college president."

"She loved him."

"That's my point."

"Your point is absurd."

"*You Always Hurt the One You Love.*"

"Who says so?"

244

"The Mills Brothers, 1944."

"That was then, this is now."

"Well, if Miss Mittelman didn't do it, who the hell did?"

"I haven't decided yet."

Bebe said my indecision over whom to nail as Loeb's killer was downright Hamlet-like. She was tired of the red herring appetizers, she was ready for the steak. "Don't tell me in all this time you haven't come up with one stinking lead?"

"I've got all kinds of leads."

"Well, which one stinks the worst?"

That was easy. I told her about the anonymous note I'd received from someone claiming to be Dr. Loeb's killer and promising to reveal himself to me in return for a hefty cash consideration.

"So who sent the note?"

"Some conman, obviously."

"Conmen can be murderers. Have you followed up on this?"

"I'd be wasting my time." I didn't mention that I'd faked greenlighting the deal by blinking my motel room lights as per the conman's request. Frankly, I was embarrassed to have given the time of day to this blatant scammer, let alone play along, albeit facetiously, with his petty prank. I'd learned my lesson years before when I gave my bank account number to a phone caller claiming there were three million dollars of unclaimed cash waiting for me in one of my ancestors' secret trusts. What you get in a gift horse's mouth is a glimpse of rotten teeth and a snort of bad breath.

"Well, *you're* wasting *my* time if you don't come up with a worthwhile book pretty quick. And by worthwhile I mean one that makes us both enough money to retire on. And by quick I mean by March 31st."

"What's the big hurry, Bebe? This is a spec project, no one is setting me a deadline, I don't have a publisher yet."

"Well, you might have a publisher."

"And I might win the Nobel Prize for Literature."

"I'm working on that. But seriously, you do have a deadline."

"Whose deadline?"

She mentioned a major publisher.

"When they haven't even read what I've written? Good joke."

"I'm not joking, they like your book so far."

"They *have* read it?"

"I've sent them what you've written to date. They have a spot on their next year's winter list so by this April they need a finished manuscript."

"Without an ending? No one knows who killed the college president yet."

"Well, find out."

"I'm trying but I can't pull the killer out of my hat."

"Try from somewhere else."

"Look, if it got me a book deal I'd confess to the murder myself."

"That's worth a shot."

"Or I'd say Dr. Loeb cut his own dick off."

"Interesting theory."

"Crimes take months to solve. Years. Some go cold and are never solved because the criminal left no traces and nobody came forward to confess."

"If yours goes cold so does your book. You need to solve this sucker damn soon to keep it red-hot."

"If we miss the winter list could they give us the following summer?"

"If we miss winter it's game over, we're out."

"Why?"

"Because another writer is on the same case."

"Shit. Who?"

She told me who.

I laughed. "He's a hack."

"A hack with a contract."

"Shit. Who with?"

She mentioned the other writer's publisher. They'd given him the same April deadline and he was on track to meet it.

"Without an ending?" I said, incredulous.

"I guess he has one."

"How could he have one if I don't?"

"He's a better journalist maybe."

"You mean he paid somebody for a tip."

"Ends justify means."

"A paid informant is a whore and I don't go to whores."

"Can't afford to?"

"Shut up." She'd struck a nerve, suggesting I was incapable of doing my own down-and-dirty research. Well, I would never pay a tipster for a spurious scoop. I got my information the old-fashioned way: I dug for it. Still, my outburst just now had been too harsh. "Bebe, I apologize for saying shut up."

She was silent.

"Bebe? I'll come down to New York, we'll discuss this over a drink."

"I can't, I quit."

"Your job?"

"Drink."

"I wish I could."

"I wish I hadn't."

"And I wish I could quit smoking."

"You did quit smoking."

"For thirty years but last night I dreamed I had a cigarette."

"You just dreamed it, so what?"

"But when I woke up this morning I lit a Camel."

"If you're trying to quit you shouldn't have cigarettes within reach. Like a recovering alcoholic shouldn't have liquor around."

"You're right."

"You know the best way to stop smoking? Never start."

"Now you tell me."

"Same for writing a book. Don't start if you ever want to stop."

"I'm not stopping."

"You're taking one step forward, two steps back. That's even worse."

It was worse. The truth was I couldn't see the light at the end of the dark tunnel that was the Loeb murder case, and the way things were going I was afraid that I would never see it and then I'd have a lot of fancy pages but no real book while my hack competitor hit the *New York Times* bestseller list. Not to be melodramatic, but how could I live a normal life after that? By normal I mean having the will to get out of bed.

"And another thing," said Bebe.

I didn't want another thing. I was stuffed with what she'd already force-fed me. "Can it wait?"

"Who's your hero?"

"Abraham Lincoln."

"I mean in your book. People want to root for a hero. You have no heroes."

"Well, Dr. Loeb is heroic."

"We meet him one minute and the next minute he's dead. A hero is the last man standing. Who's your last man standing?"

"It's too early to tell."

"Wrong, it's too late. Here, I'll give you a hint: Teddy Roosevelt."

"He's not in my book."

"What Teddy *said*, his most famous quote."

"*Speak softly and carry—*"

"No, this one: *The hero is the man in the arena with a bloody face who wins in the end or fails by daring to be a hero.* I'm paraphrasing."

Was she ever.

"But you get my point."

I did get it: Dr. Loeb was heroic only as a martyr, not as the savior of my book which needed someone at the end to reveal its cell-level putrescent truth and thereby restore a traumatized society, and my readers, to their pre-trauma state of robust mental health. Plus hit the top ten in Amazon's book sales ranking.

But none of my subjects measured up. Conclusion: I had to be my own hero by solving the mystery myself. But apparently the only way I could solve it by April was by getting Dr. Loeb's killer, whoever that might be, to flat-out confess.

So be it that Bebe Spinoza called me Hamlet. That great Dane was a ditherer until he most emphatically was not, so I would gladly wrap myself in that noble prince's cloak. "*The time is out of joint,* Bebe. *O cursèd spite, that ever I was born to set it right.*"

"Now *you're* paraphrasing."

"You think so? Look it up."

That night a brilliant idea erupting from my subconscious jolted me awake from troubled sleep. The idea was to send a mini-questionnaire to every resident of Glenfarne and every professor and student at Ballyvaughan College. The question would be: "Did you kill Amos Loeb?" Below would be two boxes, one labeled YES, the other NO. I'd include a self-addressed stamped envelope. I wrote down the idea then lay back upon the pillow and slept like a swaddled infant for the rest of the night. When I found the note in the morning I said to myself, "Who wrote this shit?"

The handwriting was mine but the idea was too oafishly simplistic for me to own up to. I ripped the sheet up. Writers who say they get their best ideas in dreams and then pitch these ideas to publishers lose their Authors Guild memberships. No one is going to confess to murder by reply mail. Therefore I would need to go out and knock on everyone's door and pose the million dollar question in person.

Stop. What the hell was I thinking? Was I still dreaming? Was I still asleep? This case was getting to me. I'd lost my appetite. My right eyelid fluttered at odd moments like it used to do when I was a kid. And now for toppers I was hallucinating totally impracticable methods of getting a murderer to confess the truth. What truth? Ah, that was the question. Did anyone at all kill Dr. Loeb? Were reports of his demise greatly exaggerated? Was he really dead?

Again, stop. Get a grip. Shave. Floss. Gargle. Brush your teeth. Take a cold shower. Then make it hot. Then cold. Then hot and cold. Drink a pot of strong tea. Meditate.

Now I felt better. Now I could think, and what I thought was yes, I could canvass the entire Glenfarne/Ballyvaughan community but that would take me far past my crucial deadline, especially since my interviews would be long and deep, eliciting more than simple yes/no answers. But who would even talk to me at this point? My initial welcome had cooled as my daily appearances at town and college events drew suspicion that I was not a truth-seeking reporter but a sinister spy of some sort. My fly-on-the-wall presence at these gatherings made people seek flyswatters. My efforts to be unobtrusive suggested snobbish disdain, if not malign furtiveness. Once the star reporter come to town, I was now a predatory scribe whose ingratiating promises to depict the locals in flattering light masked my true intention to roast them in a bilious final report.

If I couldn't interview every living soul in town and on campus, I could reach back out to people with whom I'd already established relationships, if sometimes uneasy ones. Crucially, all these people were connected to knives in one way or another. Knowing which of these people Chief Roby still considered persons of interest and which he'd ruled out would narrow my focus and save me precious time as April loomed and I raced to beat the clock.

Firing Line

Dr. Loeb's murder had been front page news not just in Glenfarne but all over the country and the world. The subsequent investigation of the murder, while lacking daily bombshells, in fact lacking much of anything newsworthy in the way of college press releases or police updates, still commanded the public's rapt attention. Chief Roby, a blusterer in person but shy in the media spotlight, shrank from this attention. Finally, though, the intense pressure for more information pushed Roby to his breaking point and he held a news conference.

"Why has the college been so secretive about the investigation?" asked a front row reporter.

"I'd say they've been cautious, not secretive."

"Is that because they're embarrassed?" the reporter followed up.

Roby pointed to another reporter. "Next question."

The first reporter wouldn't be dismissed. "Excuse me but the male president of an elite, venerable, and for most of its history all-male college was castrated. That's pretty ironic, right?"

"What do you mean?"

"Ironic means contrary to what was expected or desired."

"I know that. You think I'm dumb?"

A reporter in the back said, "Is the college hiding the truth? And if so, why? So as not to inspire copycat behavior all over academia?"

"Are you being funny?"

"No, sir."

"The college isn't hiding anything."

"What about you, Chief Roby?"

"Me?" Roby appeared puzzled, as if he hadn't recognized his own name.

"You were an eyewitness to the attack. What did you see?"

"I did not witness the attack. I arrived a moment after it."

"And what did you see at that moment?"

"I saw what everyone saw."

Questions now shot from all directions:

"What's the background to this crime as you know it?"

"Was the attack premeditated?"

"Was the motive personal or professional?"

"Whoa, boys," Roby said, regaining his composure. "I'm making a thorough investigation and will announce my findings at the proper time."

"But as for the attacker himself, whom at least do you suspect?"

"Or herself."

"Pardon?"

"The attacker's identity, and thus her gender, are unknown at this juncture."

"Well, if you could hazard a guess."

"A police investigator *concludes*, he never guesses."

"Then what is your conclusion?"

"I will give you my conclusion, gentlemen, when I have all the facts."

"What facts do you have at present?"

"Those are sealed for now, as I said."

"All right, just your impressions then. What was it like to see a man knifed in the groin and lying dying at your feet?"

"He didn't die until a month later."

"But to witness such a horrific assault—"

"I *didn't* witness it."

"Seriously? You were right there at the site."

"I was near the site but facing away from it."

"Why was that?"

"I was scanning the crowd for troublemakers."

"As the chief of police you were securing the event."

"Exactly."

"That's ironic, wouldn't you say? That you were securing an event disrupted by an unprecedented security breach?"

"The breach came from the other direction. I don't have eyes in the back of my head."

"Were you the only security officer present?"

"Dr. Loeb had his own private guardian."

"What's his name?"

"His name is Ben Marble and if anyone allowed a breach of security, he did."

"So you're abdicating your own responsibility?"

"I'm just one man."

"You're denying any personal guilt."

"Look, I'm sworn to protect this community, with my life if necessary. Amos Loeb was a member of this community so I would take a bullet for him."

"But not a knife."

"Hey, screw you. *I* didn't maim the sonofabitch."

Chief Roby ended the presser right there. I didn't blame him. These hankering scribes get a bit cheeky now and then and forget their place. The First Amendment is fine but at times you have to slap a muzzle on the Fourth Estate and let law enforcement do its work, though that doesn't restrict judicious writers from taking hard evidence and witness testimony and turning them into art.

I caught Roby on his way out of the room. Even though I had no idea what he'd been doing in the way of an investigation, I said I admired all his hard work. Then I showed him my personal list of suspects and asked him to edit out any he thought beyond all suspicion.

"That one," he said, pointing to the first name which was Tom Dunraven's.

"You're sure Dunraven didn't kill Dr. Loeb? Why is that?"

"Because Ben Marble thought he did."

"You disagree with Ben?"

"Disagreeing with Ben is always smart."

"But I thought you'd come around to his conclusion about Dunraven. You said Ben was smarter than you thought."

"I wasn't thinking straight. Look, you want a rule to live by? Put this in your book: Whatever thing Ben Marble thinks, don't think that thing yourself. Whatever he does, do something completely different. You'll be all right."

"Okay, then what about these other names on my list? Any I should throw out?"

"You trying to do my job?"

"I'm trying to document it so you get full public credit when you solve the case."

"So just interview me. Why talk to all these other people?"

"So when one of them turns out to be the culprit I'll have all the personal background I need to portray him fully and accurately in my book."

"Or her."

"What?"

"A dame could be the culprit."

"You think?"

"*Cherchez la femme.*"

"Meaning ... ?"

"Some people claim there's a woman to blame."

"Who says that?"

"Jimmy Buffett."

"Who's Jimmy Buffett?"

"You city slickers, all you know is Rossini."

"*You* know Rossini?"

"Not personally."

"Of course I know Jimmy Buffett, *Margaritaville.* But then he says it's not a woman, it's his own damn fault."

"He's lying. It's a woman."

"So a woman killed Dr. Loeb, you think?"

"Fifty-fifty odds." A brilliant deduction.

"If it's a woman then which one?" I tapped my list. He tapped a specific name.

"But that's your wife."

Roby just smiled. I pocketed the list and turned to go. "Hey, wait," said Roby, "I know you've been trying to interview me all this time."

"I have but you've been too busy."

"Sorry about that. So interview me now."

"I just did."

Roby was a useless source. His suggestion that his wife Kandy had killed Dr. Loeb was obvious payback for her telling Avital that he was the killer. Classic marriage-on-the-rocks tit-for-tat. I discounted both spouses' allegations because they cancelled each other out.

Cherchez la femme. Leave it to the notoriously misogynistic French police to come up with that sexist conceit, and how fitting that the wife-abusing Grayson Roby would repeat it. How did I know Grayson beat up on Kandy? I didn't but her saying she walked into a door didn't convincingly explain the bruises on her face. I'd love to be a fly on the wall of their house in the evenings. I'd get enough material for another whole book.

But that was for later. For my current book I needed someone's murder confession ASAP. My book was sunk without one, as Bebe said. If I couldn't get a confession immediately I'd welcome a good lead on the killer's identity from some Deep Throat who freely sang the truth instead of pimping it out.

The Drop

I KILLED AMOS LOEB.

I will sign a confession for you with my real name for a ten percent cut of your book royalties and fifteen grand upfront.

Bebe now knew that I'd received this scammer's anonymous confession to the Loeb murder, with his proposal to reveal his identity if I reimbursed him for his trouble. Ashamed that I'd paid the slightest heed to the proposal, I hadn't told Bebe about blinking my motel room lights to signal my acceptance of it. I'd also been too ashamed to tell her one additional thing: that the creep had taken the bait. I haven't told you this until now either, lest you think *I* was the fish on the hook.

Anyway, the morning after my light-blinking I found a second note under my door. Unfortunately, I'd fallen asleep by the time it arrived so I didn't catch the scammer delivering it. The new note directed me to place the fifteen grand down payment in the hollow of a particular tree at a particular time at a particular location which was indicated on the enclosed hand-sketched map.

Of course I had no intention of paying the gentleman a cent. What I did was write him a note promising payment as soon as I could spring $15,000 from the firm that managed my irrevocable trust investment account. I placed my reply note in the designated tree and waited for my correspondent to pick it up. When he arrived I would nab him and force him to confess that he was either a shameless con artist or Dr. Loeb's killer in fact. Of course that meant I had to stake out the tree until he showed up, and so I did for the rest of that day and into the night until I apparently dozed off because when dawn broke the note was gone.

A week went by and I took my correspondent's silence to mean he would wait for his payday. Meanwhile, I pondered who among my current list of local suspects might have written the note. He must live in the vicinity or be a visitor to the vicinity since he had hand-delivered the initial offer to my motel and then retrieved my reply in a nearby forest.

I've been calling my correspondent "he," but that is not to suppose his gender. There were actually a good many more women whom I suspected than men. My use of the male pronoun to designate a murderer of as-yet undetermined gender is for grammatical convenience only, with no disrespect meant to the fairer sex. I could call my correspondent "they" but that would connote multiple killers. Calling him "she" would imply bias toward a female culprit. Alternating "he" and "she" would only confuse the issue. The pronoun "it" would absurdly denote an insentient murderer, though anyone cold-blooded enough to murder the great Amos Loeb would have to be insentient to a degree.

These myriad new lexical options to choose from make writing books hard work these days, almost as hard as writing replies to *soi-disant* killers' ransom notes. Regarding which, having promised to purchase a killer's self-revelation, I now had to fulfill my promise, or confirm that I still intended to fulfill it while stalling for more time to catch the killer for free. My request for another week's delay brought the following reply:

> One more week okay. But after that if you don't pay I withdraw my offer.

He was calling my bluff and since I wasn't going to pay him to reveal himself it was pointless pretending to him that I would pay. In my next note I said I was tired of playing this cat-and-mouse game and therefore I quit.

This came back:

I'm tired of playing, too. I'm also tired of life on the lam. I know they'll get me someday but in the meantime I want to have a good time and good times cost money so if you don't give me any money for revealing myself as Amos Loeb's killer I might as well kill you.

I phoned my agent. "Bebe, what should I do?"

"He's bluffing."

"What if he isn't?"

"Then pay the bastard."

"I don't have that much money." I asked Bebe if the publisher who liked my early chapters might advance me the advance they were going to pay me eventually anyway.

She said she'd phone them and see. Not a minute later she called me back. "Good news," she said.

"Great, how much will they give me now?"

"Nothing. But the good news is they still like your book and they look forward to seeing it finished."

"I'll be killed before it's finished. Did you tell them that?"

"I didn't have to."

"You didn't mention that my life is at stake here? You didn't make that clear to them?"

"It was clear to them already."

"That I'd be dead without an immediate advance? Why was that clear to them?"

"Because they hear it from writers every day."

I spat out a few obscenities which Bebe curtailed by suggesting that in lieu of a cash down payment I could offer the killer a doubled royalty cut.

"Let him write his own book," I said, "and earn his own royalties."

"Then offer him just a couple more percentage points."

"Hell, no."

"It's your funeral."

Bebe was right, unfortunately. While I still doubted that my correspondent was Dr. Loeb's killer I couldn't risk blowing him off because if he was Loeb's killer then he wouldn't be squeamish about blowing me away. Worse, I'd lose the confession I needed for my book.

There was no way I could come up with $15,000, though. However, by selling a few precious belongings I scraped together $4,000 and I put this amount in the tree as a sign of good faith that I'd pony up the rest shortly.

Twenty-four hours later no one had picked up the money. No one showed up the following day, either. During this time it rained and soaked all the bills. Now, instead of a killer's confession I had soggy legal tender and, assuming my pen pal really was a stone-cold killer which I still doubted but now couldn't afford to deny, I had a target on my head. Or my crotch, more probably.

I took the money home and dried it out and placed it back in the tree, this time with an extra thousand I scavenged from my savings account. This time it was taken away, with a note to the effect that the remaining $10,000 was due in a week, or else no deal.

Normally, of course, one would take a threat like this to the police who would provide you with protection while they hunted the felon. So why didn't I take this to Chief Roby? Because I couldn't yet rule out that he was the felon himself. Not because Kandy said he was but because Loeb's affair with Kandy gave Grayson a clear revenge motive. In his policeman's weapons arsenal he certainly had the means to commit the crime. And since Ben lived here in Glenfarne, Grayson had an opportunity to kill him every day. Only one problem: Roby was a wuss who couldn't kill a bumblebee. Look how Kandy manipulated him into springing Avital from custody. Kandy told me Grayson's Glock didn't even have bullets in it. In that marriage she not only wore the pants, she probably packed the only loaded gun.

So maybe Kandy killed Dr. Loeb? Why, because she was jealous that he'd cheated on her with Avital? But Kandy told Avital she didn't care about that. Kandy's affair with Loeb had been of the body, not the heart. She was Loeb's mere mistress, not his wife. Lucy Loeb was much more the wronged woman, in fact she was a classic case, and so Lucy more likely killed Amos Loeb than Kandy did.

So I put it to Lucy, I said, "Lucy, did you kill your husband?" This was after we'd shared a fifth of Johnnie Walker at her home one afternoon. She'd agreed to a short interview but with Johnnie's help it stretched into the early evening and that's when I popped the big question. She asked me to repeat it, and again I asked her if she'd killed her husband. She threw back her head and laughed. I hadn't known she was capable of laughter. "Are you seriously asking me that," she said, "or is that Mr. Walker talking?"

"Both."

"Well, the answer is no."

I'd have pressed her further if at that moment Grayson Roby hadn't walked in without even knocking. He said he'd seen a strange car parked out front and thought he should investigate. I told him the strange car was my strange car and there was nothing to investigate.

"Grayson," said Lucy, "this is the writer who's writing about my husband's murder."

Grayson said, "Yes, we've met."

"He wanted to know if I did it."

"Did you?"

"Yes, but I told him no."

"You shouldn't lie, Lucy. You should always tell the truth."

"Why?

"It's the easiest thing to remember."

The two of them chuckled like naughty schoolchildren. It was a cheap joke and worse, it was stolen from David Mamet.

Grayson then told me that he actually stopped by here every day to check on Lucy in her bereavement. A widow was such a fragile creature, prey to those who would take advantage of her in her helpless misery, and vulnerable to her own morbid thoughts.

I left these two to themselves and departed for my strange car for the strange drive home.

I'd never had the slightest suspicion that Lucy Loeb was my cash-for-confession correspondent. I'd visited her just to find out who she thought it might be, but alas she had no idea. Thus my life-and-death challenge remained to find out who was sending me these desperate, threatening notes and put him out of business before he did the same to me. Or she did. Or they did. Or it.

I needed a rest. But there was no rest for the weary and in the coming weeks as one person after another refused to sit for a follow-up interview with me and my writing deadline loomed and the threat on my life hovered like a thundercloud overhead, the wearier I got, and the wearier I got, the less I was able to sleep.

I'll pay you the rest of the $15,000 but only if you can prove who you say you are.

That would get him. Unless this joker could prove that he was Dr. Loeb's killer with evidence like, say, the fatal knife with traces of Loeb's blood on it, then I wouldn't pay him another cent.

When I arrived back at the motel ten minutes after dropping the above message in the tree, I found a small box on my doormat. Opening it, I beheld a plastic Ziploc bag containing a blood-flecked knife. A note said, "I've got another one to use on you."

I replied three days later:

Here's $10,000 more. Happy? Let's get this damn thing over with. Give me a call.

A hastily arranged reverse mortgage on my place back home had netted me enough to pay the purported killer his whole fifteen grand. I sequestered myself at the County Mayo Motel and waited for the phone to ring.

That same night it did, but it was only Ben. I told him I had to get off the line because I was expecting a call from Dr. Loeb's killer.

"Speaking," Ben said.

PART FOUR

An Ancient Artifact

I had a funeral to attend so I cut the call from Ben short. But I'd heard all I needed to hear. Ben's revelation that it was he who had murdered Dr. Loeb was certainly shocking. The shock was not of the unpleasant kind, however. It was sweet because now I had my book.

"Esther Mittelman was a brave and good woman," intoned Rabbi Meir Bloch minutes later in the little chapel-cum-temple at the Melton D. Trucks Funeral Home. "She was a loving wife and a caring mother. And she would have been, if fate had allowed, a grandmother also. Ah, what a grandmother would have been this woman. Still, she was a very Grand Mother. No one should disagree."

No one disagreed, least of all the daughter of the deceased who sat well forward of me, sobbing into a hankie. I could see Avital sobbing because there was no one between the two of us to block my view. In fact, besides Avi, myself, the rabbi, and the dearly departed there was no one else anywhere in the chapel. Esther had been a very recent arrival in Glenfarne. Nobody had known her here so nobody was grieving her passing except for those here assembled, a group which increased by one with the tardy arrival of Madeline Vlasic, Esther's nurse at the hospital where she'd spent her last days. I knew Nurse Vlasic by sight. She'd greeted me upon my arrival there the day I paid Esther a visit. Madeline's "greeting" had been a who-the-hell-are-you glare, an order to stay no longer than ten minutes and, when she learned I was a writer, a demand that she be a character in my book.

Rabbi Bloch finished speaking then regarded his watch with alarm.

"Am I late?" Madeline said as she settled beside me, her ample flanks overflowing her chair and bunching up against mine.

"I think *he's* late," I said, indicating the rabbi who, after giving a quick consoling nod to Avital now darted out the door.

"That woman, a precious gem," said Madeline.

"And now so all alone," I said, assuming she meant Avital.

"Ah, but she will be joining her husband where she is going." Madeline meant Esther obviously, who had expired the previous week with Nurse Vlasic holding her hand and singing *In the Sweet By-and-By.* The coroner offered simple heart failure as the cause of death, but Esther's recent rejection of all food and drink indicated suicide. Nurse Vlasic had phoned Avital to come quickly because Esther was dropping fast, but Avital arrived too late to bid her mother farewell.

"Will you excuse me for a moment?" Madeline said. She rose and went to Avital and whispered in her ear. Avital half-smiled then resumed weeping. Madeline returned to me and sat back down. I stood up. "I was a monster," Madeline said.

I assumed she meant she'd whispered something monstrous to Avital just now. "Don't worry," I consoled her, "it's hard to say the right thing sometimes."

"Like when?" Madeline said.

"At a funeral."

"Maybe for some people."

"I'm sure she understood."

"Who?"

"Avital, when you just spoke to her."

"Understood?"

"Whatever monstrous thing you said."

"I meant I was a monster to you."

"To me? When?"

"At the hospital when you arrived to visit your mother-in-law."

"She was not my mother-in-law."

"I was gruff as a goat."

"You had a right to be. I came barging in there, I could have been anybody."

"But you weren't anybody."

"I beg your pardon."

"You were a writer. How's your book?"

"Nice to see you, Miss Vlasic." I turned away.

Madeline grasped my shirtsleeve. "Could you stay another moment, sir?"

"Actually, no."

"There's something perhaps I should tell you."

Obviously, she was going to offer me choice anecdotes from her life to help me write about her. "I'm sorry, there's no room for you in my book, Miss Vlasic, it's full up."

"It's not about that, it's something else."

"All right. Quick."

"Do you want to sit down while I tell you, or should I stand up?"

My hesitation in answering spurred her to rise just as I was descending to sit. Now I gazed up at Vlasic's massive head which obscured the ceiling bulb whose light, defrayed through her frizzy coiffure, glowed like the corona of an eclipse.

"Well, just before she died your mother-in-law said to me—"

"Excuse me, she was not my mother-in-law."

"Whose was she?"

"No one's."

"Pity."

"Gosh, it's two o'clock." I stood back up. "Got to get back to work."

"Can I catch you later?"

"I'll be working."

"All day?"

"And all night."

Ben's bombshell had given me my book's ending but now I had to finish writing the damn thing, and write it fast to land the publisher Bebe Spinoza had on the hook. Before heading to the funeral I'd given Bebe a quick ring to say the Loeb case was solved and I'd mail her my completed manuscript by the end of the month.

"Which month?" she said, clearly doubting I could deliver.

"This month, March."

"That's too late." She said the other writer had promised his publisher a March 20th delivery date. If my manuscript wasn't on Bebe's desk by the 15th I'd lose out.

I rued the working time I'd lost by attending Esther Mittelman's funeral but since I'd known Esther personally, albeit only slightly, and since Avital was my dear friend, I couldn't in good conscience skip the sad event.

"Do you work on Sundays?" Nurse Vlasic asked me.

"Indeed I do."

"No time off for church?"

"I pray by my bed."

"So I can't reach you by phone."

"Send me a letter."

"Where?"

"At my motel"

"Which motel?"

I told her and she winced in sympathy. I gave her a wrong room number in case she decided to drop by for a face-to-face chat. If she did she'd get a good fright from the wacko she'd meet in number 133.

"A letter is better than a phone call, anyway," Nurse Vlasic said. "It can be a written record for legal purposes of what I have to impart."

Fourteen days and just as many all-nighters later I sent my finished manuscript to Bebe by express courier. Beware the Ides of March? With my magnum opus now put to bed, I welcomed them.

I'd promised Ben that I wouldn't identify him publicly as Dr. Loeb's killer until April 1st so that he could enjoy a full month at large and at ease under the sun before he was arrested. But the promise was verbal, not signed and notarized for obvious reasons, and since I'd just blown Ben's cover to Bebe anyway and thus to the prospective publisher, I had no compunction about outing him to Grayson Roby so that he could alert the Connecticut police. Certainly the publisher would want official confirmation that Ben was Dr. Loeb's killer before committing to my book. Thus Ben had to be apprehended and locked up right now, not two weeks from now. Delaying Ben's arrest would let the other writer grab the brass ring first.

Roby just nodded when I told him about Ben's confession. "I'd pegged him all along," he said, without explaining why if he'd pegged him he hadn't nailed him to the wall. Roby thanked me for the information about Ben and picked up the phone to call Connecticut. As I turned to leave, he said to me, "Hey, wait, check this out." He was referring to a cardboard box on his desk. I recognized it as the Special Delivery package sent to Dr. Loeb by Jasmine Elm that I had seen in Loeb's office closet. Roby said he'd kept this item after clearing everything else out of that office.

"Where did you put everything?" I said.

"Gave it all to his wife."

"But you didn't give her this package."

"She didn't want it."

"What's in it?"

"Nothing."

I hefted the package. "Doesn't feel like nothing."

"It's a little statue, sent by that Jasmine Elm woman."

"So send it back."

"Why bother? It's just some tourist trinket, not even in one piece."

"What do you mean?"

"Look." Roby pulled from the box a small terracotta male figure.

"Looks in one piece to me."

"No dick."

"Excuse me?"

"Look, the dick's broken off."

I peered more closely and saw that the short protrusion at the scrotum wasn't a complete penis, but rather the jagged-edged remnant of a larger male member that had been severed near the root. "Priapus," I said.

"Who?" said Roby.

"This is a statue of Priapus, a Greek fertility god always shown with a huge permanent erection. I saw one at a museum once."

"This guy's erection isn't permanent."

"No, it's been cut off."

"Like Loeb's. Ha-ha."

"Ha-ha."

Then a thought hit us both, probably the same thought, that Jasmine Elm had killed Dr. Loeb. We caught each other's eye for a queasy moment, then quickly shook our heads. "Nah," we uttered simultaneously.

"What are you going to do with this thing?" I said.

"Chuck it out. Unless you want it."

"I don't want it."

Roby barked into the phone: "Hello?" He pounded his fist on his desk. "Fuckers've got me on hold." He picked up the statuette. "You sure you don't want this? Maybe it's from prehistoric times, might be worth something."

"Not with no dick."

"Right, probably worthless."

"The dick's not there in the box somewhere, is it? Might have broken off in transit."

Roby looked in the box. "Nope, gone for good."

"Like Loeb's."

"Ha-ha."

I didn't laugh this time. "Well, see you around, Chief Roby." I started toward the door.

"You know," Roby said, "once upon a time I was sure that Jasmine Elm did kill Dr. Loeb."

I stopped. "Why?"

"We both know why. She was mad at him."

"Everyone was mad at him."

"Some loved him. Ben sure did. Which makes Ben killing him so hard to believe. But I guess you always hurt the one you love."

"I guess you do."

"Did Ben tell you why he killed Loeb?"

"Yes, he did."

"Was it out of love?"

"In a way."

"How did he put it? What were his words to you?"

"You'll find out in my book." I opened the door.

"Look at this postmark," said Roby, halting me by slapping the box that had contained the statuette. "October 5th, 1988, just a few days after Elm's appearance at the college that was such a disaster. She blamed all that on Loeb, you know."

"I know."

"He didn't protect her. He didn't even show up. She was at the kids' mercy. Maybe that's what he wanted. That's why he didn't show up."

"Eh?"

"He didn't show up on purpose, so she wouldn't be protected from the rabid kids. Loeb would get his revenge on her that way."

"He had Ben there to protect her."

"Alone, but that was the Roman Colosseum in there, he needed backup."

"Why wasn't there backup? You, for instance."

"I was out on a call." I guess I looked skeptical because he said, "Emergency call, a 10-54. You know what a 10-54 is?"

From researching a piece on old TV cop shows I knew my police codes. "It means livestock on roadway."

"A flock of sheep got out of somebody's pen, they were blocking the ramp to the Interstate." To the phone Roby squawked: "Damn it, pick up." He eyed the statuette again. "Maybe I should get this appraised."

"No, you were right, it's a trinket. Worthless."

"Yeah, worthless." He dropped the statuette back into the box. "But why do you suppose Jasmine Elm sent it to Loeb? Was it a warning?"

"Your guess is as good as mine."

"We'll never know, will we?"

"See you later, Grayson."

Roby snapped to the phone: "Yeah, hello, this is Police Chief Grayson Roby in Glenfarne, Vermont. I've got some information for you."

I waved goodbye to Roby.

He waved back. "Don't be a stranger," he said.

Bad Both Ways

Q Good morning, Mr. Marble.

A *Officer* Marble.

Q Officer Marble. My name is –

A Don Turley, I know, from the probation office.

Q So you know why I am here to talk to you.

A To see if I'm insane.

Q That has been addressed already.

A I'm not insane. That's not what I pleaded.

Q That is true. You entered a straight guilty plea.

A I'm not going to change my plea.

Q It will not be changed.

A I'll take my punishment.

Q The question is what that punishment will be. My report, based on what you and I discuss here today, will help Judge Lombard determine your sentence.

Q You want her to go easy on me.

A My report will enable her to sentence you fairly, reasonably, and humanely, with a full view of who you are as a human being.

A She knows what I am.

Q Yes, and my report will enhance her awareness of not just *what* you are, but *who* you are.

A She'll still give me life. And she should.

Q We can hope for twenty-five to life.

A I killed two people.

Q I understand that.

A More than two people if you include the kid in Boston.

Q You were never charged with murder in Boston. Your record as a police officer there shows several reprimands for excessive use of force, but lethal force in only one case.

A Which was in self-defense.

Q So the official investigation states.

A So why did they fire me?

Q I cannot answer that.

A They said I was sick.

Q Your medical evaluation was not conclusive.

A They said I heard voices.

Q Did you?

A Sure, I did. Who doesn't?

Q Do you still hear voices?

A All the time. Don't you?

Q Whose voice do you hear?

A He doesn't give his name.

Q Is it a male or female voice?

A Male definitely.

Q What does this male voice sound like?

A Muffled, like he's talking through a towel or something.

Q A towel?

A Like you put over the phone when you don't want people to know who's calling.

Q He wants to be anonymous.

A He doesn't fool me, I can tell who he is.

Q How can you tell?

A Towel or no towel, I'd know Dr. Loeb's voice any day.

Q What does Dr. Loeb say?

A Depends on the day.

Q Say the day you went to Connecticut to see Tom Dunraven.

A He said Tom Dunraven must die.

Q Dr. Loeb told you to kill Tom Dunraven?

A Absolutely.

Q Why did he tell you to do that?

A Because he thought Dunraven had killed *him*.

Q But he was wrong. *You* killed Dr. Loeb.

A As things turned out I did. But I didn't mean to *kill* him.

Q Nevertheless, Dr. Loeb is dead because of you.

A In Dr. Loeb's mind it's because of Tom Dunraven. That's what Loeb thought.

Q How could he think that? He saw *you* attacking him.

A He didn't see me. I came up from behind him, I put my hand over his eyes. Plus, it was dark. Dr. Loeb assumed I was Dunraven.

Q Why?

A Well, who else would I be?

Q You could be you.

A I'm the last person I'd be. In his mind, anyway. I was his protector.

Q My notes show that consequent to that fatal incident in Boston you were dismissed by your department, and very soon thereafter you were hired by Dr. Loeb to be his personal bodyguard at Ballyvaughan College in Glenfarne, New Hampshire.

A Vermont.

Q Why would a college president need a bodyguard?

A People wanted to kill him, or said they did.

Q Who wanted to kill him?

A Old farts.

Q Specifically ... ?

A Guys who'd gone to Ballyvaughan and didn't like how he was changing it. Guys like Dunraven. They raved and ranted and a few sent death threats. Loeb pretended he didn't care but he was scared spitless. That's why he hired me.

Q Why did Loeb assume it was Dunraven in particular who attacked him?

A At the president's mansion, the night before the attack, Dunraven had physically threatened Loeb to his face. No one had done that before, not to his face.

Q Loeb told you about the incident.

A I *saw* the incident, I was there.

Q Did Loeb then give you a special order to watch Dunraven?

A Yes, he did, the next morning.

Q And so you did.

A I do what I'm told. What *he* tells me to do, anyway.

Q He told you to protect his life.

A From Dunraven.

Q From the old farts, any of them.

A But now Dunraven specifically by name. Result: Dunraven does not kill Loeb. I did my job.

Q By making sure Dunraven didn't kill Loeb?

A That was job one.

A But then *you* killed Loeb.

Q That's another story.

Q And Loeb thought Dunraven was his killer. And then Loeb, from the grave as you claim, told you to kill Dunraven.

A He didn't ask, he told me to.

Q And you felt you had no choice but to obey?

A Given it was Dr. Loeb talking, you bet the hell I obeyed.

Q Even though you knew that you were Loeb's killer, not Dunraven. And so on Loeb's orders you'd be killing an innocent man.

A Orders are orders.

Q Even from a dead man.

A Loeb was more the living dead, you could say.

Q Because he talked to you.

A Yes, and I was honored. That he would take time out from his heavenly rest just for me, it made my day.

Q: You could have come clean to Loeb, told him it was you who killed him, not Dunraven.

A Let him know that his dear friend and protector had betrayed him? Not a chance. He'd be shattered. He'd be tormented for eternity. Amos deserved to rest in peace. With the life he'd led, except for a few slips, he'd earned an undisturbed afterlife. Plus, he wouldn't have believed me. He'd have told me to get Dunraven anyway.

Q Let me ask you something rather complicated. After assaulting Dr. Loeb did you ever, even for a few moments, forget what you had done?

A That's not complicated. Yes.

Q At what point did you forget?

A The minute I did it.

Q You decided to forget? Or the memory just vanished on its own?

A Oh, I decided to forget. How else could I live with myself?

Q You mean your guilt would have driven you to suicide?

A For sure.

Q But the guilty memory came back.

A It always does.

Q And you haven't committed suicide.

A Yet.

Q In fact you tried to monetize your guilt, and to use the money you received for your own enjoyment.

A Spend it until I got caught.

Q You expected to be caught.

A Maybe I wanted to be. Stop me killing folks. Seemed a habit with me, once I started with that kid in Boston.

Q Did Dr. Loeb tell you to shoot the kid in Boston?

A I hadn't even met Dr. Loeb yet.

Q You met him that night.

A I saw him, I saw the trouble he was in, I got him out of it. I didn't "meet" him, we didn't have a conversation, he didn't tell me to shoot anybody.

Q Why *did* you shoot that young man?

A Kill or be killed, I figured.

Q He was threatening you?

A He was threatening Dr. Loeb.

Q How was he threatening him?

A With a gun.

Q Did you see his gun?

A He said he had one.

Q The official investigation found him to have been unarmed.

A Look, a cop has to take action when he thinks it's a life-or-death situation, he can't wait for an official investigation. People don't understand that. They want us to negotiate with these psychos, get them talking about what they want to do then talk them out of it. Folks say thou shalt not kill but that just works in church, not in the street. They tell us be like London Bobbies and don't pack heat. I say fight fire with fire or get out of the kitchen. But I'm no gun nut. I don't believe the Second Amendment means every first grader up to your Aunt Daisy can pack an Uzi with a bayonet mount. That's for the men in blue.

Q What's for civilians? A knife?

A Depends how they use it.

Q Tom Dunraven, say.

A He *didn't* use it.

Q Thanks to you. Because you used your knife on Loeb first, and then you used it on Dunraven.

A Just doing my job.

Q Your job was protecting Loeb's life. But you *took* his life.

A Before I took it I protected it. That was my job. Serve and protect, the cop's motto.

Q You see the irony here?

A What irony? I did what I was trained to do, I was a cop. My granddad was a cop, my dad was a cop, and then me. Officer Marble, Ben Marble. All in the family. But I'd've been a cop even if it wasn't in the family because it's the best job in the world. Who else gets to drop a dope kingpin and the next minute stop traffic so ducks can cross the street?

Q You had a good relationship with Dr. Loeb at Ballyvaughan?

A We were hand in glove.

Q No animosity?

A Until the end, no.

Q The end, when you killed him.

A I didn't *mean* to kill him, just cut him.

Q Inflicting a wound of that sort, you must have anticipated –

A It was only aggravated assault.

Q Which converted to murder when the victim died a month later.

A I understand that, Mr. Turley. I know criminal law as well as you do. I took the course at the police academy.

Q As far as I can see, you have expressed no remorse for your crime.

A I expressed regret.

Q That's different.

A It's no different. You feel bad both ways.

Q You feel "bad" that you killed Dr. Loeb?

A Bad in one way, good in another.

Q Explain that, please.

A I feel bad because he was a friend of mine, good because he had it coming.

Q Why did he have it coming?

A Because of what he did.

Q What did he do?

A He took my girlfriend.

Q Who was your girlfriend?

A I told that to the detective already.

A Now tell *me*.

Q Her name's Avital Mittelman.

A Tell me about your relationship.

A That's a sore subject.

Q Why is it a sore subject?

A I was going to marry her.

Q You'd proposed to her?

A I was going to, I'd bought her a ring. I was just about to give it to her. Lucky I didn't.

Q Why is it lucky?

A She did the dirty on me.

Q What did she do?

A Cheated on me the worst way you could cheat.

Q With Dr. Loeb, you mean?

A That's what I mean.

Q How did you know she'd been cheating?

A I saw her.

Q Where?

A At his house, the president's mansion.

Q You were present?

A Not inside the mansion, I was outside.

Q What were you doing at the mansion?

A Protecting Dr. Loeb, that was my job. So when my girlfriend drove up and parked in his driveway and went in the mansion I had to be alert.

Q For what?

A Anything.

Q You saw her as a threat?

A *He* was the threat, it turned out.

Q A threat to whom?

A My girlfriend.

Q How did you know that he was?

A I saw him.

Q You went inside?

A I stayed outside, I saw him through a side window.

Q You saw him threatening her?

A She didn't need any threatening, she looked pretty happy doing what he had her do.

Q Which was what?

A She was on her knees in front of him, he was standing, pants down, put it like that.

Q Did you intervene?

A I wanted to intervene, I almost did, but I knew if I did I'd kill him on the spot.

Q You killed him later.

A I didn't want to, I tried a long time not to, but after I saw him do what he did with my girlfriend I knew that someday I would.

Q There was yet another individual whom you planned to kill.

A Who?

Q Mr. Maeck.

A That damn writer? I was bluffing, he didn't get the joke.

Q He paid you $15,000 not to kill him.

A Sucker.

A You'd told him if he didn't pay you'd kill him with a knife.

A I *should* have killed him.

Q Why?

A He broke our deal.

Q What was your deal?

A My part was I'd tell him I killed Dr. Loeb so he could finish his book. His part was he wouldn't turn me in until he finished the book and sent it to his publisher a month later. Meanwhile, I'd have a month of fun with his money. I went to Compo Beach.

Q Where's Compo Beach?

A Connecticut. Westport, Connecticut, next town to Southport.

Q It was March. Not exactly beach weather.

Q You're right but there's great restaurants in the neighborhood.

Q So how did Mr. Maeck break your deal?

A There was another writer writing about the same case. He and my guy Maeck were racing to see who'd finish and get published first. So Maeck picked up the pace and finished two weeks before he told me he would, so instead of turning me in end of March he leaked my name on the 15th. Police nailed me in my bungalow. I still had half my money left.

Q So Mr. Maeck betrayed you and now you want him dead.

A Damn right, he owes me two weeks. By the way, you're pronouncing his name wrong.

Q How is it pronounced?

A Rhymes with dreck. But who cares? I haven't heard that he got the book contract anyway.

Q I've heard that a deal is in the works.

A Good, I'll get my ten percent.

Q Which you can't spend in prison. So why sell your confession in the first place?

A I told you, so I could live it up while I was still free.

Q But why bargain for just a month of freedom? Why not more?

A It turned out being just two weeks.

Q I understand that. But why didn't you bargain for six months, say? Or a year? Or hell, when your time was up, why not bolt the country, fly to Burundi or somewhere, a place that wouldn't extradite you? Why not stay on the lam as long as possible?

A That's no life.

Q You enjoyed your time at Compo Beach.

A I did in the restaurants but not at night in bed.

Q Why not in bed?

A Nightmares.

Q What kind of nightmares?

A About getting caught. I woke up in a sweat, I wet my goddamn bed.

Q You never dreamed of eluding capture?

A Never. I knew someday they'd catch me.

Q How did you know that?

A Sooner or later every fugitive gets caught.

Q Some don't. There are warehouses filled with cold cases.

A They're cold for the police, but in the culprits' consciences they keep burning.

Q So your conscience made you confess?

A A cop can't have a conscience?

Q I didn't say that.

A Mine was killing me.

Q Because you'd killed a friend.

A My best friend, who trusted me with his dying wish. Well, his wish after he was dead.

Q Which you heard loud and clear in your head.

A Well, not so clear with the towel. But clear enough.

Q You heard his voice from the dead.

A Like I'm hearing yours right now.

Q Do you hear it now?

A I hear you fine.

Q I mean Loeb. Are you hearing Loeb's voice right now?

A It never stops, I'm always hearing it.

Q What's it saying right now?

A That's private.

Q Do you ever respond to the voice, or do you just listen?

A Just listen.

Q You never talk back to it?

A No.

Q Would you like to?

A I can't.

Q Let's say you could. What would you say to it if you could?

A Shut up.

Q Okay, fine, we'll pick this up tomorrow.

A Not *you* shut up, Mr. Turley. I didn't mean *you.*

Q Who did you mean?

A Him.

A Dead Letter

Time flies when you're having fun and it creeps when you're miserable. It should be the reverse but that's not how God planned it which proves there is no God, not a loving one anyway, as Ben told me his father disabused him every night before bedtime. "If God loved us, Benny," he said, "he'd put gold coins in Cracker Jack boxes and make it rain rupees in Bombay."

Ben asked him, "Does the Devil love us?"

Replied the father, "I'll tell you when I'm dead."

The father died a year later and Ben is still waiting for an answer.

In his first year of prison confinement Ben certainly had more misery than fun so time for him was a creeper. Actually, Ben was less miserable than just deathly bored. My occasional visits to him were his only relief from the grinding tedium. "How's Amos?" he would greet me, either forgetting that he'd murdered him or making a very sick joke.

"He's in the pink," I replied, though bronze was the correct tint for Dr. Loeb's sculptural incarnation, a larger-than-life statue that was unveiled at the Autumn Inferno rally on the first anniversary of the fatal knife attack. The statue was on the exact spot in front of Founders Hall where Loeb had fallen.

I returned to Glenfarne for the event to pay my respects to the man whose murder had inspired my book. Would that it had inspired some publisher to publish the book, but alas, the publisher Bebe Spinoza said had been slavering for it stopped slavering after reading my completed manuscript. It was too long and too contrived, they said. Not heartfelt enough. I should juice it up and present it as a pure novel instead. They suggested very significant and very specific revisions, all of which I rejected outright, with the result that they dropped my book from their winter list and, as it turned out, all future lists. The other writer's book wasn't published either when it was found to contain multiple fallacious assertions, such as that Ben Marble didn't kill Dr. Loeb at all, and that Tom Dunraven in fact did.

Throngs descended upon Glenfarne for the big Loeb memorial event, people who'd known Loeb as friends, people who'd worked with him, and a huge number who'd never met him but admired him from afar. Charlie Cubbage came, less to honor Dr. Loeb than to reminisce about the good times he'd shared here with his friend Tom. Faye Foxley came. Piggy was already on campus as a Ballyvaughan freshman. Grayson Roby didn't show, having left town after Kandy Roby withdrew her complaint of spousal battery on condition he grant her a divorce and disappear from her life. Kandy herself attended the unveiling, not, as she would say later, out of special fondness for Loeb but out of duty as he'd been one of her dozens of lovers, though apparently not her favorite. Of Loeb's statue she would say that she liked him better in bronze than she had in the flesh.

Anton Wohlgemuth, now a star professor at the Yale School of Drama, sent his *freundliche Grüße* from New Haven. Lucy Loeb stayed home, either nursing her sorrow privately or, more likely, roasting more beef for Loeb's ghost. Provost Lou Pinto, who'd served as president of the college *pro tem* after Dr. Loeb died, read a vitriolic condemnation of the board of trustees for passing him over for the permanent job in favor of a plutocrat with no academic credentials who reportedly aspired one day to be President of the United States. Lou's partisans in the crowd hooted and hissed the new college president's name until Lou fell silent, not because he stopped speaking but because his mic cord was cut.

Jasmine Elm also came back to town, not to attend the unveiling but to ask for her dickless statuette back, claiming it was a priceless ancient Greek artifact. Lucy Loeb directed her to the town police station where Grayson Roby, half out the door on his way out of town, greeted her with the news that he'd dumped the thing at the county landfill.

Rally night was freakishly cold which is saying a lot for Glenfarne where by this date ponds often froze solid and their ice cracked in the night like thunderclaps. It seemed cruel to unveil a statue in this weather. I was shaking and my toes and fingers were numb and as the bronze was bared I imagined how Loeb felt up there stripped of the cloak that had been concealing him. Could a statue die of hypothermia? If it could, would an enormous bonfire made of railroad ties bring it back to life? Amidst the blubbering histrionics of this night, these seemed legitimate questions.

I had arrived in Glenfarne just moments before the start of the ceremony, and checked into the County Mayo motel after it was over. Along with my room key the desk clerk handed over an envelope which had arrived for me just after I'd checked out back in the spring. I hadn't left a forwarding address so the motel had held the envelope until such time as I might return to enjoy once again their splendid hospitality.

In the upper left of the envelope was the name Madeline Vlasic so upon entering my room I dropped it, unopened, into the wastebasket. After a refreshing shower I flopped onto the bed and turned out the light and fell asleep, but for just ten minutes as the alarm on the night table, having been set for 11:30 p.m. by the previous guest, jangled me awake. Unable to sleep after that I turned on the TV and flitted through televangelists' rantings, wildlife documentaries, and commercials for blenders, tort law firms, hair re-growth tonics, and depilatory creams. Reading is my best soporific but I'd brought no reading material so, desperate, I plucked Madeline Vlasic's envelope from the wastebasket. But I didn't want to read a rambling discursion on the life of a psychiatric nurse, or more probably a mash note since Nurse Vlasic had clearly taken a shine to me from the start. Her bluster at the hospital had been obvious camouflage for the thumping of her heart. Her initiating haunch-to-haunch contact with me at Esther Mittelman's funeral had showed that her fervor hadn't cooled a bit. I admit that I was flattered by this fervor but, desperate as I was for a woman's touch since my dead-end affair with Avital, I wasn't attracted to a woman with a tattooed spinach leaf on her left cheekbone and day-old shellfish on her breath.

I dropped the envelope back into the wastebasket but then, not wanting the housekeepers to find it and read its contents, I decided to burn it and so, with the Bic I carried for my Camels, I did.

Or tried to. An instant after the paper ignited I pinched the flame out, ashamed to be showing a well-meaning if tiresome letter writer such rank disrespect. The least I could do was quickly scan her message before destroying it.

Dear Mr. Ma

The remaining letters of my name were burned away but the message below was intact:

As you know. I wanted to tell you this in person but it's better you have it in writing to refer to as you write your book.

Lose the preamble, sister, cut to the chase. I started to flip the letter back into the wastebasket but the next words I glimpsed held me back:

I killed Amos Loeb.

What?

I severed his genitals ...

No. What was she talking about?

291

... and though I did not mean for him to die he's dead now

so I can die in peace.

Wait a minute, Ben Marble killed Amos Loeb. What the hell was Madeline Vlasic doing saying that she herself was the killer? What gave her the right?

I re-read the outrageous statement and in doing so I noticed that it was in quotation marks. Madeline Vlasic was quoting someone other than herself. She was relating what another person had said to her. But who had said it?

Madeline's next lines set me straight:

These were the last words Esther Mittelman said to me. They were the last words. I am quite sure, she ever said on earth.

Well, Esther Mittelman lied. No, I take that back. Calling her a liar maligns her memory. She didn't lie, she just had a Freudian wish-fulfilling false memory, as Avital said she often did. Esther's bogus confession was typical of someone so disturbed that she imagined talking to her dead husband's ghost. Plus, the old woman was planning her own suicide so what could she lose by taking the rap? You'd think Madeline Vlasic with all her training and experience with delusional patients would have understood that. I re-flicked my Bic and burned the whole letter to ashes.

Beyond Belief

Ben escaped from jail after serving ten years of his mandatory life sentence. He did so through a stroke of the same freakish good luck that had enabled him to escape from his automobile submerged in the river at the end of Part One of this book. I haven't yet told you how Ben survived that near-death watery calamity, though I've been promising you that I would. I wish that I could tell you now but I've been advised that my account might, by its sheer implausibility, start readers doubting other astonishing occurrences I've related.

Ben's prison break made headlines so of course you know the overall facts of that caper. What you don't know are its miraculous details which were not reported because they were not known at the time. Indeed, they have remained unknown to the public to the present date. I know them because Ben revealed them to me in a letter he sent me soon after his escape, or I should say he delivered to my home personally so as to avoid a postmark on the envelope, and under cover of darkness so I wouldn't see his face.

Ben accepts that he will now be a fugitive for life with all the stresses of living under an assumed name with a radically altered appearance, always keeping to the shadows as he darts from one hideaway to another. But at least he is no longer a cell-bound prisoner, nor a prisoner of conscience since he has once again suppressed the memory of all that he did, and has thereby quashed his guilt.

Call Ben an evil man. Call him barbarous, damnable, and sick. But don't call him submissive or meek. Don't call me those things either because when I'm struck down I strike back. Best case in point is this book which, after its rejection by that publisher in 1989 and its subsequent dismissal by every other publisher in New York, after which Bebe Spinoza dropped me as a client and I perforce became my own agent (thus saving an agent's 15% commission on advance and royalties by paying it to myself, albeit that 15% of no advance and no royalties isn't very much), I pressed on through the ensuing three-plus decades, earning a living by polishing rich kids' college application essays, writing grant applications for nonprofits, and substitute teaching at the local high school, all while keeping hope alive for the eventual publication of my magnum opus.

But time was running out. Finally in desperation I revisited the suggestions for revisions made by all those dismissive publishers and, gritting my teeth, acted upon some of them. My concessions were minor; I didn't overhaul the whole book. But by tweaking lines of dialogue here and there for heightened emotional effect and by adding a sensational section on Ben's prison break, I secured at long last a brave and wise publishing firm, ironically one that had originally rejected me but that now, with a new chief editor in place, had come to see the light.

The book in your hands is the result. I wanted it to contain the explanation of how Ben survived his ordeal in his overturned car in the river but the publisher, fearing logical challenge to my account of that miraculous event, did not. The publisher did love the new and sensational chapter I wrote about Ben's prison escape and believed that it guaranteed a bestseller in itself. I believed it did, too, and so it pained me greatly to withdraw that section from my final manuscript, thus depriving you of the pleasure of reading it. I withdrew it not to preserve my book's overall credibility, but to avoid giving clues that would lead to Ben's recapture. Am I thus aiding and abetting a fugitive? Am I now complicit with a triple murderer? You make the call on that. As Ben's probation officer said, there was *what* he was, a murderer, and there was *who* he was, which to me was a friend. Plus, Ben said he wouldn't be at all happy if I revealed how he escaped from prison, and he made a familiar threat to me in case I did let it out.

Full details on both of Ben's miraculous escapes will appear in a future edition of this book, I promise you that. The current version is not quite as fine as I want it to be but, as I'm sure you understand, I take what I can get.

CPSIA information can be obtained
at www.ICGtesting.com
Printed in the USA
JSHW021908090423
40062JS00002B/2